READERS LOVE MIA PAGE!

'This is everything I want in a book.'
★★★★★

' A cosy, feel good story.'
★★★★★

'I loved this book and the characters! Bookish vibes and Enemies-to-Lovers,100% Amazing!'
★★★★★

'Such a fun read'
★★★★★

'Loved the sweet build-up of the romance.'
★★★★★

'I couldn't put it down! The twist at the end was excellent. So, worth reading.'
★★★★★

'A funny and warming story thoroughly enjoyable read. Would highly recommend.'
★★★★★

'Mia Page totally blew me away.'
★★★★★

'I loved this book . . . the romance, the drama, the back and forth of the will they won't they?!'
★★★★★

'Such a cute book!'
★★★★★

'A wonderful, warm, comforting novel that was a joy to read. I can't wait to read more from this talented author.'
★★★★★

LOSING THE PLOT

Mia Page is a pseudonym for Claire Handscombe, a British writer who moved to Washington, DC in 2012, ostensibly to study for an MFA in Creative Writing, but actually – let's be honest – because of an obsession with *The West Wing*. She is the author of *Unscripted*, a novel about a young woman with a celebrity crush and a determined plan and *Girl, Unstrung*, a YA novel about a teen violist, and the editor of *Walk With Us: How* The West Wing *Changed Our Lives*. Recently back in London after three happy years as a bookseller at East City Bookshop in DC, she also writes the *If You Love That, Read This* newsletter, and hosts the Brit Lit Podcast.

ALSO BY MIA PAGE

Bookishly Ever After

MIA PAGE

LOSING THE PLOT

avon.

Published by AVON
A division of HarperCollins*Publishers* Ltd
1 London Bridge Street
London SE1 9GF

www.harpercollins.co.uk

HarperCollins*Publishers*
Macken House, 39/40 Mayor Street Upper
Dublin 1, D01 C9W8, Ireland

A Paperback Original 2026
1

First published in Great Britain by HarperCollins*Publishers* 2026
Copyright © Claire Handscombe 2026

Claire Handscombe asserts the moral right to be identified as the author of this work.

A catalogue record for this book is available from the British Library.

ISBN: 978-0-00-858737-6

This novel is entirely a work of fiction. The names, characters and incidents portrayed in it are the work of the author's imagination. Any resemblance to actual persons, living or dead, events or localities is entirely coincidental.

Set in Sabon LT Std by HarperCollins*Publishers* India

Printed and bound in the UK using 100% Renewable Electricity at CPI Group (UK) Ltd

All rights reserved. No part of this publication may be reproduced, stored in a retrieval system, or transmitted, in any form or by any means, electronic, mechanical, photocopying, recording or otherwise, without the prior written permission of the publishers.

Without limiting the exclusive rights of any author, contributor or the publisher of this publication, any unauthorised use of this publication to train generative artificial intelligence (AI) technologies is expressly prohibited. HarperCollins also exercise their rights under Article 4(3) of the Digital Single Market Directive 2019/790 and expressly reserve this publication from the text and data mining exception.

*This one's for you, the reader of romance novels.
Thank you for making this community so much fun!*

Chapter One

JESS

Jess can't concentrate this morning. The next-door neighbours have been drilling through the wall again, but if she's honest, that's not the real reason she's distracted. The real reason is the email on her phone, burning a hole in her pocket. Well, that and the few affiliate pounds that have just landed in her bank account.

Under these circumstances, there's no point trying to work. She might as well do what she always does when she's feeling flush: head to her favourite bookshop for a browse. See what's new (as if she didn't have an encyclopaedic knowledge of that already). See what's old, that she might have missed. Chat to her favourite booksellers. (They're all her favourite. How could anybody who has chosen to spend their life around books possibly *not* be her favourite?) She has to while away the time somehow until the big important meeting that the email in her pocket has summoned her to.

And as big important meetings go, this one is a whopper: she's been invited into the hallowed offices of one of London's biggest publishers by a man whose name she recognises from a million acknowledgement sections, because of course she reads those. You'd be crazy not to: authors thanking their pets, their kids, the random man in the corner shop who always remembers to keep their favourite wine in stock. You find out who is related and which authors are friends and who is secretly annoyed with whom. (You have to read between the lines for that one, but that's the most fun part.)

The man who has invited Jess into his office is none other than Nathan Thomas, Senior Acquiring Editor at a major imprint, aka a man who has the power to make dreams happen. Jess imagines him in a high-ceilinged room, surrounded by manuscripts, pointing randomly with a sparkly wand and saying, 'I'll have this one . . . and this one . . . and that one.' Obviously, that isn't how it works, she knows: it's bound to be all staring at a screen and reading emails, like almost everyone else's office job, with maybe the occasional glamorous lunch charged to the company credit card.

But Nathan Thomas remains a fairy godmother of sorts, granting wishes at what seems like random, and for as long as Jess remembers, *her* greatest wish has been to write a book. Or rather, to actually have the self-discipline to finish one. At the last count, she had twenty-seven first chapters sitting in her metaphorical bottom drawer – some on her computer, some in her grandparents' loft, some lost in the depths of the boxes under her bed alongside postcards from her mum and essays from school and cinema tickets from her university days.

Jess is, she admits, a little confused as to why Nathan has summoned her. She has worked closely with his colleagues in marketing on giveaways and paid collabs for Instagram, and she's got the collection of tote bags to prove it. It's not impossible that she's mentioned the twenty-seven first chapters she has to the marketing people, in the course of a wine-fuelled brainstorming meeting. Or, come to that, the fanfic she wrote when she was heavily into her *Younger* phase, inventing romance plotlines and subtly correcting some of the inaccuracies about the publishing industry that bugged her most about a TV series she otherwise loved.

But Nathan is a Serious Editor of Serious Fiction, and that probably isn't how people like him choose books to publish. *Oh, you've always wanted to write a novel, have you? Dabbled in fan fiction? Well, here's a hundred thousand pounds and a contract.* From what she knows of the publishing industry, it can't possibly be that simple.

A Tube journey and a bit of a walk later, Jess is standing in front of her favourite bookshop. She scrolls through her phone to Nathan's email, rereading it for clues for what is probably the fifteenth time that morning.

From: Nathan Thomas
To: Jess Martin
Subject: A project

Dear Jess,

My colleagues in Marketing have passed your email address onto me – I hope that's okay.

I wanted to be in touch directly because I have a project that I'm hoping you'd be interested in. My team have told me that your emails frequently make them laugh, and your writing style should be bottled. They've also mentioned that you know the book market inside out across an impressive array of genres.

Based on all this, I believe you'd be a great fit for this particular project.

If it suits you, I'd be delighted to meet you – let me know when works for you.

Kind regards,
Nathan

Making people laugh is Jess's favourite thing. Being praised for her writing style by a man of Nathan's standing is a very, very close second. Her cheeks have ached from smiling since she first received the email a week ago.

And now she's smiling all over again, because she's in one of the places she loves most in the world: a bookshop with bright blue walls and tables stacked with new releases. The low hum of customers talking to each other while they browse, even on a weekday. And there, face-out among the fiction shelves, a book she's just written the most fun kind of review for: the ten-out-of-ten-would-recommend, five-stars-and-then-some kind. Her favourite romance author has once again knocked it out of the park with her latest, a gender-swapped retelling of *Persuasion*, and Jess is excited to hit submit on her review and get to tell the world about it. And of course to humblebrag about having read an early copy – that part of her job never gets old. The early copies, of course. The free books. Not the humblebragging and the slight sense of superiority she feels about it. Perish the thought.

Jess runs her index finger across the spines of the books. She pulls a few off the shelf at random, opens one and inhales. It's the best smell in the world; she can't help spinning with delight. And as she does so, she catches the amused eye of someone smiling at her from the other side of the bookshop. Not just *someone*: a very handsome man. A man, in fact, who seems to have leapt straight off the pages of the books she has just reviewed. If she was going to cast anyone dreaming of the day his beloved would return from her years of training to sail across the Pacific, then it would be him. Speaking of clichés, he is one himself: tall, dark, handsome. His hair is slightly unkempt in the way of hair that started out perfectly combed but has had a hand run through it repeatedly, probably in the throes of creative thought. He clearly hasn't had time to iron his shirt, probably because his brilliant mind is occupied with far more important things. Love, perhaps. His faraway beloved. Or else, not that at all: philosophical questions like how to salvage democracy from its current downward trajectory; how to save the world from itself. Could she get away with sneaking a picture of him and posting it on her Instagram story, suggesting that if he makes you swoon, then the book she's reviewed is definitely for you? Probably not. Cursed be privacy laws. And cursed, she supposes, be basic human decency.

Oh, crap. Now he's caught her looking. His deep brown eyes on her send a jolt of electricity up her spine. Jess clears her throat, looks away, thanks the gods of Next and birthday vouchers for sending her the turtleneck she is wearing, which covers up her chest and the blush she can feel creeping up it. She risks another glance, and he is still looking. Is it hot in here? It must be hot in here. It's easy to overdo the heating in March, when the weather is all over the place. But taking off the turtleneck is out of the question. All in a rush, the book still in her hand, she moves towards the till. Does she actually want to read this? Jess isn't sure. But she has to do something with this random burst of energy coursing through her. Moving seems to be that thing.

But Jess hasn't thought this through. She knows that Amy, the only bookseller on the floor, is currently mid-conversation, recommending what to read after the latest Sally Rooney to an earnest young woman carrying what is already a perilously large stack. So the till is empty and now, as well as hot and bothered, Jess also feels stupid and redundant, trying to avoid tapping her fingers and instead seem nonchalant and chill for this audience of one – this audience she isn't sure is even an audience, for surely the tall, dark, handsome man has better things to do than check up on how patiently or impatiently she is waiting for the bookseller. From behind her honey blonde fringe, she sneaks a glance in his direction – only to find him gone. Had she imagined him into existence? She wouldn't put it past herself. She's often been accused of spending so long with her nose in a book that she loses touch with reality.

Beside her, someone clears their throat, and she turns her head despite herself.

It's him.

Patches on his elbows, his coat and laptop bag over his shoulder.

Presumably, coming to buy a book of his own, before he heads out to save the world from itself or deliver a philosophy lecture or whatever.

Not such an unreasonable thing in a bookshop.

And yet, Jess is startled. She suppresses a gasp. Choirs of angels launch into song, or perhaps that is just in her mind. In the film she is mentally casting. Because after all this time of reading about other people's meet-cutes, is she finally having one of her own?

'Hi,' he says, having successfully caught her gaze and held it.

She has nowhere to go. She is stuck. She can barely hear him over the choir of angels, but she knows social conventions. She knows how she is expected to respond.

'Hello,' she says back, and then, in a moment of supreme inspiration, 'I love it here.'

'So lovely, isn't it? It's one of my favourite bookshops.'

'Oh, really?' It seems like she would have noticed him if she'd seen him before. And if he's here enough for it to be one of his favourites, and she's here enough for it to be one of her favourites, then it stands to reason that she should have seen him. As is so often the case, the filter that separates thought from speech in most normal people fails Jess. 'I haven't noticed you here before.'

The tall, dark, handsome stranger smiles. Just a twitch of a smile, like he knows she let this slip out by accident.

'I-I mean . . .' she stammers, as she often does in lieu of that filter operating properly. 'Not that there's any reason I would have noticed you. Just – you know. If we're both here a lot.'

'So you come here often?'

His handsome face contorts into a self-conscious wince at the cheesiness of the line. Jess bites her lip, suppressing a giggle. She doesn't know what to say next. And neither does he, apparently. The silence between them stretches past uncomfortable and into unbearable. But then, at last, Amy makes her way back to the till, apologising profusely for the delay.

'No worries,' Jess says, handing over the random book she'd picked up in a rush of energy. Its cover looks promising. This novel will be fine. It will be good! Maybe she'll discover a new favourite author. She reaches down to the counter to pick up a bookmark. And so, at the same time, does the handsome man.

The choir of angels starts up again as their fingers brush against each other.

'Ah,' he says, snatching his own bookmark away. 'Sorry.' He drops his hand by his side and flexes his fingers one at a time, as if trying to cool them down from the same heat that is spreading through hers. 'Alex,' Amy says. 'We've got the book you ordered. Let me find it.' She hands Jess's book to her and disappears behind the counter.

Alex, Jess thinks, once this has filtered past the choir and she gets to hear it. *That's a nice name*. Not that it matters, since she will be forced to abandon this bookshop forever and never see him again. He clearly wasn't lying about being a regular, since they know his name, and she can't risk another encounter like this one. It's all so unbearably awkward. She'd always imagined that when the universe handed her a meet-cute, she would handle it with grace. In this moment, it seems unclear where she would have got that impression.

'Thank you,' Alex says to Amy, once she's returned with his book. And maybe also to Jess for keeping her company at the till?

'You're welcome,' she says, just in case, and he looks at her oddly, then rearranges his features into a smile. He nods, in that vague acknowledgement of a goodbye you do when you aren't sure if there was enough of a meeting to warrant one but you'd feel rude just slipping away. She nods back. She can't help turning as he walks towards the door, just to see what the view from the back is like.

It is very pleasing.

Such a shame she will never see him again.

Chapter Two

ALEX

The last thing Alex needed on the way to his meeting with Nathan was a distraction. Never mind a distraction in the form of a pretty blonde with, enigmatically, a pencil threaded through her hair, a smile that spoke of mischief, the kind of changeable eyes that seemed to suggest a deeply active mind – hazel, he supposes, technically, but mesmerising swirls of blue and green and gold would be more accurate. He will never see her again and determine this exactly, since returning to that bookshop is clearly out of the question now, but that is not the point. His hand still feels . . . odd, somehow, from where his fingers grazed hers by the bookmarks.

Yet Alex is a professional, and while he and Nathan have known each other since university, he likes to project professionalism when they are meeting for work. Seriousness. Gravitas. If he's honest with himself, this is the image he likes to project always – competency. It's just that he has to work harder at it with the people who've known him the longest. People talk, sometimes, of being able to relax with long-term friends, but Alex finds the opposite is true: he has to work against the grain so that his guard does not come down lower than he is comfortable with. And comfort is not a feeling with which he is very familiar.

But 627 steps after the bookshop, he feels his heartbeat slowing at last. Pushing the door into Nathan's familiar office, Alex breathes deeply. This is where he feels anchored, reassured. Nathan will tell him his book is on the right track and provide some pointers for the first round of edits. For storyline and subplots to develop, so he can counter his tendency for terseness.

Nathan rises from the seat behind his mahogany desk and walks around to half-hug him, half-clap him on the back.

'Alex!' he exclaims. 'Always a pleasure.'

'Likewise.'

'How have you been?'

Alex considers this. Considers, as always, whether the person asking is actually asking because they want to know, or merely performing the rituals of civilised society. He decides that while Nathan is a friend, now is perhaps not the time to break the news that Alex has finally taken his advice and found a therapist's phone number in a serious-looking directory.

'Oh,' he says vaguely, in case actual news is required. 'You know . . . New niece. That kind of thing.'

Nathan looks faintly amused, as he so often does in conversation with Alex. 'That *kind* of thing?'

New nephews and nieces are forever being born into Alex's family. Engagements and weddings are constantly being celebrated; add to that birthdays and graduations and christenings, and it's rare that a month goes by without what some might consider fairly epic family news. Consequently, each piece of that news feels slightly less epic than it might do to others. He'd be in a permanent state of rapture if he allowed himself to get too emotionally involved in each event. And that wouldn't do for his state of mind, or for the level-headedness he needs in order to create quality work.

'Yes.'

'Step-niece? Half-niece? Niece-niece?'

Alex's friends are more interested than he is in making these distinctions, fascinated as they are by his somewhat comically large family. Now that they are all adults, it would be churlish to make distinctions between those of his siblings who shared both parents pre-divorce, the siblings who came into his life fully formed once each of his parents remarried, and the siblings who were born thereafter. He's lived with all of them at various times. Wiped the tears and put plasters on the grazed knees of all of them, changed and bounced the youngest to sleep. Baby Elizabeth is technically a step-niece, but this could not be less relevant. Cradling her tiny body last week, he had felt no less protective or proud than a month earlier when his nephew Oliver had been born to Alex's technically full-sister Susannah.

'I lose track,' he says, playing into the familiar joke of his university friends and signalling, he hopes, that these distinctions are irrelevant.

'Fair enough.' Nathan gestures to a cluster of armchairs in the opposite corner of his office. 'Sit, sit.'

On the low table in the midst of the armchairs sits a distressingly high stack of dazzlingly white printed paper. He doesn't remember his novel being *this* long.

Nathan clears his throat. 'So,' he begins, and Alex feels his heart rate increasing again, a bead of sweat making its way down the centre of his back. 'How do you feel about this book?'

Alex doesn't think it matters much how *he* feels. He's not particularly interested in discussing that. He wants to know how Nathan feels or, rather, what he thinks. But he plays along.

'I'm just glad it's finished,' he says, trying for the easy laugh, not wanting to give anything away until he can tailor his response to Nathan's opinion.

'But beyond that?' It's clear that Nathan isn't going to let him get away with glib evasiveness. His family is one thing; their work together is another.

As Nathan well knows, Alex has found this book harder to write than the others. Perhaps the pressure of his literary success has finally caught up with him. After all, Alex's career path has been an usually smooth one so far: a critically acclaimed debut; the sophomore slump successfully vanquished and the third book a triumph, longlisted for a couple of admittedly minor prizes and selling like the proverbial hot cakes after a mention in *The Guardian*'s summer reading recommendations. The other shoe was bound to drop sometime.

'I'd like to hear what *you* think about it,' Alex says.

'I think . . .' The pause tells him all he needs to know. Nathan was the one to call this meeting; he's had ample time to figure out what to say. If he's still unsure how to phrase it, something must be very wrong. 'I think it's quite . . . dense.'

'Rich and complex?'

'There is definitely richness and complexity,' Nathan says. The care with which he is framing each sentence is the opposite of reassuring. 'But it is also quite heavy.'

Alex imagines the sound his manuscript would make if it were dropped from a great height – or even a relatively small one. It would land with a great *thonk*.

'I see.'

'Your novels all have depth, Alex. They all have emotional resonance, wonderful characterisation, and an exploration of the issues facing today's society.'

Alex nods. While pleasing to hear, this is not news. Not for nothing has he been called 'the Millennial Jonathan Franzen', after all.

'But they also all have wit, and warmth, and a lightness of touch. This one feels . . .' Nathan trails off, no doubt hoping Alex can fill in the blanks for himself. But Alex refuses to make this easy for him. 'Feels . . . ?'

'Well, somewhat lacking in those areas.'

Alex can feel his own shoulders slumping. He has worked so hard on this book – harder than on any of the others, and for much longer. It's been four years since his last hit. A couple of years after his third book, fans started idly wondering on social media – and sometimes messaging him to ask – when his next one would be coming. A year after that, a Google Alert drew his attention to a journalist's throwaway comment: 'It may be that we have seen the last of Alex Maxwell, brilliant though his writing was.' And now nobody seems to wonder anymore. The literary world has moved on, has found new idols to worship, new books for the beach, new tellers of epic family stories with serious messages but a *lightness of touch*. They're assuming, perhaps, that Alex has given all that he had to give and that three novels is the limit. He had been assuming the opposite: that he was merely getting started.

'I see,' Alex says now.

To be fair, it is not easy to write about a plane crash with wit and a levity. It is even less easy when, at night, your dreams begin to fill with images of your own family on a plane, different combinations surviving, others having to make do with a forever changed life. Until now, the complexity but also the love of his family have always been an inspiration for his exploration of relational themes. This time around, though, it seems more of a hindrance. He doesn't know what's changed. Perhaps his therapist will tell him. Or perhaps his therapist will nod and smile and politely ask, *But how does that make you feel?* It's enough to make Alex shudder.

'I have a solution for you, though,' Nathan says brightly.

They've tried several solutions together already, in the course of drafting this book, with Alex fighting every day with the blank page, only to find that what he's written is . . . well, stodgy at best. They've brainstormed; they've gone for long walks in the sunshine and shorter walks in the rain; Nathan has recommended books that discuss narrative techniques and novels that exemplify those techniques, and Alex has read the ones which he didn't find frightfully patronising. Nathan has tried chivvying Alex along and he's tried giving him space. He's suggested plot points and added helpful comments in the margins of the occasional chapter that Alex sent him to ask if it was landing right (*no pun intended*, he has been careful to add). Yet the result of all of this is a less than satisfying novel. Yes, it's only a first draft – and a first draft's only job is to exist – but still, Alex can *tell*. And so, apparently, can Nathan. Besides, it's not a first draft in the true sense: in the four years he has been working on this novel, Alex has tinkered, rewritten, deleted, inserted. He's edited as he's gone along. This is just the first draft that *Nathan* is seeing in its entirety.

'Before you start working on my editorial suggestions, I want you to try something different. Something – maybe a little unorthodox?'

Alex feels his frown deepening. He is a proponent of the orthodox, of doing things properly, in time-honoured ways. He is not a proponent of change. But he takes a deep breath and prepares to hear Nathan out. He is, after all, not unreasonable.

'The solution is about to walk through the door, actually. She's a brilliant writer, with different sensibilities to yours. She'll help you inject some levity into the book. Some romance, even.' Alex takes a deep breath. Romance? He knows, of course, what's selling right now, and that readers have always yearned for love stories: hence, Jane Austen's perennial success, for example. But must *everything* be about romance? Before he has processed this, let alone had time to argue, he registers in quick succession: a knock, a bright: *Come in*, and what must surely be an apparition. Because there, improbably, inexplicably, is the girl from the bookshop.

Chapter Three

JESS

Well, this is unexpected.

Behind the door is not only Jess's potential fairy godmother, albeit with no wand, sparkly or otherwise, but also . . . the hottie from earlier. Alex. She swallows hard. She'd pinch herself, if there was a way to do so surreptitiously and not look like a clichéd character in a badly written novel.

'Hello,' she says, levelly, waiting to be introduced.

Nathan stands to his feet and extends his hand. 'Very nice to finally meet in person,' he says, shaking her hand firmly but not aggressively. His grip is the trustworthy type. The 'you're in good hands' type of grip. She couldn't tell you what kind of grip Alex has, though. She only knows that something like electricity is flowing through it. What is the universe playing at, exactly? Has she, in fact, hit her head and woken up in a romcom, like in the plot of that Rebel Wilson film?

'This is Alex Maxwell,' she vaguely hears Nathan saying. 'One of my superstar authors.'

'Lovely to put a name to a face,' she says, smiling.

Alex remains impassive, as though he's never seen her before. Is it possible he has a twin, who is somehow also called Alex? Or that the door to Nathan's office is in fact a portal to another universe, and Jess has landed in one in which she and Alex have never met before? In this moment, it feels as plausible as any other explanation.

She waits for all to become clear.

Nathan gestures to an armchair, and she does as she's told and sits down.

'I wanted to invite you here today because I have a proposition for you. An invitation, really, more than a proposition.'

Jess looks to Alex. There is nothing to read on his face at all.

'As you know, Jess, my marketing team speak very highly of you. They love the humour in your book reviews and enjoy the way you write about the bookshops you visit around the world. I also happen to know that you can write dialogue in a way that really sparkles. And rumour has it that you'd be interested in trying your hand at your own novel.'

Jess's heart, which had begun to pound in her ears, increases its volume. Between that and the choir of angels, she is having a lot of trouble hearing Nathan, never mind processing what he says next. Sparkling dialogue? Is he talking about her fanfic? Has he *read* her fanfic?

'I can't offer you your own novel, not yet. But what I can offer you is the chance to work with this great writer.'

'You mean,' Alex chimes in, the words *great writer* having seemingly summoned him into the conversation, 'as a mentor? I'd be honoured. Though I'm a little busy at the moment—'

But Nathan interrupts him with a shake of his head. 'No, not exactly. Jess would be a kind of editorial consultant.'

Jess watches Alex's mouth fly open in shock. Then notices herself noticing his mouth, and scolds herself internally. Then realises her own mouth is open, and promptly closes it.

'What exactly did you have in mind?' Alex asks.

'Well,' Nathan begins. 'Jess is witty. She has a lightness of touch even with serious book reviews. She writes brilliantly in the voices of characters she hasn't created herself.' So he *has* read her fan fiction. Or at least somebody on his team has. Should she be embarrassed? Worried about Alex judging her even more than he already is? *Focus*, she tells herself. 'And, if her social media is to be believed, she reads 150 books a year, and writes about many of them, too. She has a great instinct for what the next big thing is going to be, and she has a good sense of what works well in fiction and what readers want.'

Alex narrows his eyes at Nathan. He does not look at Jess. 'What kind of books?' When Nathan doesn't respond immediately, he repeats himself. 'What kind of books does she read?'

Jess doesn't love being talked about as if she isn't there. She also doesn't love where it feels like this is going. 'I read all kinds of books,' she says. 'I read lit fic, and non-fiction, and YA, and fantasy, and thrillers. And yes, I read romance.'

She forces herself to look straight at him when she says *romance*. Not in a flirtatious way, but in a I-refuse-to-be-shamed-about-this way. It is ridiculous in this day and age that being shamed for reading any genre of novel is still something that she – that anyone – needs to fight against. 'Romance powers the publishing industry,' she says, her argument long ready and long rehearsed for precisely this kind of situation. 'It's the sales of writers like Emily Henry and Jasmine Guillory that fund the publishing of obscure lit-fic novels about white men walking around Hampstead Heath thinking deep thoughts.'

She sees a smile playing on Nathan's lips, and buoyed by this, she continues her spiel. 'And there's a special kind of skill involved in following a template in genre fiction but making it your own. Whether that's when somebody is murdered, and we have to find the killer, or these people are in love – can they make it. The reader knows what the ending is – in fact, they pick the book up precisely because they know the ending, but they want to see what new twist on the journey the author is going to provide for them on the way there. And on top of that, lots of romance writers are funny. Which, let's be honest, is something we all need from the world right now – a bit of laughter.'

She leaves a pause. 'But I read all kinds of books.'

Alex finally looks at her full in the face for the first time since the bookshop. 'You feel passionately about romance, though, by the sound of it.'

The word *passion* does something to her insides that she wishes it wouldn't in this particular context. She *is* passionate about romance, as it happens. But she is also defensive of it, and she knows that defensiveness is not a good look – not for herself, and not for the genre.

'I think it deserves respect.'

'And would you say it's your favourite genre?'

'I read everything.'

'But your favourite?'

He's got her there. Because she knows that if she says *yes*, she will lose whatever respect he has for her, her well-constructed speech notwithstanding. But if she says *no*, she will lose her self-respect, and that's far more important.

'As it happens, yes.'

He turns his attention back to Nathan. 'And you want us to work together?'

'I do.' The eye contact between Nathan and Alex lasts. And lasts. Jess suspects they are having an entire conversation with that eye contact. A conversation that mostly consists of Alex begging, 'Please, no, anything but this, anything but her.' So much for that meet-cute in the bookshop; so much for her bumping her head and landing in a romcom. He doesn't even seem to remember her. He certainly has no respect for her.

Nathan clears his throat and speaks again. 'I think your book has a lot of potential, Alex. You know that. Some great characters, some great social issues, some masterful sentences. It just needs – a bit of *je ne sais quoi*.'

'And you think she—'

Jess clears her throat. Inserts her name. 'Jess.'

'Jess is the one to do that.'

'I think Jess could help you add an interesting dimension to your writing. I think you could learn from each other. So yes, in answer to your question, you would be mentoring her, in a way.'

'And she'd be mentoring me.'

'Think of it as helping you to get in touch with your emotions. And find your lost sense of humour.'

'I haven't lost my sense of humour.'

A snort escapes Jess's lips before she can help it. This whole conversation is so evidently devoid of humour that it seems absurd he could think of himself as someone with any sense of what's amusing. She's heard Alex Maxwell's name, of course, though she hasn't read his books. She's heard it in conjunction with phrases like 'surprisingly funny' and 'warm and witty' and even 'emotionally intelligent'. All of which makes her wonder if his novels are ghostwritten. Or maybe co-written by another unsuspecting romance novelist plucked from obscurity, and perhaps thereafter murdered and buried in his back garden.

'I think,' she says, because this is becoming unbearable, 'that this maybe isn't going to work.'

Alex nods emphatically, but Nathan is not to be moved. 'Nonsense. He just needs a moment to get used to the idea. What I have in mind is for you, Jess, to take this novel away, have a read, think about where it can be improved – sorry, altered . . . supplemented, if you will, with a romantic plotline. And also suggest some jokes – anything to make it lighter.'

'There's not a lot that's funny about a plane crash,' Alex says.

'There's humour in everything,' Jess says. 'Throughout history, that's how entire peoples have survived their hardest periods. With dark humour.'

'Exactly,' Nathan says, obviously pleased that she seems to be joining in with his beating Alex into submission. 'I'm looking forward to seeing how you draw out a love story from this plane wreck.' Is he referencing the plot? Or the book itself? Who knows. 'That might mean writing or rewriting some passages, amplifying some characters. Maybe working with Alex on the structure a bit. And you could also tease the book on social media, get people excited about what's coming next from him.'

Jess knows she should say no. She can tell already that Alex is going to be impossible to work with, and not just because she is distracted by his inconvenient good looks. But there's a fizz of excitement deep in her belly. She *wants* this. It sounds like an adventure. To take a stodgy lit-fic novel and make it into something people are actually tempted to read? To add a love story where there isn't one already? Yes, please.

She's learned, though, not to show her hand too quickly. If you're too obvious about your enthusiasm, there's a danger that you'll be expected to do something *for the love of books*, rather than for money or for reward. And it's not that she wouldn't do something for the love of books alone, but she also needs to eat. Pay rent. Live in London, where even the air seems to cost money.

So she takes a deep breath and she asks a question that doesn't come naturally. 'What's in it for me, though?'

'I would have thought *that* was obvious,' Alex mutters.

She chooses to play his game. 'Aside from learning from a master, obviously.'

Nathan smiles. She gets the sense he is enjoying this back-and-forth far too much. 'You'll be mentioned in the press release that goes out to the media, and the collaboration will be pitched as one of the unique things about this book – something that reviewers and podcasters will pick up on. I'm aware you're pretty well-known on the bookish internet already but this'll elevate your status even further. Pretty prestigious, don't you think? Might lead to a book deal of your own someday.'

She waits, hoping her excitement isn't too visible. Because she needs something else, too.

'And, obviously, generous remuneration.'

Jess lets her grin out at last. 'Now we're talking,' she says. She's already spending the advance in her mind: a bigger flat, more bookshelves, a foodie holiday for herself, a cruise for her grandparents.

Alex clears his throat. 'And what's in it for me?'

'A better book. Jess's contacts to help you sell it. Is that somehow not enough?'

'My books sell fine,' he says. 'And when a successful literary author brings out a long-awaited next novel, there's always a flurry of reviews.' Jess isn't sure how she manages not to roll her eyes. *Successful literary author.*

She would bet that foodie holiday that she knows what Alex is thinking – that he doesn't need Bookstagram; that's for the lesser writers, the author of commercial fiction. Of romance novels, say. For someone like him, *The Guardian* is enough.

'Reviews don't sell books like they used to,' Nathan says. 'And anyway, we're going for better than selling *fine* this time around. We're going for stratospheric.'

A smile escapes from Alex, too. Jess is vaguely aware that Nathan is playing both of them to perfection to get to the *yes* he is aiming for. But the thing is, she'd love to write a novel. Much as she'd never admit it to Alex, working alongside someone like him *would* be a good place to start. If only he weren't so rude and pretentious. The patches on his elbows should have clued her in.

Trust the universe to finally send her a meet-cute, but get the details so very wrong.

Chapter Four

ALEX

'You can't be serious about this,' Alex says, the moment Jess is out of the door, her fading footsteps communicating that she is also out of earshot.

The only plausible explanation is that this is a threat. A bluff. Either Alex gets his act together, finds the humour that can supposedly be extracted from this serious plotline, or Nathan imposes an 'editorial consultant', whatever that is. And not just any 'editorial consultant', but a distractingly pretty one with mesmerising eyes and a worrying penchant for fluffier books – he won't dignify those books with the word *literature*.

'As serious as a plane crash,' Nathan says, the shadow of a smile playing at his lips.

'Very funny.'

'It's not meant to be funny,' Nathan says. 'And to be clear, neither is your book. I'm not expecting you to transform it into a laugh-a-minute romp. Just to raise the odd smile, that's all. So the reader isn't relentlessly attacked by grimness.'

'Relentlessly attacked? You really hated it, didn't you?'

'Sorry.' Nathan offers up a tight-lipped smile. 'I didn't mean that quite the way it sounded. The book isn't grim. At all. It's got the makings of something great, maybe better than all your other books so far. But it is . . . well, fairly cheerless.'

Alex refuses to do the undignified thing of going round in circles – a plane crash! It *is* cheerless! – like a pampered toddler throwing a tantrum. If anyone is pampered here, it's – what's her name again – Jess. Who else gets a leg-up in the publishing industry handed to them on a plate like that? She probably doesn't know what it's like to have to battle with anxiety. To be ready at any moment to be interrupted because one of the many members of your unwieldily large family needs something from you. Alex has had to navigate all of that. He has had to work hard. He had to read craft books, study for an MFA, write two novels that went nowhere before he finally got a book deal. Jess takes a few photos, posts them online, and hey presto, she is now – in, what, her mid-twenties – deemed to be the saviour of his below-par prose?

'She had a *pencil* in her hair, Nathan. She was putting her nose in books and *smelling* them.' What had seemed charming and whimsical at the bookshop feels like something else now – evidence that she is not serious enough for this kind of project. 'She'll probably want everyone on the plane to survive. Land on a tropical island flowing with milk and honey and live there happily ever after.'

'I doubt that.'

Nathan turns away from Alex, then stands and moves towards his bookshelf. He runs his fingers along the spines of a row of books – twenty-nine of them. Pulls out a worryingly orange book, and another with a bright green cover.

'I want you to go away and read these.'

'Romance novels?'

'Yes. Very good ones. They're warm and witty.'

It's not an accident that Nathan has used this phrase. *Warm and witty* was one of his favourite compliments for Alex's second novel from a notoriously hard-to-please reviewer at *The Times*. He and Nathan had read the review together. Alex is not the type to dance around a room in glee, but if he had been, that would have been the moment. *Warm and witty*, he had repeated, in awe of this victory, this welcome into the literary firmament by one of its staunchest and most intimidating gatekeepers. *He's deployed an alliteration*, Nathan had pointed out. *That's how you know he really means it.*

'Nathan,' Alex says now – the pain, he hopes, evident in his voice. 'Please.'

'These romance novels are surprisingly humorous. They've also got emotional depth and they don't ignore the realities of life. So yes, they're stories with happy endings. But that's not all they are.'

Nathan holds out the books in Alex's direction, nodding at them, a clear instruction for him to take them.

'Haven't I suffered enough?'

'If you *have* suffered, then some people might say that maybe that's precisely why you need romance novels.'

'Some people, like Jess?'

'Maybe some people like me, too. It would do you good to read something fun. And I don't just mean that it would do your *writing* good. I mean *you*.'

Alex chooses not to interrogate this odd assertion in this particular moment. He'll return to it later, in his mind; he knows this already. But there are more pressing issues at hand right now, in this conversation, than whether or not he should read romance novels to 'heal his soul' or 'open himself up to the possibility of love' or whatever the claim is that people make – that even sensible, reliable, serious Nathan seems to be making. He sighs heavily, deliberately, as he takes the books.

'Look, Alex.' Nathan twists his wedding ring, clockwise and then anticlockwise. In other men – men like Alex – a gesture like this might reveal suppressed anxiety or marital trouble. But Nathan is one of the most confident people Alex knows, and one of the most happily married. *I pray every day for you to have what I have*, Nathan had said to him after too many glasses of prosecco at his second book launch, nodding in the direction of his wife, Priya. For Nathan, playing with a wedding ring is just playing with a wedding ring. That simplicity, that innocence – they are things Alex deeply admires. Maybe even envies, if he's entirely honest.

'I know it's hard,' Nathan says now. 'You've written these brilliant books, and you've spoken out about not believing in writer's block, and now here you are, having taken four years to finish a book because you've struggled with writer's block. I know you hate asking for help. I know you hate accepting it when it's being offered to you. But I also know you wouldn't want to put anything out into the world that isn't your best work – isn't as good as you can possibly make it. And here I am, offering you a solution. Offering you, potentially, a lucrative book deal for the next novel, if you can get the nuances of this one right.'

What Nathan is *not* saying is abundantly clear: their continued partnership is also at stake. This stings Alex perhaps more than anything else – the idea that he could be dropped not only by his publisher, but by one of his oldest friends. Partnering with Nathan in his writing career has had nothing but upsides for both of them until now – aside, that is, from the creeping, niggling fear that Alex has, at best, jumped the queue by knowing the right people, that he's a nepo-writer of sorts. Now he is seeing other issues: the fear of letting Nathan down, of disappointing him and even, perhaps, being exposed as a fraud to him. Anyone can write three great books. That's just dumb luck. But if you can't sustain it for the long term, did you ever really know what you were doing? Was Nathan right to take a risk on him?

Besides which, more prosaically, royalties from his last three books can't keep him fed and watered forever. There have been translation deals in Italy, Germany, even in the difficult-to-crack literary market that is France; this past year, he received the maximum amount allowed from the British library system on the basis of how many people have borrowed his books. But all of that, he knows, will eventually slow to a trickle. He might have to give up skiing trips. He might have to eat out less often, forgo the black daal from Dishoom which he likes to consume no less than monthly. He might even have to move away from Hampstead, and that can't be countenanced.

So he sighs, and he says, 'Fine.' And then he says, 'But I can't be held responsible for my actions.'

There's that smile again, at the corner of Nathan's lips. 'Deal,' he says, holding out his hand for Alex to shake.

'Deal,' he replies, against his better judgment.

Chapter Five

JESS

All day, Jess feels unsettled. The builders have mercifully paused whatever torture they're inflicting on the walls next door, but still, she is just as distracted as if a drill were currently perforating her brain. Her latest book review is coming out flat, uninspired, when this particular book deserves so much better. It deserves to fly off the shelves, and Jess wants her review to inspire that kind of shopping spree. But all she has is a load of clichés – clichés, in fact, like *flying off the shelves*.

It's no mystery why she's so frazzled. She's tried all her usual techniques to move past how she felt in the meeting with Nathan – patronised, rejected, disbelieved, with hope waved in front of her eyes and then immediately withdrawn when it became clear Alex couldn't work with her. She's put on her favourite feel-good 90s playlist full of the songs she and her mum used to dance around the house to when she was growing up. She's looked at TikToks of Europe's most beautiful train journeys. She's clicked around Pinterest, looking for inspiration for her next holiday, the one she's hoping to convince her best friend Lily to take with her before – after three years of marriage – she inevitably disappears off into the land of People With Children.

And still, Alex's words and attitude bother her. It bothers her that he looks down on romance, even though she should be used to this kind of attitude in the book world by now. It bothers her that he doesn't seem to understand the role of humour in fiction, and in life. And it bothers her that this cutie from the bookshop has turned out not to be the man of her dreams, after all.

It's probably for the best. He's older than her – she'd have guessed thirty-three, but Google has put her right: he's thirty-five. The dimple she's seen in photos gives him a boyish feel, and ridiculous elbow patches notwithstanding, he looks good for his age – for any age – with no sign of hair loss or male pattern baldness. A little bit of grey, perhaps, but if anything, the salt-and-pepper specks in his almost-black hair are annoyingly attractive. He'll be wanting, no doubt, to settle, to have kids. She's only twenty-eight, and not ready for that yet. True, the hustling for freelance gigs and the running around the country to bookshops events and festivals can get a little stressful, a little exhausting. It's also true that in the not-too-distant past, she'd stood inside Waterstones in front of a face-out copy of Sophie Kinsella's *The Burnout*, swallowing back the prickle of inconvenient tears which she managed to stave off with the hasty booking of a solo holiday to Corfu. But she's not ready for the settling, for the kids. It feels like there are more adventures to be had out there in the big wide world first.

Yes, it's definitely for the best that Alex isn't The One. But it still bothers her that the universe played this cruel trick. There were choirs of angels, after all. Does that not count for anything anymore?

Thank goodness for Lily, who has responded to her SOS WhatsApp with a good-natured series of GIFs and an invitation for dinner. *Gareth's out at a work thing this evening*, she's written. *I'll make you your favourite pasta dish and we can talk, or watch* The Great British Sewing Bee, *or have* The Great British Sewing Bee *on in the background while we talk. Whatever you like.*

Lily, as always, is a gem.

* * *

As promised, Lily has made what she calls her Magic Pasta – magic because it's so simple, yet so tasty. She refuses to divulge exactly what's in it – beyond bacon, courgette, cream, herbs of some kind – even though it has now served its ostensible purpose: she'd always said the only way to get the recipe was to marry her, and Gareth had taken her at her word. Lily made it for him on their third date, and now here we are, four years later, Lily successfully coupled up, Jess still begging for the recipe so that she can work her own magic on an unsuspecting man.

She takes a deep breath and begins this particular instalment of recipe begging.

'So,' Jess says, twirling her fork in the linguine. 'I thought I'd found a worthy recipient of your find-a-husband pasta.'

'Magic Pasta,' Lily corrects. On this, she is very particular. The proper terminology must be adhered to.

'Magic, find-a-husband pasta.'

Lily takes a sip of wine, perhaps fortifying herself. 'I feel we're getting sidetracked onto your usual pleas for my recipe. Tell me about this worthy recipient.'

Jess has saved all the crucial information for a conversation in person. Her WhatsApp was deliberately cryptic. 'Not worthy, as it turns out.'

'Okay.'

'I almost got a book deal today.' It is only a slight exaggeration of the facts. And Jess has always wanted to say, 'I got a book deal.' This is close enough.

'That sounds exciting. But what does *almost* mean?'

'It's a long story.'

In preparation, Lily refills their wine glasses, and then Jess talks. She is aware of the length of her own monologue, and regularly checks Lily's eyes for signs of glazing over, but she seems to be following, with appropriate *oohs* and *aahs* and cries of, *That's outrageous*, and, *How could the universe be so cruel?*

'But you're going to do this, right?' Lily says, once Jess pauses for breath and a large swig of Pinot Grigio.

Jess looks at her sternly, the *were-you-even-listening* look that Lily has always called her teacher glare.

'I mean, obviously he's an arrogant sod, and he is rude and unappreciative, and he doesn't understand the importance of the romance genre and thinks he is superior because he writes literary fiction . . .'

Fine, so she *has* been listening after all.

'But, like, Jess, what an amazing opportunity! You've

always wanted to write a book! This is definitely a step in the right direction.'

Jess was afraid of this. Afraid of herself, too, and her own propensity to cave, especially when something new and fun is involved. Especially when that something new and fun is a man whom, despite her misgivings about his personality, she quite enjoyed looking at.

'He clearly doesn't want me to help. When I think about having to be in a room with him, trying to convince him that I know what I'm talking about, that my ideas are good ones . . . well, the words *blood* and *stone* spring to mind.'

'It's not like you to shy away from a challenge.'

Lily knows how to push all Jess's buttons. Words like *shy*, words like *challenge*. She is right, of course. Jess had just let her irritation with Alex momentarily cloud her judgement. She takes a sip of wine, tries the idea out in her head. Of course she can do this. She is more than capable of rising to this particular challenge. Of wearing Alex down, if that's what it takes, until he holds his hands up in surrender and utters the magic words, 'Fine! We'll try it your way!' And he'll see, Nathan will see, the world will see, that she actually *does* have what it takes. That her hours of reading books weren't just about escapism – there's nothing wrong with escapism, anyway; she lives for it – but that they were teaching her something, making her into a great writer.

By the end of the evening, she and Lily are toasting Jess's imminent success. Alex's, too, of course. But mostly Jess's.

Chapter Six

ALEX

Alex's feet take him back to his favourite London Bridge café almost against his will. Certainly against his better judgement. But he's been summoned by an email from Jess to discuss their working arrangements. and while he's still not so much on the fence about them working together as firmly on the *no, thank you* side, he has to admit that he wants to see her again. He's fascinated by her, in an academic sense. And character study is vital for a writer.

The more he has thought about Jess, the more intrigued he has been. Intrigued about whether all that carefree jollity is a front, or authentic but living in her alongside deeper, more complex emotions. (He has seen her Instagram posts and read her Substack, and surely nobody can be that enthusiastic about everything all of the time.) Intrigued about why Nathan thought that Jess, of all people, might be a good match for him (purely authorially speaking, of course). Intrigued – and despite himself, impressed – by her strength and passion when she defended romance novels in conversation with him, sure in her convictions, even if he does still think those convictions are misguided. He's always preferred people who have that kind of determination, especially when they can back it up with their own internal logic, even if that logic is a little bewildering. All of this is infinitely preferable to people who just glide through life seemingly unaffected by anything, even though deep down he aspires to be one of those people. It just seems as if it would be a lot easier, somehow. Probably less suited to being a writer of renown, though. So here we are.

And here, also, standing at the counter, waiting for her coffee, is Jess. A cardigan shot through with embroidered daisies that would look ridiculous on anybody else. Her honey blonde hair swept up in a messy-but-classy bun-like style. Big hoop earrings last seen on his parents' Kylie Minogue tapes from the Eighties.

He clears his throat next to Jess.

'Hello,' she says. Something behind her usual cheerfulness: resignation, maybe.

It's fair enough, in a way. He hasn't exactly been kind to her so far. It's not, after all, her fault that his first complete draft was a depressing mess, drastic times calling for drastic measures – and it's not her fault that Nathan deemed her to be the appropriate drastic measure. And Nathan has so often proved to be wise, in life and in writing. Maybe he should give him a chance with this seemingly crazy idea.

But for now, how to keep this conversation going? To avoid an awkward silence, or worse, tedious small talk about the weather, Alex reaches for observational humour. 'I don't mean to alarm you,' he says, 'but there's a pencil in your hair.'

Others may have smirked at this line. But she grins, seemingly all joy. 'I know,' she says. 'I put it there myself.'

'I see.' He nods. But he has to ask. 'Why?'

'To hold my bun together.'

He feels himself frowning, his forehead creasing. From his years growing up with many sisters, he is all too familiar with scrunchies and hairgrips and multicoloured multipacks of elastic bands designed for ponytails. He's even done his fair share of hair brushing and, at the peak of his pseudo-parenting, French braids. He always admired the ball girls at Wimbledon, though, how tidy their hair was. He never quite got it that even on any of his sisters. But then, that would have required them to sit still.

In all his years as a makeshift hair stylist, though, he'd never come across the pencil as a hair accessory. At the bookshop, it had seemed as if the pencil had been stuck in her hair just for somewhere to put it between markups of a book she was reviewing. This time, though, it seems more complex than that, more deliberate.

'How does that work?'

Flat white for Alex, the barista calls. He nods, but does not take it. He is very distracted. Because Jess has taken down her bun. She's holding the pencil, and he very much hopes that isn't so that she can stab him with it.

She shakes her head, as if to dispel that notion, and

her waves of blonde hair fall around her face, brushing each of her shoulders in turn, then her neck, then her shoulders again. He is, somehow, transfixed. Unable to swallow, though he desperately needs to. This close to her, he notices her freckles for the first time, a dusting across the bridge of her nose and along her cheekbones. He clenches his fists, defending himself against the instinct to reach out and touch them.

She turns to face away from him, so he can watch as she puts her bun back together. He grits his teeth together, further defence for his heart and his hormones – this time against the curve of her neck, more freckles where it meets her shoulders, as she puts the pencil in her mouth and lifts her hair into a ponytail. She wraps it around her finger – and he sympathises. In this moment, it feels like she could easily do the same thing to him. She twists her hair up, threads the pencil in, out, in, out.

Jess spins around to face him. 'See?' she says, brushing back the strand of hair that has fallen out and now frames her face. 'Easy.'

'I see,' Alex squeaks out, like a teenager whose voice is still in the process of breaking. He clears his throat, finding the lower register. 'Thanks for . . . that.'

Flat white for Alex, calls the barista again, in the tone of someone who is trying hard not to sound irritated because of having to repeat herself. *No, no, no*, he thinks. *Don't break the spell.*

And it does, in this moment, feel like a spell. True, he was attracted to Jess when they first met in the bookshop. But that was *then*. That was before she had become an instrument of torture. Is it possible that her hair alone would be capable of entrapping him like this?

'So,' she says. 'Have you decided?'

'Decided what?' Alex is having trouble accessing his thoughts. On account, perhaps, of blood having rushed away from his brain and towards other places.

'Are you going to let me work on this novel with you?'

'Your hair is trapped in your earring,' he says. Which does not answer the question, but does buy him time. And does also give him an excuse to reach forward and gently remove the forward-falling strand, brushing her cheek as he does so. Her skin is so soft.

She looks up at him, her eyes full of – something. Asking, perhaps, to be taken seriously enough to work with him. In this moment, it feels impossible to deny her that.

'I think that would be fine,' he squeaks out. He has got to get control of his voice. Of his mind. Of himself.

'Good,' she says. She seems to be satisfied, and he wishes the same were true of him. 'I can work with *fine*.'

'So when do we start?'

Jess picks up the coffee that's been called for her – another flat white, though he's surprised that he doesn't add sugar. If pressed, he would have guessed she'd have sugar in her coffee, marshmallows in her hot chocolate, strawberry sauce on her ice cream.

She leads him to a table. 'That's what we're here to discuss, isn't it? Get your diary out.' She reaches into her backpack for an actual, physical notebook – colourful and loud, of course. Then she retrieves her phone from her pocket and hands it to him.

'Put your number in there,' she says.

It shocks him how easily he obeys, unthinkingly and without argument. Is this how their relationship is going to be from now on? *Let's hope not*, he thinks. *This spells trouble.*

Chapter Seven

JESS

Today's the day Alex and Jess are officially starting work, and Jess has taken maybe a bit longer than usual to pick her outfit. It's that awkward, not-quite-spring time of the year, when she digs her coldish-weather clothes back out for one last outing before she moves on to her summer wardrobe. Boots, scarves, layers. Soft jumpers. Merino wool. Looking good helps Jess to feel good, feel confident. It has nothing to do with Alex himself, of course. The electric shock that Jess felt when Alex's finger brushed her hair away from her earring was probably just static. He is not handsome enough to tempt her into trying to impress him. And if she *does* impress him, she'd like it to be with her writing, not for how good a messy pencil bun looks on her or for her ability to pick a colour palette. She only wants to teach him a lesson about who deserves to be taken seriously. She doesn't care what he thinks about *her*, only that he is put in his place and that his arrogant assumptions are corrected.

But choosing the right scarf (maroon and white gingham) to go with the new boots she picked up in an end-of-season sale (dark brown knee-highs, block heel) and the right in-between-the-seasons coat (dark denim), then hunting around for her tortoiseshell glasses . . . All of this has taken longer than Jess planned, and she's running a bit late. So she doesn't have time to do much more than glance at the postcard she picks up from her doormat. Her mum is in Santorini this time, having a wonderful holiday, enjoying the sun, and all the rest of it. Nothing fundamentally different from the postcards Jess has been receiving all her life: the primary way in which her mother has conducted a relationship with her since Jess moved out to go to university. They are punctuated with calls that always seem to end before Jess has fully updated her mum on her life, with a quick 'must dash, love' and some air kisses down the phone. At least it makes for a fun collection of postcards on her fridge. She'll find a spot there for this one later. But for now, she's more excited about wearing her boots for the first time. She eyed them all winter and was thrilled to see them on sale. She's glad she's getting to wear them before the days get warmer and she's back to Mary Janes and sandals.

But it turns out that wearing a pair of boots for the first time is maybe not the wisest choice for travelling across London, from Pimlico to Hampstead (of course Hampstead; where else could Alex be expected to live?). Definitely not the wisest choice if you're trying to rush down the Tube stairs because you have a hunch that the person you're meeting is the type not to suffer unpunctuality gladly, and you don't want to give him the upper hand by starting off on the wrong foot.

And it's exactly that kind of tangle of limbs that gets Jess into trouble as she twists her ankle on the last step down and has to cling on to the banister to stay upright and avoid, if at all possible, landing on her tailbone.

It's fine, it's fine, it's fine, she tells herself, checking around her and feeling grateful that nobody was there to witness her humiliation. After a second or two of deep breaths, it really does seem fine. The ankle seems fine while she sits on the Victoria Line to Euston; it twinges a bit on the escalator at Warren Street when she changes to the Northern Line; it seems fine again while she is sitting on the least dirty seat she can find on the next train. But by the time she's got out at the station at Hampstead and walked up the steep hill immediately outside, she thinks she might be about to die.

And when Alex opens the door to his – of course! – adorable house (a yellow door!), it's all she can do to keep from falling into his arms and begging him to carry her over the threshold. She thinks it takes a lot of self-control not to groan when he points to the stairs. Apparently, not even a three-time-bestselling author can afford an entire house in Hampstead; he has a flat, like everyone else she knows, though he doesn't share it with anyone, which deserves some credit. But then, he's in his mid-thirties, and maybe that's just what being in your mid-thirties is like – being a proper grown-up. Jess knows she is lucky to be able to afford Pimlico at all, never mind alone and in her twenties – a combination of hard work, unexpected professional success, and, let's be honest, help from her grandparents. They like having her close by, and she likes being able to hang out with them and with Ivy, her little cousin who often stays with them. And, of course, she loves Pimlico. Who wouldn't? It's central – easy to get everywhere on the whizzy Victoria Line, the station a three-minute walk away from her flat. But Pimlico is also quiet, with the friendly feel of a village where the local newsagent calls you by name and the owners of the legendary greasy spoon know to always give you extra mushrooms.

'Are you okay?' Alex asks, an unusually kind concern in his voice. Or perhaps it's not unusual. Perhaps it's unfair to judge him based on just two meetings, one of which was a contentious one with his editor. But whether or not it's unusual, it's certainly unexpected. 'You look a bit pink.'

'I'm fine,' she says. 'I was hurrying to get here on time, and that hill . . . you know?'

Alex looks at Jess intently, as if trying to decide whether she's lying, and then gestures for her to go first up the stairs. Gallantry, she chooses to think. The kind of good manners that comes from being educated at one of those fancy private schools. (Westminster, to be precise, not that she has memorised his Wikipedia page.) Nonetheless, she's aware of his eyes on her as they walk up the stairs, assessing, she hopes, her clothes (good), or noticing how flattering this corduroy skirt is on her curves (also very good, if she does say so herself), rather than how pathetically she is hobbling.

'What's wrong with your ankle?' he asks, when they're two steps up and she finds herself, again, clinging to a banister as if her entire life depended on it.

'Oh, nothing. These are new boots and they're taking some getting used to, that's all.' Jess winces. Hardly the put-together, super-professional image she was hoping to put across today.

'Looks like a little more than that.'

She's not sure how to respond. To reiterate the lie, or to call him out for being a know-it-all, or, better, to thank him for his concern? Surely the latter is most appropriate, but it sticks in her throat a little, and it doesn't convey cool, nonchalant, and in-control in quite the way she intended to during this first meeting, just the two of them. So she goes with awkward silence. Always a great option – works in almost every circumstance.

'Sit, sit,' he says when they get to the top of the stairs and he opens the door for her, seemingly unfazed by said awkward silence. 'And maybe take those boots off?'

It takes every clenched muscle in Jess's body for her to control her face, so as not to give away how much it hurts to remove the offending boot. Sitting on a chair next to hers, Alex indicates his lap.

'Let me see.'

Surely, he can't mean . . . But she searches his face, and it seems as if he does indeed mean it. He nods, points at his lap again.

'My bark is worse than my bite,' he says – maybe an apology of sorts? 'I promise.'

She can't help but smile, even as she gingerly places the offending foot on him. She thanks the gods of weather for the fact she's wearing tights – it's been far too long since she shaved her legs, and imagine the mortification of *that*. Unless he can feel her hairy legs *through* her tights? Oh no, he can't, can he? She would *die*. She is pretty much dying now. She's burning up. She's probably caught a chill, like a heroine in an Austen novel who can't go out for a stroll without courting death. Will she have to live in this Hampstead flat for the next month while her ankle heals? That's probably not how these things work in the twenty-first century.

Or maybe she's burning up for other reasons. Her foot feels electric where it is touching him.

'May I?' he asks.

She isn't sure, exactly, what he is asking. But she nods, because in this moment, she'd probably say yes to anything. She is wondering if she has also somehow hit her head and concussed herself so badly that she has forgotten it happened? She is feeling oddly woozy.

He cradles her ankle with care, feeling for pain points.

'Ouch,' she says, when he finds one.

'Sorry,' he says. And then, 'Good news. It's not broken. Just sprained or twisted.'

As far as Jess knows, Alex doesn't have any kind of medical training, but there's something authoritative about his voice, and she can't help but trust him, or at least believe he knows what he's doing. He lifts her leg gently, stands, and places her ankle back on the chair. 'Stay with it up like that,' he says. 'I'll go and get some ice.'

He returns with a green Birds Eye packet, which for some reason makes her smile.

'Rice,' he says, somewhat absurdly.

'Pretty sure those are frozen peas.'

The crease of concern between his eyebrows disappears, replaced by faint crow's feet as he smiles. All of these, signs of age and wisdom. And experience tending to the injured, apparently. Oh, and the dimple: there it is, finally, in person. Not just a rumour or a photo on the internet. 'No, I mean, RICE. Rest, Ice, Compression, Elevation.'

'Ah.'

He hands her the peas. 'You have to give it time to settle.'

'How do you know this stuff?'

He shrugs. 'Lots of experience looking after younger siblings with minor injuries.'

And then, just like that, the moment has passed.

'Now,' he says. 'About this book.'

Chapter Eight

ALEX

The sight of Jess hobbling, visibly injured, has done something to Alex's insides that he wishes it hadn't. The fact that she was trying to hide it from him made it endearing, somehow. Why she'd insisted on impractical footwear is beyond him, though. They're nice boots, and he has to admit that they complement her outfit, but surely, getting places efficiently and uninjured should be the main priority when it comes to what you wear on your feet.

He doesn't, of course, convey any of this to Jess. Instead, he brings her tea, gives her some cushions to further elevate her foot, and checks multiple times that she is comfortable, until she seems almost annoyed with him for continually asking. Alex knows he can be accused of many things, but ungentlemanly behaviour is not one of them.

'So,' she says, reaching for her tote bag and pulling out a wad of pages that he recognises as his novel. They'd been pristine when Nathan had handed them to her – shiny and bright and full of potential – but now they're crumpled and scribbled on. He wouldn't be surprised if they were out of order, too. 'Yes. Your book.'

Alex holds his breath, waiting. *Is approval from others something you look for, do you think?* his counsellor had asked him in their last session. *Doesn't everybody?* he'd replied. He isn't sure why Jess's approval, in particular, matters to him, though. Perhaps for the same reason that he'd been struck dumb by the way her hair had brushed her shoulders at the coffee shop. Perhaps because she is only the second person to have read this particular book. Perhaps because she'd clearly sensed his disdain for the kinds of novels she loves, and may want, in retaliation, to express her disdain of literary fiction in general, and his writing in particular. Which would be fair enough. But probably just because what she thinks, and her suggestions, and her ideas, are going to shape not just the novel itself from here on in, but also the next few months of his work, of his *life*, and determine how miserable or otherwise he is going to be.

Jess tucks a strand of hair behind her ear. There's no sign of a pencil holding her bun up today. 'Well, first, let me say – I really enjoyed the read. I thought it was very immersive. I sat down to have a flick through for half an hour after our meeting with Nathan, and when I next looked up, it was dark and I realised my stomach had been rumbling for ages.'

He should take a moment to savour this. After all, isn't this what every author wants? For their audience to be so caught up in the story, or in the prose – or preferably both – that they forget they are reading, lose track of time, miss their stop on the Underground? But he knows what she is doing: the compliment sandwich that he remembers all too well from his studies in the US. An attempt to lower his defences by starting with something positive. Any minute now, she will launch into what is, he thinks, mistakenly termed *constructive criticism*. It has always felt destructive to him.

'I also thought the premise was brilliant. It reminded me of those old epic disaster films from the Seventies – you know, *The Poseidon Adventure*, *The Towering Inferno*. You get to know people's backstories, and you worry about them, you get emotionally invested, you want them to get out alive. Also, the best episodes of *Casualty*.'

He can feel his eyebrows responding. *Casualty*? The trashy weekly soapified drama about a hospital? He wants to respond, but he has been trained. In writing workshops, you sit in silence while the compliment sandwich is delivered by person after person around a round table. Only at the end are you allowed a few cursory words, which must include *thank you*, even when you want to murder everyone for how profoundly they've misunderstood what you were trying to do and ruined it in your own eyes as well as everyone else's.

'But I've noticed,' she says, and the *but* is his sign to brace himself, to roll himself up into a ball like a hedgehog, spikes out, to protect himself, 'that all the characters with the most interesting backstories are men. I also wonder if third person omniscient is the way to go with this one. Have you considered multiple-point-of-view?'

Has he considered . . . As if he doesn't think of every possible option before putting pen to paper.

She is looking at him as if expecting a response. As if this isn't a writing workshop in Iowa but a collaboration between two people who don't need to abide by esoteric and slightly brutal rules devised in the Forties by some random academic.

'I didn't want to write from the point of view of women. Get accused of – you know. Coopting an identity not my own. Et cetera.'

'Yeah, I can see that. Lucky you've got me, then.'

'Got you?'

'To help write the women.'

'Help write the women?'

'Is it me, or is there an echo in here?'

Alex makes a show of looking around the room. Then, despite himself, wanting in on Jess's pathetic attempt at a joke, 'Is it me, or is there an echo in here?'

She shakes her head in despair at him as you might at an unruly four-year-old. Which, as far as Jess is concerned, is perfectly fair: his childish joke deserves it.

'Sorry,' he says. 'I just thought – I saw your role as more editing, not actually writing, *per se*.'

He knows that bringing out the Latin is borderline insufferable. It's a move he learned a long time ago in an attempt to assert intellectual and educational dominance. It's also one that Elodie, his first serious post-university girlfriend, called him out on more than once. It wasn't what led to their breakup, but it also wasn't *not* what led to their breakup.

Jess tilts her head and widens her eyes.

'My role?' she repeats.

'There really is an echo in here.'

She presses her lips together, as if attempting to keep herself from saying something she'll regret later. Not that he is looking at her lips or has any interest in them. She doesn't break eye contact; she is daring him to speak. To say more. But he knows better than to do that.

'Nathan seemed to think,' she says eventually, and he is disproportionately glad of this small victory, of Jess being the one to give into the urge of filling the silence, 'that I should have considerable input into the crafting of this book.'

She waits for him to respond. When he doesn't, she shuffles in her chair, rearranges her ankle slightly, winces. If he didn't know better, he might suspect this to be a ploy for sympathy, or at least for him to back down in deference to her pain. And though he *does* know better, something twists in his insides again.

'Fine,' he says, reluctantly. He knows he is being played, but he has no more control over the situation than a pawn on a chess board does.

'Fine, as in, you'll let me help write the women?'

'Fine as in I'll let you try and help me write *something*.' He knows he doesn't really have a choice; Nathan has made that much abundantly clear. He is just having trouble letting go of the illusion of control. 'We can discuss the finer points later.'

He looks at her expectantly, nodding at the manuscript. He can't bring himself to ask for more of her 'constructive criticism', but he knows there is more, and he might as well get it out of the way now.

'I also think . . .' She takes a deep breath, a sign perhaps that she is expecting him to push back on what she going to say. Or maybe she is expecting him to push back on everything. Which would not be entirely unreasonable, as expectations go. 'I think they should all survive the plane crash.'

'All of them?'

Jess nods, her blonde hair bobbing on her shoulders, which increases the earnestness of the moment, somehow.

'That's very romance-ending, happily-ever-after, Jess.'

He has never used her name out loud before. He likes the way it sounds, likes the way it feels, the *s* landing softly on his tongue.

She doesn't rise to the obvious bait. 'Just because they all survive doesn't mean they don't have issues,' she says. And then she says some other things, but he doesn't really hear them, because the sentence has landed, somehow, deep in his gut, the way a punch might. His ears ring; he feels, inexplicably, as if he were underwater.

When he emerges, she is drawing her substantial remarks to a close.

'What do you think?' she says.

'About what?'

'What I've just said.'

He has no choice but to hedge. 'It's a lot to consider.'

'I know. And I know it's not easy to hear criticism from – you know, a reader of inferior genres.'

It's a dig, and Alex shouldn't bristle, but he does. The

usual internal hedgehog pose he adopts when hearing feedback on his work doesn't seem to be working when it comes to Jess.

And that, no doubt, is going to be a problem.

Chapter Nine

JESS

It's hard to stay frustrated with someone so good-looking, someone who has so tenderly cradled your ankle and produced peas from the freezer to reduce the swelling. But Jess is giving it a good go, nonetheless.

As she talks about Alex's book, she can see him physically retreating, his shoulders slumping. Shouldn't he be used to having his work closely examined? From what she understands of weird writing courses like the one he went on in America, you're supposed to sit there and take it while a room full of people lob their feedback at you, then graciously thank them for stamping on a piece of your soul, and then go away and incorporate their suggestions into another draft of your piece of writing.

Isn't that exactly what they're doing here? And she is just one person. One person, whose criticisms he should surely be able to easily dismiss, since he seems to think she knows so little about what constitutes good writing. She knows writers can be tender-hearted and sensitive – although she's seen no evidence of either trait in Alex so far – but she would have expected him to have grown a thicker skin by now. And she is being honest, but not unkind. She's even looked up how to do the compliment sandwich!

'Sorry,' she says, and he looks up, startled.

'About what?'

What she really means is that she's sorry in the general British sense of wanting desperately to clear the air and not being exactly sure how. She's sorry if she's made things awkward. But mostly, she's sorry they're in this position, the two of them. Sorry she ever opened Nathan's email and took his offer seriously. But she can't really say any of that – not without making things even *more* awkward and weird, so she goes with a true *sorry*, an apology *sorry*.

'I'm pretty sure I sounded snarky back then, but I know I don't enjoy hearing other people pick apart my work, either. You've poured a lot into writing this book, and it is good! A lot of it is working really well.'

'Working really well,' he repeats. '*Working*. People used that word a lot on my MFA course.' He does air quotes with his fingers and puts on what is a truly terrible American accent. '*The present tense is not working for me. That character's motivations are not working for me.*'

Jess can't figure out what his tone means. Is he sad? Bitter? Nostalgic for the days when he was the golden boy with a whole literary future ahead of him, rather than stuck in the mire of trying to sustain his career? She also can't work out why she cares. Or whether she *should* care.

But if they're going to work together – if she's going to be, essentially, his voice – she should probably take some time to get to know him. Understand how he ticks. Understand . . . well, the character's motivations. Whether or not they 'work for her'.

'Did you enjoy your course?'

It's such a bland question; she hears that as soon as it's out of her mouth. But she's got to start somewhere.

'*Enjoy* is an interesting word,' he says. She waits for more, but he clearly enjoys being a man of mystery. She waits a little bit longer. Then she gets tired of waiting.

'Say more about that,' she says.

He laughs. 'You sound like my therapist.'

She would definitely like him to say more about *that*. A therapist? What does Alex have to be in therapy for? Writer's block, perhaps? It did take him forever to write that not-exactly-brilliant first draft. And she's also, despite herself, a little impressed. In her admittedly limited experience, it's pretty unusual for a man not only to take responsibility for his mental health and go to therapy, but also not to be afraid to admit it to a near-stranger, even if – as Jess suspects – it did slip out accidentally. If Alex was anyone else, she might even find it a little bit attractive. But if she did, that would make this whole situation very awkward indeed, so it's just as well it's not the case.

'The course was good,' Alex says at last, probably realising Jess isn't just going to drop this and move on. 'I learned a lot, including more about literary theory than I ever wanted to. I made some good friends. And I loved living in DC. It's a really beautiful place. So much history, and beautiful architecture. The restaurant scene is incredible. Lots of amazing bookshops, even if my favourite one did close, because the guy who owned it decided to be a piano teacher instead.'

He's the happiest she's seen him yet, when he talks about DC. His face opens up; his dimple pops. She'd like to ask him more about that. But she's curious about something else, too.

'You didn't want to go to Iowa?' She's showing off. Letting him know that she, too, knows about American MFAs. She knows that Iowa is the birthplace of the writing workshop that the Publishing Industrial Complex has come to accept as normal, when it seems to Jess that it's really, really not. She knows that Iowa is the Harvard of writing courses, still *the* place for aspiring literary writers of a certain type. Exactly Alex's type, in fact.

And just like that, the light has gone from his face again. 'That *was* the plan.'

'Or, you know . . . somewhere closer to home. I've heard that the Creative Writing MA in Norwich is good. The Iowa of the UK, I think someone called it.'

'Norwich?' His tone suggests Jess might as well have mentioned the moon as a suitable place to study creative writing.

Her tortoiseshell glasses have slid down her nose a little, which is perfect for looking at Alex over the top of them in the manner of a stern schoolteacher wanting to correct a mistake.

'What, is the University of East Anglia not good enough for you? You know, the place that trained Kazuo Ishiguro?'

To be honest, she'd live in Norwich now if she could. London is convenient for getting to all the places she wants to go to. It's been home forever. It's also where Lily lives, where a lot of her university friends have ended up. And, of course, where her beloved grandparents still have the flat she spent so many nights in as a child, just down the road from her tiny Pimlico flat. But she prefers the pace of life in Norwich. It's slower; it gives you time to appreciate things. Between the UEA's prestigious writing course, the National Centre for Writing, and the brilliant independent bookshops, there's all the literary culture anyone could ever want – and it's all within easy walkable distance. She loves getting around on foot, rather than faffing around with Tubes and buses and trains. When she studied there, she would look forward to wandering through the market, picking out flowers, a different kind every week, though she secretly always wanted tulips.

'It's not that. It's—'

His phone lights up on the table next to him. He glances at it. *Georgina*, it says. A sister, or stepsister, or maybe half-sister, Jess knows. Nothing suspicious. 'Sorry,' he says, once. And then again, 'Sorry. I have to take this.'

Jess tries not to let her irritation show on her face. *How convenient,* she thinks, *for him to get out of that conversation.*

While he's gone, she lets herself stew a little bit. There have to be easier ways to write a book. Easier than repeatedly meeting up with someone who clearly thinks she's his intellectual inferior and trying to get him to understand that a little bit of lightness improves a book, that the darkness is only beautiful by contrast.

Jess read Alex's book through once, with the critical eye of a reviewer. She liked it. A solid four out of five stars. But not one that would have Bookstagrammers reaching for the usual complaint that Goodreads won't let them have half stars, which is a shame because this one is really a four and a half. No: this one is firmly a four. Which is fine! It's more than fine. But she knows Alex can do better. Nathan clearly knows it, too.

So she reads it again, paying particular attention to the female characters she was intrigued by. Thinking of new characters she could write into the story. Colour coding, underlining, scribbling, mind mapping. And then she got to work, with her own scenes.

Or tried to.

Everything that came out was . . . blah.

Which is infuriating, because she knows she can do this. She knows she can write, be funny, inject humour into serious thoughts. Maybe the pressure to prove herself is getting to her. Not that she cares about proving herself to Alex. Clearly, nothing she writes for him will ever be good enough, 'strike the right tone', 'blend with his writing'. *Et cetera*, as he would no doubt say, with his pompous Latin. But she does care about proving herself to Nathan. Proving herself to *herself*.

All of this feels incredibly fraught. She has a job she loves. She loves touring bookshops to review them on her newsletter and post pictures to her social media. She loves interviewing authors for her podcast. She loves tracking her affiliate links, noticing them getting clicked, people buying books she's recommended – books that deserve to be better known, books that aren't just the ones that everyone is talking about, the ones with the posters on the Tube. Does she really need to get involved in the writing of one? Enjoying other people's books – getting paid to enjoy them, no less – seems so much easier. Maybe some dreams are meant to stay that. Just dreams.

If only she didn't have Lily's voice in her head: *It's not like you to shy away from a challenge.* Jess has always loved her own sense of adventure, of get-up-and-go, the thing that propelled her to start her own business as a bookish influencer when her friends were getting worthy or well-paid, but slightly dull-sounding, jobs as teachers or management consultants or investment bankers. She wants every day to be different, every week to be slightly unpredictable. The emails that come from nowhere, asking her to jump on a train to chair an interview panel at a romance readers' retreat. The publicists sliding into her DMs to offer her an early copy of the hottest debut novel of the moment. The endorphin rush of hitting *post* on social media and watching the likes come in. When she graduated, she figured that if it didn't work out, she'd have the rest of her life to choose something worthy or well-paid instead. But it's worked out so far. And now here she is, in the home of a super successful, if marginally annoying, bestselling author. Not just to interview him or bask in reflected glory, but to *help* him. Twenty-one-year-old Jess would have squealed in glee.

Twenty-eight-year-old Jess is less sure, however.

Behind her, Alex clears his throat, his phone call finished.

'Sorry about that,' he says. 'Just my sister arranging babysitting.'

Jess does her best to smile less tightly than she naturally might. He made it seem so urgent. Was he so desperate to get out of the conversation? Or just unable to say no to his siblings? 'No worries,' she says.

'So what were we saying?' he asks, sitting opposite her this time.

She shuffles her foot on the chair, rearranges the packet of by-now-entirely-defrosted peas. 'You were telling me that Norwich is inferior.'

'I don't believe those were my actual words.'

'It was in your tone, though.'

He rolls his eyes. Actually rolls his eyes. Jess can't believe the rudeness, the condescension. But with her ankle the way it is, it's not like she could make a dramatic exit, even if she wanted to.

'Maybe we should go back to the book,' Alex says.

'Probably best.'

He makes eye contact and holds it for a long time, in a bizarre kind of power play. She focusses on the deep chocolate of his eyes (Lindt 85 per cent, if she had to pick), resisting the urge to look away. Whatever is happening right now, it feels important that she not be the first to flinch.

'You've made a lot of great notes for me here,' he says, pulling his gaze from hers and looking down at the stack of paper. 'I think probably the best thing is for me to have some time to digest them, and then I'll be in touch?'

Jess can't tell if he is fobbing her off. But it doesn't matter, in this moment, because it means one thing: she gets to leave this flat, hobble down the stairs and back to Pimlico, back to her rainbow bookshelves and her Instagram props and her makeshift podcast studio – safe, solid ground, where she doesn't need to prove herself or justify her existence or sit around being condescended to.

'Sure,' she says. She hands him back the defrosted peas with a smile she hopes is both apologetic and thankful.

Alex offers her his arm to lean on as she makes her way to the stairs. She does her best to ignore the jolt of electricity that shoots up her hand when she leans on him. She is starting to wonder if he is, in fact, radioactive, and that's why there seems to be so much electricity around him? If those two things are even related.

She's never been much for the sciences. Probably best not to think about it too hard.

Chapter Ten

From: Alex Maxwell
To: Jess Martin
Subject: Your feedback

Jess,

Thank you so much for the detail and attention with which you read my novel. If anything I say in this email seems less than grateful, I apologise in advance. I am genuinely impressed with, even touched by, the care you took. (As well as intrigued and somewhat amused by the colour coding.)

However, I must disagree with several of your observations. The women are not just *there in the background*. They play an important role, even if they don't narrate *per se*.

The scenes you have inserted, even allowing for the fact that they are first drafts, do not work for me as either a writer or a critical reader of the novel as a whole.

As for the repetitions you suggest may grate on a certain kind of reader, they are what's known as *anaphora* and *epistrophe* – deliberate figures of speech to create a certain style.

I must also re-iterate that having all the passengers survive seems profoundly unserious, and something that belongs in a romcom novel with a cartoon cover (no offence intended) rather than in the kind of thoughtful literary fiction that my readers have come to expect from me.

Along the same lines, though I admit the jokes you've inserted do represent the right sort of dark humour for the story in question (and though, I further admit, they raised a smile with this reader), they are nonetheless inappropriate for this kind of work.

All best,
Alex

PS: I trust your ankle is healing well.

From: Jess Martin
To: Alex Maxwell
Subject: Your feedback

Hi Alex,

My ankle is doing much better, thank you. I appreciate both the peas and the RICE advice. The offending boots have been temporarily confined to the naughty step in the shoe cupboard to think about what they've done.

It really was a pleasure reading your novel – I wasn't just saying that to make any constructive criticism more palatable.

I'm sorry that we disagree so much on so many fundamental elements of the book and on how we can work together to elevate it. How do you propose we move forward?

Best wishes,
Jess

From: Jess Martin
To: Alex Maxwell
Subject: Your arrogance

Alexander,

Obviously, I'm never going to send this, but just typing it is helpful to get it off my chest. Maybe it's the writer in me – the writer that you clearly don't think exists or has any value, but that's your prerogative.

It isn't charming to phrase an email like a character in a Dickens novel would. Get with it. This is 2026.

My suggested scenes had clearly written all over them 'obviously, you can write these much better, this is just a broad-brush suggestion'.

Also, saying 'no offence' after something offensive doesn't make it any less offensive.

Also, also, your constant use of Latin is not endearing or impressive. It's irritating and pompous. It so happens that I have an A Level in Latin, but I don't feel the need to constantly brandish it around like some kind of blunt weapon.

Also, also, also, I know what anaphora and epistrophe are, and I understand the Rule of Three. I just don't necessarily think a novel is best served by making constant use of the same figures of speech over and over again. Yours certainly isn't.

Your name, by the way, is an anagram of Relax, Edna. I wish you'd take that advice. Maybe you'd be happier. Maybe we all would.

Yours disrespectfully, because frankly that's all you deserve,

Jess

From: Jess Martin
To: Alex Maxwell
Subject: Jess Martin has attempted to recall an email

From: Alex Maxwell
To: Jess Martin
Subject: Too late

J,
It is nice to know what you think of me. Not that I was really in any doubt, but if those doubts had existed, it would have been a relief to have them assuaged.
A.

From: Alex Maxell
To:
Subject: My arrogance, apparently

Jessica,

At least, I assume it's Jessica. Although I wouldn't put it past you to be above having an actual full name. Full names are very *normal* and *boring*, after all.

I actually *am* never going to send this to you, because I am not careless enough to accidentally press send. See how I haven't added your email address into the required field? That is to doubly make sure that if I *do* accidentally press *send* – say, because fury is preventing me from thinking logically – I am protected from my own stupidity.

One day, we will look back at this whole *débâcle* and laugh, and laugh. (I'd normally add a third *and laugh* but wouldn't want to offend your sensibilities by overdoing the Rule of Three.) What larks! We could have been rich and famous, both of us successful authors and perhaps even friends! But instead we are both stubborn and arrogant in our own endearing ways. It will make for a great story. Though perhaps we'd rather have the success, fame, and friendship*? I suppose we'll never know.

*Yes, that's an Oxford comma. Deal with it.

All my worst,
Edna.
(What is this relaxing of which you speak?)

From: Jess Martin
To: Lily Saunders
Subject: FW: Too late

Lily! Help!! Look what I accidentally just sent to Alex. Now what????
J xx

From: Lily Saunders
To: Jess Martin
Subject: FW: Too late

Lol. xx

From: Jess Martin
To: Lily Saunders
Subject: FW: Too late

What's that supposed to mean???

From Lily Saunders
To: Jess Martin
Subject: FW: Too late

I'm surprised you don't know what lol means in this day and age. xx

From: Jess Martin
To: Lily Saunders
Subject: FW: Too late

I do know what lol means! I just don't know what it means *as a response to what I've written*. I'm genuinely in pain here. Help me!!! Please??

J xx

From: Lily Saunders
To: Jess Martin
Subject: FW: Too late

Sorry, J. I was teasing, but I see now that this is not a teasing kind of situation.

Sadly, short of inventing time travel, I don't think there's much either you or I can do about this. Agree it's mortifying, though.

Your name on a book would be pretty cool! And you're always saying you'd love to treat your grandparents to a cruise – maybe the money from this novel could help with that? I suppose what you need to think about is whether you want the book deal badly enough to put up with Alex (and with the embarrassment of his knowing what you think of him). As I understand novel writing, it's not a quick process – you'd be spending a lot of time together. Maybe weigh that up, alongside the benefits.

Seems to me that there's a lot of pride at stake on both sides. Maybe some prejudice too. Make of that what you will.

I have to run, but call me later?

Toodle-pip, my lovely! Try not to stress, it will all be fine. Eventually, anyway xx

From: Alex Maxwell
To: Nathan Thomas
Subject: Impossible

Nathan,

I cannot work with Jess. She is impossible.
Alex

From: Jess Martin
To: Nathan Thomas
Subject: Update

Hi Nathan,

First of all, I want to say a massive thank you for entrusting me with the mission of working with Alex Maxwell. It was a huge privilege for me to be invited to take part in the project, and despite a shaky initial meeting, I was more than happy to go ahead and take on this assignment.

However, it's become apparent that we are deeply incompatible, both as people and as writers, and that the aforementioned mission is, in fact, impossible.

I hope you'll be able to find a different solution for improving this novel, which I do think shows a lot of promise – I enjoyed reading it.

All my apologies, and all best wishes,
Jess Martin

From: Nathan Thomas
To: Alex Maxwell; Jess Martin
Subject: Meeting

Dear Alex and Jess,

Thank you for your separate emails updating me on the situation. I propose that we meet at your earliest convenience.

Would 9 a.m. this coming Monday suit?

Kind regards,
Nathan

Chapter Eleven

JESS

This time, Jess wears flat shoes and allows plenty of time. There won't be a repeat of the helplessness of the last meeting, even if her ankle does occasionally throb, making her wince. She won't let Alex see that. She won't show any signs of weakness whatsoever. Although, admittedly, perhaps turning up at the meeting with Nathan is a sign of weakness in the first place. She'd meant her email resigning from her assignment as Alex's editorial consultant to be strong, to be final, and she imagines she's been summoned in order to retract that resignation. She also imagines that Alex will be there for similar reasons.

Shockingly, she arrives before he does.

'Should we wait for Alex, or . . . ?' She feels mildly traitorous starting the meeting without him, though she's not quite sure why.

'No, no,' Nathan says, opening his office door wide and gesturing for her to come in. 'This has actually worked out well. There are some things I probably need to explain before he joins us.' He pauses, a verbal paragraph break, and then launches into the reason for wanting to see her. 'The thing is, I've known him a long time, Jess. I don't know if he's told you, but we've been friends since university. And I know him well enough to know that he's embarrassed about needing help. His first three books came relatively easy to him, and he got used to that. He wrote some pretty cocky pieces about how you should write every day, how writer's block is a fallacy – you know, all the classic arrogant young-male-writer stuff. And then he found himself in a situation where he had to swallow some of his own words. It's not easy for him. And those MFAs, well . . . they can be useful, but they can also breed a certain kind of contempt in writers, especially writers who were prone to contempt in the first place, to superiority about a certain kind of book.'

None of this is news to Jess. 'Yes. That's why I don't think this is ever going to work. This partnership, I mean.' She feels her own ears getting warm, probably pink. '*Writing* partnership.'

'I think it can,' Nathan says. 'I think you can be good for him, help him to lighten up. And if you don't mind my saying so, I think he can be good for you, too. He knows how to structure a story and develop characters – you'll learn a lot from him. And having his name attached to yours will definitely help, as and when you're looking for your own book deal one day. I think you just need some time to get used to each other. If you can learn to see under that veneer of arrogance, which is really just a veil over his own embarrassment – and if he can get over his sense of superiority . . .'

'How long do you think that's going to take?'

Conveniently for him, Nathan is saved from having to answer that question. There's a knock on the door, and a flushed and flustered Alex trudges in.

'I'm sorry,' he says. 'Signal failure. Bloody Northern Line. I really tried to get here on time, but . . .'

Jess finds his grovelling apology a little baffling. Signal failures and other Tube-related delays are a common source of lateness in London, and people understand. Besides, it's only a few minutes, and it may be a work meeting, but it's a work meeting with an old friend.

'Alex, it's fine,' Nathan says. 'We've all been there with rush-hour Tube journeys.'

'And just, like, the Northern Line in general,' Jess adds. An olive branch she is offering: *We're all in this together. We're just the same, you and me. Two aspiring writers just trying to make it through London life unscathed.*

'Yes, well. Nonetheless, I apologise.'

Nathan gestures at an armchair, inviting Alex to sit down.

'I gather that this writing partnership has been off to rather a rough start?'

'That's one way to put it,' Alex says.

'We don't agree on anything,' Jess adds.

'Alex often doesn't agree with me when I'm editing him, either,' Nathan says, ostensibly speaking to Jess, but looking straight at Alex. 'But he usually comes around.'

'You're my editor,' Alex says. 'I don't have a choice.'

'Yes, well.' Nathan clears his throat. 'I'm afraid you don't have a choice with this, either.'

'I don't follow.'

'It's time to stop dilly-dallying around with this novel. If you're serious about it, then I want you to work with Jess on it. If you're not, and you want to work on something different – that's fine. But obviously, that will impact when we pay you the next instalment of your advance.'

Jess watches Alex. His Adam's apple bobs up and down as he swallows hard.

'I see.'

'And Jess – this could be the start of a brilliant writing career for you. I know I mentioned having your name in the acknowledgements and the marketing. But how about on the cover, as a co-author?'

Jess pretends not to notice Alex's sharp intake of breath. And she knows full well that Nathan is playing her, appealing to her dreams to get her to agree not to throw in the towel. But knowing his tactics doesn't make her immune to them. She is already visualising her own novels piled high on the tables at her favourite South London bookshop, the one with bright blue bookshelves where she first laid eyes on Alex.

'So, here's what I propose.'

Jess has a feeling that whatever Nathan is about to say, it's more likely to be an order than a suggestion.

Nathan reaches into his leather satchel, and pulls out a set of keys, which he slides on the desk towards the two of them.

'I've got a lovely little house not far from London. I Airbnb it out usually, but it's clear for the next couple of weeks. I want the two of you to go and spend a weekend there. Jess – it'll be a great place to take some pictures for Instagram. Maybe even pictures teasing your collab. Get readers excited. Re-engage Alex's fanbase.'

'*Tease our collab?*' Alex has brought out the air quotes again. 'Is that some sort of TikTok language?'

Jess closes her eyes, takes a deep breath. She doesn't dignify this question with a response, and neither does Nathan.

'I want you to come back from Godalming with an action plan, a full plot summary, some new chapters, some rewritten ones.'

'That seems like a lot for one weekend.'

'You can go for longer if you like,' Nathan says, smiling. 'As I said, it's free for two weeks.'

Jess and Alex make eye contact for the first time since the beginning of the meeting. She can see her own horror reflected in his eyes.

'A weekend seems like plenty of time to get all of that done,' she says quickly, to assuage the fears of both of them.

'That's what I thought,' Nathan says. There's a twinkle in his eye that seems to indicate he is enjoying this far too much. 'I'll email you both the address.'

With her peripheral vision, Jess tries to decipher Alex's body language. He's picking at his cuticles. He opens his mouth several times as if about to protest, and then closes it again, having presumably found nothing to say – or at least nothing that he is comfortable saying in front of Jess. She almost feels sorry for him in this moment, until she remembers that she is trapped too. *Forced proximity*, Lily will no doubt say when Jess reports this conversation. *I love it.*

Jess loves it too. It's one of her favourite tropes. Inside the safety of novels, though. Not in real life. Especially not *hers*.

Chapter Twelve

ALEX

Alex waits for the door to close and stares hard at Nathan, hoping to communicate with his eyes what he doesn't want to risk saying out loud, in case Jess can still hear him. Though why he should care what she thinks is beyond him. And it's not as if they aren't aware what they think of each other at this point, anyway. Her email didn't *say* she found him pompous and arrogant (just his Latin), but it may as well have done. He knows how to read between the lines, particularly when the lines are practically jumping off the screen and punching him in the face. And as for what Jess knows of his opinion – well, it's not as if he has been subtle.

Nathan pretends not to be able to translate Alex's stare.

'Are you enjoying the romance novels I lent you?' he asks, all innocence, as though he hasn't just lobbed a grenade into Alex's creative life, into his hard-earned sense of order, into what's left of his inner peace or whatever it is that the therapist is trying to get him to achieve.

Truth be told, he has not given the novels a second thought. He's dumped them in a heap on his bedroom floor; he isn't sure they're worthy of the effort of rearranging his bookshelves so that they will fit there. The only time he remembers them is when he trips over them on the way to his sock drawer, cursing himself for his uncharacteristic messiness.

'I haven't had much of a chance to look at them,' he says.

Which is not quite true, and Nathan knows it, and Alex knows that Nathan knows it.

'How about in between bouts of staring blankly at your computer screen, hoping inspiration strikes? Would that be a good time?'

The truth is, Alex has been too overwhelmed to do much beside stare at the screen. He's finding it hard to focus, having to read even the most basic sentence two or three times to fully grasp its meaning. A layer of undefined emotion hovers somewhere above his head, raincloud-like, whether he's sitting at his desk or pouring milk on his cornflakes (even spilling it! Which he never does! He has been pouring milk on cereal his entire life; how is it that he is suddenly unable to do so without splashback?).

It could be that he's annoyed at Jess for all her criticism of his novel. Or that he's found himself unable to draft the scenes Jess has suggested, and that he's irritated with himself for succumbing to writer's block, the scourge of inferior writers. Or that he's disconcerted by the discomfort and the disorder of delving into his emotions with his therapist. He hates the messiness of that. He'd thought he was above letting emotions interfere with his writing, with his *life*. He's always been very good at compartmentalising: accessing memories and feelings from his childhood when at his desk, bringing messy families to life, then stuffing them back in a metaphorical suitcase that he zipped up tightly until he needed it for the next writing session.

But now, he seems to have no control over any of it. He wakes up in the morning – or, worse, the middle of the night – remembering a dream involving his parents throwing things at each other in his childhood kitchen, or his stepsiblings measuring the exact dimensions of their bedroom so that each one had precisely the space allocated to them. Or he catches a scent on the Tube, and it reminds him of the strong perfume his stepmother wore when she first entered their lives, and his stomach curdles – a visceral reminder of the confusing mix of emotions from back then: he liked her, but he felt guilty that he liked her, and also felt guilty that he felt guilty. In those moments, he is angry: angry for the child he was, who just needed someone to listen to him, to help him parse all the changes in his family; angry *at* the child he was, for bottling it all up; angry, shamefully, at his siblings, because they were the reason he bottled it up, so that he could hold it together for them, be strong for them, be there for them.

All of this is messy. He doesn't like mess.

And then there's Nathan's insistence on these romance novels, on his working with the distracting presence that is Jess. And now on putting her name on the cover alongside his, their literary fates forever entwined, as a romance novelist might put it. How is he supposed to concentrate when she's so infuriatingly pretty? And, worst of all, when she's so infuriatingly right about his novel?

He stares blankly at Nathan, willing his brain to form a coherent response that doesn't make reference to any of this.

'I've been busy,' he says eventually, all too aware of how ridiculous and faintly pathetic it sounds.

'Busy sulking that I'm imposing a co-author on you?'

It's a reasonable guess. Alex nods.

'All right. Well, I'm not having this conversation again, so I suggest you get over it.'

Alex opens his mouth to argue, but is rescued by his phone ringing.

'Do you need to get that?' Nathan asks, nodding towards the corridor, signalling, perhaps, that their conversation is at an end and it's time for Alex to step out.

Reaching into this pocket, he brings out his phone and a quick look at the screen confirms what he suspected: his sister Louisa needs him for something. 'Probably not,' he says, for no good reason. But then the reason occurs to him. *You're punishing her*, says the voice of his therapist in his head – and maybe that's true.

Alex thinks often about what would have been different if Louisa hadn't called him that time, right as he was about to kiss Elodie, to tell her he loved her for the first time. His phone rang, as it always seemed to, and Elodie couldn't take it anymore, and who could blame her? Always playing second fiddle to his needy family, so large and sprawling that it was like a constant game of whack-a-mole: as soon as you'd dealt with one problem, with one person's neediness, up popped another. These are all things Alex understands now, thanks to the therapist Nathan convinced him to try. He couldn't have put any of this into words at the time.

'Okay,' Nathan says now. 'Well, I should probably get on.' He gestures vaguely at a pile of paper next to his laptop. 'These manuscripts won't edit themselves.'

Of course. Nathan's other authors. After all, he doesn't just sit around all day waiting to read the latest instalment of Alex's brilliance.

'Right,' Alex says, taking the sledgehammer-subtle hint. 'I'll be off, then.'

'Have fun in Godalming,' Nathan says, and Alex wonders if there's the trace of a glint in Nathan's eyes. 'Just not too much fun, okay?'

Alex feels his cheeks unexpectedly burn up. 'What's that supposed to mean?'

'Nothing,' Nathan says. 'Just try not to kill each other, that's all.'

Alex is almost certain he can manage that.

Jess: I have some news

Lily: Good? Bad? Both?

Jess: Mostly bad.

Lily: ??

Jess: Remember Alex?

Lily: The arrogant Latin-deploying author you're definitely not going to work with?

Jess: Except I am. Going to work with him. I'm being shipped off to Surrey to an Airbnb in the middle of nowhere with him to get this book done.

Lily: I don't think you need a ship to get to Surrey from London.

Jess: Fine. 🙄 I'm being trained off, then.

Lily: Love it.

Jess: Do not say forced proximity.

Lily: Forced proximity.

Jess: 😊

Lily: You know what you haven't mentioned?

Jess: What?

Lily: Whether he's hot.

Jess: I said I wanted to make Magic Pasta for him. Draw your own conclusions.

Lily: Well, then. Forced proximity sounds like no bad thing.

Jess: There won't be pasta.

Lily: There are other ways to win hot men over.

Jess: Great. Now you've got me thinking unthinkable thoughts.

Lily: 😁

Chapter Thirteen

JESS

It's been a few days since Jess called in to see her grandparents, and that seems like a worthy excuse to delay boarding the train for a weekend away with the man whom the universe had tantalisingly dangled in front of her as her potential soulmate and then cruelly whipped away. Or perhaps it was a mercy. Who can tell?

It was back in the Eighties that Grandpa Alan and Grandma Val bought their flat on the Lillington Gardens Estate, mere footsteps from Pimlico Tube station, in the Eighties, and they've lived there ever since. (If Jess's mum is to be believed, they had briefly, in gratitude, hung a portrait of Margaret Thatcher in the hall above the shoe rack, but quickly and quietly removed it when the miners' strike began.) Jess often calls in on her way to or from the Tube, whether for mundane daily travel or various adventures for work or play, or the many things that blur the boundary between them – like trips to Bath, one of her favourite places: once she's chaired an author event at Topping & Co, she can get lost in the rabbit warren of Mr B's Emporium of Reading Delights for several hours. If she gives her grandparents enough pre-warning of her visit, there is often a Tupperware of baked goods waiting for her to pick up: an added bonus.

And yes, here it is, on the kitchen counter: flapjacks, this time – Jess's favourite. She pretends, as she always does, not to notice. She'd never want her grandparents to think she has an ulterior motive for visiting, beyond her grandma's effusive hugs and slightly wet cheek-kisses, and her grandpa's sweet if often misguided advice, usually dispensed while he scratches his bald patch.

'No Ivy today?' she asks, peeking round the corner into the lounge to see whether her little cousin is ensconced in her favourite armchair with a book or a game on her tablet.

'Not today, no,' Val says, and a smile escapes. The smile surprises Jess: she has never heard her grandparents say anything but kind things about Ivy. Ivy's mum has chronic fatigue and Val is happy to be able to help out. But this blink-and-you-miss-it smile at the corner of Val's mouth tells a slightly different story: one of relief at the lack of responsibility today. After all her years looking after her own daughters, then Jess, and now Ivy, it's fair enough to want a rest. Val has more than earned it. A twinge of guilt twists in Jess's gut: if she was around more, off on fewer adventures, she'd be able to step in. And it wouldn't be a hardship, not really: she loves seven-year-old Ivy, who's affectionate and talkative and never gets tired of a game of Connect Four. Val moves on quickly, before Jess can properly parse or interrogate any of this. 'So where did you say you were off to this time?'

'Have you got time for a cuppa, love?' Grandpa Alan interjects, ushering Jess towards the living room in anticipation of her *yes*. Jess makes a show of checking her watch, though she's never been known to reject a cup of tea and has built this exact thing into her schedule.

'Always, Grandpa,' she says.

His eyes crinkle, as if he never gets tired of being given this noble title. 'Coming up,' he says, and shuffles off into the kitchen.

Val is looking at Jess expectantly. 'I'm off to Godalming,' she says. 'I'm being locked away with another writer until we come up with a half-decent plan to improve his novel.'

Val raises an eyebrow. 'That sounds . . . slightly unorthodox.'

'It's definitely an unusual tactic.'

'It also sounds like the beginning of a murder mystery.'

Jess chuckles. 'It *is* very possible that one of us may not emerge alive.'

Val's expression turns to concern. 'You know him, do you, love? Joking aside, I'm not sure I like the idea of you being alone in a house with a strange man.'

'Oh, he's not strange.'

It's true. Alex is many things: arrogant, slightly awkward, weirdly old-fashioned, judgemental. But not *strange* as such. And definitely not creepy.

'Oh?'

The curiosity in Val's voice triggers an instant blush: Jess can feel the warmth creeping from her forehead down towards her cheeks. Thank goodness for her grandpa, saving her with the cup of tea he hands her: something to focus her hands and her senses on.

'I know him a little,' she says quickly. She can't quite meet Val's eyes, which is ridiculous. What does she have to hide? Precisely nothing. She thought she liked Alex; she now realises she doesn't. All she has to do is survive a weekend without killing him. And then, maybe, what she gets paid will mean she won't need to say yes to as many events and can be around more for Val and Alan and Ivy.

'I see,' Val says, her smile more evident than the earlier one. This smile tells Jess that her grandma has already drawn her own conclusions.

'We're just writing together. And I wasn't joking about one of us killing the other by the end of the weekend. He's pretty annoying.'

'I see,' Val says again, her smile broadening. She will clearly not be talked down from the conclusions she has drawn. And Jess does not want to fall into the category of She Who Protests Too Much.

So she doesn't protest. Instead, she throws her grandma a crumb. 'I'm not saying he's *not* good-looking.'

'Just . . . not your type?'

'Something like that.' *Something very unlike that, actually*, the voice in her head rebukes her. *You know you can't resist a man with a dimple. It's not nice to lie to your grandmother*. 'There's more to life than looks,' she says eventually. Not a lie. Not the whole truth. This is the best she can manage right now.

'I see,' Val repeats. Her lifelong trick: say as little as possible and leave silence for Jess to fill. It usually works. 'Well,' she adds, when nothing else is forthcoming. 'Keep me posted, okay? And be careful.'

'I'll make sure he stays away from sharp knives.'

'With your heart, I mean.'

Jess slurps the last of her tea, hiding her face in the mug for as long as she can get away with. 'I'd probably better be going,' she says, jumping up. Her grandma is kind, caring – as she always has been. But Jess feels squirmy and uncomfortable at the thought that there is anything to be careful about. It's fine. It's all fine. Alex has shown himself to be utterly unattractive as a person, whatever the outside packaging might imply. She's surely not so easily swayed as to go back on this realisation.

'Wait,' Val says, as Jess is already halfway out the door with her wheelie suitcase. 'I've got some flapjacks for you.'

It's a sign of how flustered Jess is that she had almost forgotten about the Tupperware in the kitchen. She needs to snap out of this, and fast.

* * *

Jess knows it's churlish to have planned to catch a train later than Alex's. There's no reason she needs to, and it would be easier to arrive together, jump in a cab together, dig around together for Nathan's spare key. It's just that it feels important to take control of this –

the one thing that's in her power – and to grab a tiny amount of space and time to herself before she is forced to share a house with her inconveniently attractive nemesis for an entire weekend. There'll be nowhere to get away from him, not without good reason. She feels claustrophobic just thinking about it.

But she's always loved taking the train, watching the bustle of London recede and give way to sparser houses and then farmland, rivers, and expanses of sky. She puts on a swelling classical music playlist or the soundtrack from the 2005 *Pride and Prejudice* film and lets herself feel the weight and excitement of starring in her own film. It's all very Main Character Energy.

Somehow, she imagines Alex wouldn't let her do any of this, any more than he'd let her get lost in the pages of her book or concentrate on flicking through the magazine she always carefully chooses before a journey. (Godalming might only be half an hour away, but it's still a journey, damn it, and she's still going to enjoy it.) Even if he didn't *actually* say anything, even if he, too, dug a book out of his bag – a thick biography of a worthy white man of Britain past, perhaps, like a Cadbury or a Colman – his, well, just *being* there would unnerve her. She'd imagine him silently judging her as she sat, quietly daydreaming or paging through the advance copy of the latest book by one of her favourite authors that had flopped onto her doormat just that morning, with most fortuitous timing.

All of this plan, though, does not account for the current state of British railways. She always, somehow, forgets the essential detail that trains get delayed and trains get cancelled, and there's rarely a seat anymore, let alone a window seat from which she can daydream and wave at the occasional sheep.

She should not have been surprised to see Alex waiting for her by the ticket gate, looking forlorn. But she always forgets this part, the part where you can't rely on anything going according to plan. Her stomach, confused, drops, and then leaps.

'My train has been cancelled,' he announces, though she's figured it out all by herself. Alex wouldn't *miss* a train. He'd be half an hour early to allow for any small mishaps, and probably because he is always hoping that, this time, the platform announcement will come a decent amount of time in advance. Then, with the smug leisureliness of the unnecessarily organised, he'd be able to stroll to the platform and onto one of the many still-available seats.

He sounds irritated, and Jess can't blame him. But while *her* irritation stems more from her vague anger at the Conservative governments of the Eighties for championing privatisation and therefore being responsible for this mess, his, she suspects, is more from the world refusing to run according to his meticulously planned schedule.

'I guess we'll just have to travel together,' she says, trying for playful, trying for a *we-all-know-that's-no-hardship-look-at-us-getting-on-so-well* vibe, and failing. Instead, she, too, sounds irritated.

* * *

By the time they board the train, Jess's irritation has turned to plain annoyance. There was a last-minute platform change, because of course there was, and now they are scrambling on behind a crowd of similarly frustrated travellers; hopes of a Main Character Energy window seat – or any type of seat, for that matter – have faded into oblivion.

'Come on,' Alex says, his long legs carrying him faster than Jess can keep up with, with her still-not-totally-okay ankle and her heavier-than-it-should-be-for-one-weekend wheelie suitcase. 'There might be more space up front.'

But there isn't.

At the front, just behind first class – the aisles are already full of people standing, having, presumably, all had the same idea. The train is about to leave, so there's no time to backtrack – the only thing for it is to stand in the delightful section right by the door and close to the toilet. The cup of tea Jess had with her grandparents before getting on the Tube to Waterloo is starting to feel like it might have been a mistake, so maybe this prime location will come in handy. It is, however, very much not in keeping with Main Character Energy. It has, instead, the energy of the background actor whose trailer is a fifteen-minute walk from the stage. Or maybe not even that. Maybe they just have a fold-up chair in the rained-upon carpark.

'Mind if I move this?' Alex asks her, motioning towards her wheelie case. She isn't sure where he can move it to, but he somehow finds a gap on the side and wedges it there. It's a Jenga move that makes more space for everyone; it's good thinking. She's momentarily impressed with his practical side – not a string she would have assumed most writers like him had to their bow. Like liquid, the crowd flows around the new arrangement, finds new spaces.

'What's in that thing, anyway?' he asks her. 'Rocks?'

After being impressed with his Jenga skills, she is now disappointed in his lack of creativity.

'Books,' she says. 'I figured, you know . . . New surroundings. A chance for a different background for some Instagram pictures.' That, and her favourite sunflower jumper knitted for her by her grandmother years ago and perfect for the unseasonably cold weather that's forecast for the weekend. It's bulky rather than heavy, so Jess brought a bigger suitcase than she might have needed to, and from there it was only a small step to filling some of the spare space with life's other essentials: a few changes of glasses (aubergine purple, jade green, yellow with black dots) and more novels than could ever be necessary for a work trip of just a couple of days.

'I see.' He nods gravely, as if attempting to project that he is taking her seriously, but she is not fooled. What Jess doesn't tell Alex is that the wheelie case also contains more changes of outfit than she could possibly need for a weekend, even if she were to change three times a day. She doesn't know what she'll feel like wearing at any given moment. And she wants, of course, to look her best – not for any particular reason, just because she feels good when she looks good, and when she feels good, she is more likely to do good work.

Jess looks around her, trying to assess how uncomfortable this train journey is likely to be. And just as she's thinking, *Okay, this is fine, it's going to be fine, we don't have to stand too close to each other; there might even be space to sit on the floor*, a seemingly endless group of what she guesses are university students piles on, right before the whistle and the closing of the doors, chatting and singing and carrying eminently spillable coffee cups. And suddenly – whoa! – there she is, pushed a lot closer to Alex than she had ever intended to be.

'Hi,' he says, amused, with something almost soft in his voice.

'Hello,' she says, in a tone that she hopes communicates, *I acknowledge the awkwardness of this situation and am deeply mortified. I assume you are too and I'm sorry about that, although not sorry in the sense that it's my fault, just in the sense that I would very much like this situation not to be happening.* A tone she hopes doesn't quite communicate what she is actually thinking, which is, *I want to die.*

Jess closes her eyes and inhales deeply, ready to let out a long breath as slowly as possible, as she learned to do in 2020 when even escaping into romance novels wasn't quite calming down her heartbeat sufficiently to fall asleep at night. But in 2020, when she did that, there was never the smell of clean laundry and cedar and fresh coffee mingling together in quite the way that Alex's scent is right now. She keeps her inward breath going as long as she can, inhaling that scent, filling her lungs with it. It's pleasant, that's all. It's calming. Maybe it's not even him she's smelling? She can't imagine ever being calm around him.

Jess exhales slowly, opens her eyes. Takes a quick look around her, matching scents with their likely sources. No, it's definitely Alex who smells so good. Why does he have to smell so good? This is unhelpful. It makes her want to rest her head against his chest, breathe him in. His red flannel shirt looks soft, too. It seems like maybe resting her head there could be quite comfortable, too. In the absence of a window seat, that's all. Main Character Energy in a different way.

Now what, though? Do they make conversation all the way to Godalming, or do they ignore how close together they are? She has, after all, stood much closer than this to many strangers at rush hour on the Tube. She's stood with her head under people's armpits and her bottom in people's faces, the breath of strangers landing in her eyes and, on occasion, in her mouth. And in those situations, she has, wherever possible, fished out her phone and pressed play on a podcast, or dug out her book and escaped into its pages, the awkwardness and unpleasantness and unwelcome intimacy of the cramped conditions fading into the background as she's focussed on something else. So it seems that maybe this is what she should do now. Except he isn't a stranger, and maybe it's rude to screen off the reality of his too-close company?

Why does nobody prepare you for these minefields? This kind of thing is what they should teach at school, with extra PSHE classes instead of trigonometry, which she has not once used since handing in her GCSE Maths paper.

Thankfully, it is Alex of all people who rescues her from this dilemma. He reaches into the backpack at his feet and pulls out a book, in a way that seems almost designed to give Jess permission to do the same. From the tote bag on her shoulder, she retrieves a proof of the newest Katherine Center novel. Bliss. Some authors never let Jess down, and Katherine Center is one of them. She knows from reading the first paragraph that this book will be no exception. Some people reach for the same TV shows over and over for comfort, the characters like old familiar friends. For Jess, it's the same authors she reaches for – their voices like a familiar soft blanket on a chilly afternoon. As she sinks into it, she's absorbed by the story, the dialogue, the characters, and the will-they-won't-they – although, quite clearly, in the time-honoured tradition of romance novels, they will.

She is fourteen pages in when groans around her alert her to the fact that the train has slowed and then come to a stop, and not in the usual here-we-are-at-the-next-station kind of way – more of an equally familiar here-we-are-stopped-for-no-obvious-reason way. She waits to catch Alex's eye and sigh in unison with him. As she's also experienced multiple times on the Tube, nothing bonds strangers like shared travelling trials. She's exchanged many a raised eyebrow with fellow commuters in her twenty-eight years on this planet. But Alex's brow is furrowed in a different way. He's concentrating on his book, trying no doubt to grasp the nuances of a speech by Winston Churchill or what the election of Barack Obama has to say about twenty-first-century America and what came next.

Except.

Those books don't usually have bright pink covers with cartoon characters.

What is he reading?

Could it be that Alex Maxwell is reading a romance novel?

Has Jess slipped and fallen into another dimension, where such things are possible? She manages, just, to keep herself from gasping. She tells herself that her movements should be gentle; she doesn't want to scare away this miracle.

Or maybe he's reading in order to find things to criticise? That seems more plausible than Alex reading a book like this for pleasure. Yes, that must be it. She breathes in again, to slow herself down. She had got far too excited at the prospect of Alex reading a romance novel for normal-person reasons. And there's his scent again. All these thoughts and feelings are giving her whiplash, and meanwhile, there he is, oblivious, reading.

Smiling?

Yes, he's smiling.

Not smirking.

So maybe he's genuinely enjoying himself after all. Maybe he's not reading for criticism.

Curiouser and curiouser.

Without warning, as if coming unstuck from deep mud, the train lurches forward. Jess's tortoiseshell glasses slide down her nose. The girl next to her sways, leaning into Jess to stay upright.

'Sorry,' she mutters, gathering herself, but Jess is feeling very forgiving.

Because, by leaning into Jess, she has pushed Jess into Alex.

His red shirt is indeed very soft.

His scent is even more pleasant up close.

And his breath on her face is definitely more pleasant than the breath of a random commuter.

'Hi,' he says again, in the soft voice from before.

'Hello,' she repeats, in her apologising-for-the-awkwardness tone, even though she finds herself not fully meaning the apology. Her heart is beating fast, unless it's his she can feel. She thinks, unexpectedly, that she'd stay in this position quite happily all the way to Godalming. All the way to the end of the trainline. *Push me again*, she finds herself willing in the direction of the girl with the headphones. *Give me an excuse to stay like this.* But the girl, of course, doesn't, and Jess has already let herself lean on Alex a fraction too long. 'Sorry,' she says, and she shuffles away from him, though not as far away as she was before.

'That's quite all right,' he says, making eye contact.

She opens her book back up, but her concentration has gone. Not even Katherine Center can bring her back from this kind of distraction. Her pre-departure cup of tea weighs heavily on her bladder, but now is not the time to give up her position in favour of the loo. She will just have to cross her legs. To think of things other than her pressing physiological need. Besides, another pressing physiological need, quite an inappropriate one, is making itself felt. Not that she should be thinking of that, either.

What *is* this other dimension she has fallen into?

And how does she get out of it? Because it's very unhelpful.

Impossibly, more people get on at the next station. There's no lurch; there's no falling into Alex's arms or being caught by him. There's just the chance to keep inhaling him from closer still, even while she pretends to read. Sorry, Katherine Center, she thinks, ashamed of disrespecting a book like this. But somehow, she feels that an author of meet-cutes and forced proximity, of denial of feelings and falling in love, would understand completely.

Chapter Fourteen

ALEX

That train journey to Godalming felt like both the shortest and the longest of Alex's life. Firstly, it is extremely frustrating that British trains do not know how to behave – to arrive when they say they're going to, and, above all, not to be cancelled. What is the point of meticulously planning your life if external circumstances will not cooperate? Or perhaps that *is* the point: meticulously planning your life with an extra half an hour's breathing space at every turn, *just in case*. It is all extremely tedious.

He had a plan. He was going to get to the station in plenty of time for a good seat with a table, get one of these romance novels out of his backpack, and give it a try with a pencil in hand and as much of an open mind as he could muster. But, instead: no seat. No way to make notes. And a very distracting blonde who probably didn't *need* to be quite so close to him at all times, but whose closeness he could be forced to reluctantly admit that he did not, exactly, hate. Reading together companionably is the best kind of friendship as far as Alex is concerned. In an ideal world, would you also be standing in a train corridor alongside far too many University of Guildford students exchanging gossip, popping bubble gum, and occasionally breaking into song? The answer to that should go without saying. Still, he is glad that Jess did not insist on small talk all the way to Godalming – or even any of the way – and he enjoyed the faint smell of apple shampoo he caught from her hair when the train's swaying delivered her closer to him. It was uncanny, in fact, that the descriptions of the heroine in this book he was reading included the pleasant smell of her hair, so that Jess's presence acted almost as a live olfactory illustration of what he was reading.

Had he known he would be travelling with Jess, he would have packed a different book – a Churchill biography, perhaps – so as not to invite ridicule. He wanted to read romance in private, decide for himself what he thought of it before risking being interrogated as to his views. But if she had noticed he was reading a romance novel, she didn't say.

Jess seems grateful when Alex lugs her ridiculously heavy suitcase down the train steps for her. She probably has eighteen pairs of shoes in there, even though she and he are only going to be holed up inside the house, arguing about the best way to rip apart his novel and start again. He has stopped short of tracksuit bottoms and ratty T-shirts and made himself bring jeans and shirts in his backpack. When he writes at home, it's all about comfort, and also all about dressing in such a way that would make him too ashamed to go out, for fear of being recognised by a reader, as tends to happen around Hampstead. He wouldn't be surprised if there had been a Londonist article forewarning residents and potential visitors to be on the lookout for writers on the Heath, because that is where they go for inspiration. Which is not untrue: he's seen Alan Hollinghurst on one occasion, Nina Stibbe on another, nodding to each of them as he passed, in an indication that he both recognises and appreciate them but feels no need to interrupt their day. It is not, however, impossible that on this trip Jess will drag him outside for a walk – not impossible that he will drag *himself* outside in an effort to gain some space away from her: breathing space, thinking space, space to express himself without being judged for his supposedly pretentious views.

'Should we call an Uber?' Jess asks, once they're out of the station.

'If I remember correctly, the house is quite close to here,' he says. When he says *if I remember correctly*, this is really just for propriety's sake. He definitely remembers correctly; he has planned every step of this journey meticulously. He just doesn't know what will happen once they actually *arrive*. That is anybody's guess. Inwardly, and not for the first time since meeting Jess, he curses Nathan and the freshers' fair at Durham where they met and became friends.

He catches her slightly wincing. Maybe it's her ankle.

'It's a twenty-minute walk, I think.'

'Yes, I suppose that's quite far with a suitcase . . .' He's not trying to be judgemental or difficult. Just stating facts. A twenty-minute walk in the out-of-London fresh air honestly sounds delightful after that cramped train journey full of hazards, like trying not to get too close to Jess despite noticing how good she smells; trying not to overthink what it means that she allowed herself to be jostled into him; trying to concentrate on his book without being too obvious about the cover.

'Oh, no,' she says. 'It's not that. It's just . . .' She's blushing now, and he's wondering if, as is so often the case, he would have been better keeping his mouth shut. 'I could really do with the loo. I had an ill-advised cup of tea just before leaving home.'

He tries not to smile at the coyness of her blush. But it also takes every bit of the self-control he has carefully cultivated over the years not to ask the kind of question he spent his teenage years asking his younger siblings: *Why didn't you go when you had the chance?* The train toilet had been literally footsteps from their standing space. In fact, they'd occasionally caught less than delightful wafts of odour from it.

'Ah,' he says, handing over the key. 'I see. Well, in that case, why don't you call an Uber, and I'll see you at the house? I'd quite like a walk.'

Jess looks relieved at his suggestion. He chooses to believe it is the imminence of the toilet, rather than the twenty minutes away from him, that has this effect.

'It's a plan, Stan,' she says. He hasn't heard that particular turn of phrase in a decade, and it makes him smile.

* * *

Alex has never been to Godalming before, but it feels oddly familiar – perhaps because it's the platonic ideal of a small British town, the kind of place Postman Pat might have driven around in his red van, with, of course, his black and white cat. Alex takes his time walking to the cottage: thirty-two minutes, to be exact. The introvert in him is mildly terrified at the idea of spending an entire weekend in someone else's company – someone talkative, someone with opinions, someone whom he very much suspects is the opposite of an introvert. Writing, more than anything, is an activity he likes to undertake in complete silence and solitude. He's never understood people who take their laptops to cafés and expect inspiration to strike with all that background noise, all those interruptions. He's also never understood the idea of co-writing – another reason this entire project seems doomed. Writing is one man – or one woman – and their notebook and favourite pen, in silence, utterly concentrated.

Alex loves the feeling of fountain pen on smooth paper, gliding along, carrying his thoughts from left to right along the page. He loves the smell of ink. The sense that these rituals link him back through time to generations – centuries! – of writers that came before him and on whose shoulders he stands. (He'd like to think that it links him forwards to the generations to come, too, but he is not so naive. They write two-thumbed on their phones; they tap away at their keyboards, easily and happily and regularly distracted by the supposed delights of the internet. If looking down on such ways of working makes him a curmudgeon, then so be it. He'll gladly be called a Luddite in exchange for knowing the joys of a quality fountain pen.)

Cafés, however, have their uses: namely, the use they were created for – the provision of quality hot beverages. Though he invested part of his advance for his last novel in his own machine, he is yet to master the art of the perfect flat white. On the way to the cottage – and only partially to delay his inevitable arrival and the onslaught of Jess's ideas and sunny enthusiasm – he stops at Gail's to pick one up. And while ordering it, he remembers that during that first work meeting – the one in the coffee shop, where she let down her hair – her order was a flat white, too. With one sugar, if he remembers correctly (which he does, but only because he has a good memory for random facts). So while he's here, buying one, he might as well buy two. If nothing else, to make up for the fact that he's never acknowledged that he remembers her as the girl from the bookshop, remembers their brief flirtation. He'd only flirted like that because he'd thought there was nothing at stake, since he'd never see her again. Flexing his chat-up muscles so that they didn't entirely atrophy. He knows he's in no fit state for a girlfriend at the moment. The way he's writing – or not writing – is not so much a signal to him that he's not doing brilliantly, as much as a giant red flag flapping in the wind and declaring that he's got some things to sort out in his mind, and probably his heart, and the few therapy appointments he's had so far have confirmed as much. He didn't expect the interaction with the blonde to have such an impact on him; he didn't expect to still be thinking about the girl from the bookshop when he arrived at Nathan's office; he certainly didn't expect her to turn up at the meeting. And he wouldn't have expected himself to behave so appallingly when she did – a spoiled brat, a *child* – but he was embarrassed, and confused, and flustered, and that combination has never worked well for him.

All in all, better late than never: Jess more than deserves an apologetic flat white. Rounding the final corner as he makes his way to Ethan's cottage, Alex hopes against unlikely hope that it will buy enough of her approval to at least start the weekend together on something like the right foot.

Chapter Fifteen

JESS

Jess is excited despite herself to discover the place for their writing retreat – the birthplace, perhaps, of a great authorial partnership. The Uber drive over to the house allowed her to clear her head and get hold of her runaway emotions – what had *that* been about, on the train? It was probably just that her penchant for Main Character Energy had run away with her. They hadn't come here for some kind of forced-proximity misadventure. They'd come to work, to be creatively productive, to talk about books and writing and plotline and characters. It would be fun! And then, at the end of it – not the end of this weekend, but the end of the whole, well, *thing* – they would have a book. Something they could both be proud of.

Something with her name on it, out on the tables at Waterstones. Something she could show to her grandparents, who had never quite understood what it was exactly that she did. They were proud of her in a nebulous kind of way – their go-getter granddaughter, whose intelligence and brilliance it was possible they overestimated – and that was lovely. But her grandpa kept getting *confluence* and *influence* mixed up and her grandma kept promising she'd 'watch her little videos one day'. Jess had no doubt she fully intended to; she imagined her opening her computer, clicking around, baffled, and then giving up and telling herself she'd try again the next day. But a book on a table at Waterstones: *that*, they would understand. Her name linked with the name of an author described in one review as *perhaps the greatest of his generation*.

The key is a little stiff in the lock, but once she pushes open the door, she gasps. The house is all wooden beams and low ceilings, cosy rugs and lamps for subtle lighting. In the corner of the living room, an open fireplace, with wood neatly stacked ready for use and instructions as to how to build a fire with maximum safety and efficiency. Jess finds herself rubbing her hands in glee, like a cartoon character in a moment of excitement. She has a good feeling about this place, about its potential over the next few days. Wandering around, she finds a cupboard full of board games – noting, happily, that they include Scrabble. She identifies the bedrooms, trying not to pre-empt a decision about who would get to sleep where, trying to set herself up for diplomacy and magnanimousness. *No, no,* she would say to Alex, *you pick*. She does like this one that she is standing in, though, with its view of the garden, the hint of blossom on some branches of the magnolia tree. Maybe they could come back in a few weeks' time, when they're in full bloom; maybe even every season, to see the changing landscape of what seems like a very pretty town and to brainstorm, novel after novel, becoming a literary power couple as leaves turn and snow falls and trees bud again.

It is possible she is getting ahead of herself.

It is also possible that she has unintentionally used the word *couple*. Only to herself, and not out loud. It is recoverable. Better to make the mistake in the privacy of her own mind and then shake her head clear of such thoughts.

It is also possible that she is still blushing at where her thoughts have gone, when Alex knocks on the door. She attempts the deep breathing again, though it hasn't been particularly effective so far today.

'Hang on,' she says, yanking the handle this way and that. There's a knack and eventually she finds it, though she couldn't say how.

'I come bearing coffee,' he says, nodding at his full hands. He must have knocked with his elbows.

Instant brownie points. She beams at him. Maybe this weekend won't be so bad. Maybe it will be great.

'That's thoughtful,' she says, taking both the cups from him so that he can remove his backpack, kick off his shoes, shrug off the journey, make himself at home. 'Thank you.'

'Flat white,' he says. 'One sugar.'

This does not feel like a coincidence. The blush that had possibly receded creeps back up Jess's chest.

'You remembered,' she says. Her voice is probably giving too much away – too much wonder, too much gratitude. Because he has, after all, only remembered her order, as any thoughtful friend or colleague might.

'Of course,' he says. 'Same order as me, but with

sugar.' He pauses, which Jess suspects is for effect. She suspects, from the twinkle in his eye, that a bad joke is coming, and she braces herself. 'I don't need it,' he says. 'I'm sweet enough already.'

She's tempted to roll her eyes. But he's just brought her coffee, so he deserves better.

Besides, she remembers how kind and gentle he'd been with her ridiculous sprained ankle that time. He may be a little prickly, a little porcupine-like, but it isn't impossible there is some sweetness there, too. Remembering her order, bringing her a drink – those are indications, too.

'I'll take your word for it,' she says, with what she hopes is a hint of playful teasing in her voice.

Jess is beginning to relax into this whole endeavour. This is someone she can work with. And this is a place she can work in – away from the distractions of London, fresh air coming through the windows along with birdsong (or perhaps that is still the angelic choir) and not the slightest distant roar of a motorway carrying commuters to and from their various grindstones. Away from everything – this feels like a great place to write. She doesn't know much about the process, but when she's imagined herself actually making progress on a novel beyond the first couple of chapters, she's pictured long sessions in coffee shops with her laptop, taking time and care over sentences, shutting out the world. She knows from the authors she's interviewed and from occasionally having witnessed it that many writers snatch time in the car, waiting for their kids after school, or squeeze a tablet onto their knees on the train on their morning commute. She admires what that says about their determination, their dedication to their craft. But she can't help thinking it's not the platonic ideal of Being a Writer. This cottage – this is far more like that platonic ideal. Just her and her book. And a tall, handsome man who brings her coffee.

Chapter Sixteen

ALEX

The flat white seems to have worked its magic. That, and the terrible joke he has been using for years – decades, even – to soften people, make them smile. It was the first thing he'd said that made his stepsister Georgina laugh despite herself after his father had married her mother. More of a snort, really, but he caught her eye and laughed back, and it bonded them. So the bad joke has become more than just a bad joke. It's become something that evokes fond memories for him, a part of his history that he usually feels vulnerable sharing, so that he surprised himself by coming out with it just now. But Jess seems to have appreciated it; Alex didn't miss the glint in her eye.

He has to admit he is impressed with her work ethic. Setting down her coffee on the table in the kitchen, she gets out her laptop, and says, 'Shall we get to work?'

'Yes,' he says, not wanting to tamp down this impressive show of enthusiasm. (Though it doesn't seem as if it's for show. It seems, like everything else about Jess, to be impressively genuine.) 'Let's. Let me just drop my bag in my room and get my bearings.'

'Sorry,' she says. 'I'm just feeling a burst of inspiration. But of course. Feel free to pick whichever room you like.'

They're both perfectly fine rooms, though one is more basic than the other, with a smaller double bed, and looks out onto the front of the house, which he guesses will be beautiful later on this month when the magnolia explodes in pink and white blooms. He hasn't read Nathan's Airbnb listing, but he wouldn't be surprised if it emphasised the other room: its views of the countryside, its sense of being so much further away from London than their short, if slightly fraught, train journey might imply. He imagines that is the bedroom which Jess would like, though unexpectedly she hasn't yet claimed it. And it feels like, despite the bringing of the coffee, which she had seemed disproportionately delighted by, he still has some ground to make up after how rudely he has behaved towards her. If they're going to be locked together in such close quarters for a few days, it's probably for the best, for both of them, that she be as happy as possible.

'I'll take the front room,' he calls from his new quarters. 'I like that it looks out onto such a pretty street.'

'It's beautiful, isn't it? Great choice.'

He thinks, though, that he can hear relief in her voice. That he wasn't wrong about her preference. That he is beginning to be able to read her. He doesn't know why, exactly, but this makes him happier than it has any right to.

'Thanks for the coffee,' she says, when he comes back with his notepad, his pen, his stack of notes. 'That really hit the spot.'

'You're welcome,' he says. 'It's the first rule of writing. You can't write without coffee.'

He has a T-shirt that says as much, bought for him by his sister Jen. *A writer is a mysterious organism capable of turning caffeine into books*. He often wears it when he's at his desk, a sort of sartorial pep talk. *Come on, Alex, you've got coffee. That's all you need to get some words out*. Or even, *Come on, Alex, this is who you are: a writer. With coffee, you can do this*. It hasn't always worked, but he goes on trying, valiantly. He doesn't wear the T-shirt out and about, doesn't want to draw attention to the fact he's an author. He'd feel silly if he bumped into one of the literary luminaries of Hampstead – people who can probably write even without caffeine or sartorial pep talks. But he also doesn't always feel like being stopped by one of his own fans, who might not be totally sure that it was definitely him without the T-shirt clueing them in. It's happened once or twice; they say nice things; they sometimes ask for his autograph (one even had one of his books with him, which was more gratifying than it maybe should have been). But then conversation inevitably turns to what he's working on now; they always feel the need to point out that it's been a while, as if he doesn't know, as if he hasn't noticed. They say it inquisitively, almost as if they're concerned for his well-being, as if they're hoping he hasn't succumbed to writer's block, which, since they're true fans, they know he doesn't believe in. He makes a joke, deflects, asks if they're writers, too. More often than not, they blush, shuffle their feet, own up to having attempted a short story or two or begun a novel. *Don't give up*, he tells them, even though he's on the verge of giving up himself, and because most people are most interested in themselves, they drop the subject of Alex's writer's block, eager suddenly to tell him about their own creative path. He's heard some seemingly endless synopses of the kind he should probably read on nights he has trouble sleeping, but he's also met some interesting people, and he loves watching the spring in their step as they walk away, newly buoyed and perhaps inspired by his words of encouragement and the idea that published writers are people just like they are, who wait in a queue at Gail's for cheesy scones on Saturday mornings, or mutter to themselves when the wait for the zebra crossing is too long, or can't help taking a picture of the London landscape from the top of Parliament Hill on a bright autumn day. But those encounters make him feel like even more of a fraud, more of a failure, and it's exhausting. Goodness knows how George R. R. Martin ever shows *his* face in public.

To his delight and surprise, Jess laughs at his quip about coffee. A bright, sparkling laugh that somehow lights up the room. A laugh he'd like to hear more of.

'Really?' she says, nodding at the stationery in front of him. 'Is the second rule expensive pens and Moleskin notebooks?'

'That's just a life rule,' he says.

She nods earnestly, as if absorbing a valuable lesson. 'I see.'

Jess closes her laptop, pushes it to one side. 'So how do you want to do this?'

He's wondered this himself – where to start. Truth be told, he wonders this every time at the editing stage. Reading through his own first drafts, he usually goes through all the stages of grief – most notably, one of sadness that the book isn't as good as he imagined or hoped – before arriving at acceptance: it's an okay draft, but there's a lot of work to do, still. And now what? That's when he usually calls in Nathan for extra wisdom and a little reassurance. *It's a first draft*, Nathan always tells him. *First drafts aren't supposed to be good. Their only job is to exist.* Alex telling *himself* this doesn't seem to cut it, but when it's Nathan, it seems to make sense.

He could start by asking Jess what she thinks of his book, but he already knows, because she'd told him in detail, through her big loopy writing on his manuscript that communicates friendliness even as it eviscerates him: *Too much description here.* Or *You've said this already.* Or *Hmm, I find this part hard to believe.* She's written him a long, thoughtful editor's note on the strengths and weaknesses of the book, what she thinks needs to be added, what should be pared back. He read it angrily once – those stages of grief, again – but after a walk around the block to clear his head, he read it again, and found himself nodding, relieved that some of his instincts about what didn't work were being confirmed and that she'd helped explain the unease he hadn't quite been able to put his finger on at some points in the manuscript.

She must take his silence now to mean uncertainty, to mean that he needs her to take charge, because she leans down into her bag and pulls out a multi-coloured block of Post-It notes. 'I brought these,' she says. 'I figured they might help.'

He usually goes for plain white index cards for novel-planning purposes himself, but maybe he can be flexible on this one tiny thing. Pick his battles and keep his powder dry for when she insists that the passengers on the plane all have to survive, deleting his favourite scene: the moving (if he does say so himself) death of a child in the arms of his mother. (His mother! A woman, let it be noted. He has not ignored women, as Jess has unfairly suggested.)

'You've come prepared,' he says. 'I like that.'

She sits up straighter, presses her lips together. He gets the sense she is trying not to show how much she enjoyed the compliment.

'I take this seriously,' she says. 'You know that, don't you?'

'Yes,' he says. He didn't need the Post-Its to tell him as much. He could tell in the meticulousness of her notes, in the care she'd obviously taken to closely read his book more than once.

'Good.' She searches out his eyes with hers. 'I know this whole thing isn't easy for you. But I feel very honoured to get to be part of your process. I hope you know that.'

Once upon a time, the way she clearly stated this might have freaked him out. But his years in America have got him used to people who freely share how they are feeling, who don't just leave it to be read between the lines, passive-aggressively or otherwise. He wouldn't say he is comfortable with it, as such. He's a long way from *that*. But it doesn't unnerve him in quite the way it used to.

'I appreciate that,' he says, forcing himself to hold her gaze. Feeling, as he does so, his stomach inexplicably lurch.

Jess is the first to look away. She picks up the manuscript. 'Maybe we should talk through it in macro terms first,' she says. 'What's working, what isn't. Which characters maybe aren't adding much to the plot and how we can introduce others that do.'

Alex clenches his teeth and counts to ten. Why does it feel as if Jess is poking at a bruise with every one of these suggestions?

'Okay,' he says, opening his notebook to a fresh page. Scribbling notes feels safe; it feels like a way to look down, for her not to see the impact her words are having on him. He is a professional, for Pete's sake. He should have thicker skin than this. It's embarrassing how vulnerable he is feeling.

He writes, then underlines: *Characters to reconsider*. And he waits for Jess to speak, for the axe to fall. When it doesn't, he looks up to find her reading, seemingly caught up in his words on the page.

'I love this section,' she says, pointing to a paragraph he has agonised over. 'I just don't think that's quite the right word here.' And the thing is, she's right. He's written *craving*, but even as he wrote it, he thought, *No, I don't think I mean that, exactly*. 'What if we changed it to *yearning*?'

He snaps his fingers three times in quick succession and she looks up, startled.

'What does that mean?' she says.

It's funny, the things you start to think are normal when you're doing an MFA. 'Oh, sorry. It means, *bingo*. It's what we used to do during discussions in writing workshops to show we agreed with what someone was saying.'

'I see.' She sounds mildly disapproving. Alex doesn't really blame her.

'So, in other words, thank you. That's exactly the word I was looking for, and I didn't even realise I was.'

Those lips of hers pressed together, again. He finds it very endearing – almost as endearing as her precision in language. It's the first time, he realises, that he's said thank you. He suspects it won't be the last. That this book will be all the better for her involvement, that if anyone can rescue him from the scrapheap of yesterday's forgotten writers, from the fear of being recognised on Hampstead Heath, it might, after all, be Jess.

Chapter Seventeen

JESS

Jess is enjoying herself. She has the flutter in her belly she recognises from when she's in the flow of writing a good review, or interviewing an author who's giving some fascinating, unexpected answers, or taking a photograph for Instagram with the light falling just right on her bookshelves. She's treading as carefully as she can, not wanting to unnecessarily hurt Alex or even cause him to bristle, if she can avoid it, but in her enthusiasm, it's possible she is not being careful enough. She makes as much eye contact as possible. She touches his arm gently to communicate, she hopes, empathy and kindness. She gets Jaffa cakes from her bag and offers them to him on a regular basis, usually just after suggesting they delete a scene she can tell he's worked hard on or questioning the existence of a particular character – the novelist, say, who seems to be a stand-in for Alex himself, the kind of meta thing authors do sometimes that works best with a subtlety he has not quite brought to it.

'Cup of tea?' she asks now, after winning a battle on deleting some paragraphs from an overly long description of the plane's fuselage.

Alex stretches, his arms high above his head, his grey T-shirt rising slightly to reveal a sliver of skin below his belly button. Jess tries not to look; it feels oddly intimate that she would know the pattern of his body hair or the exact colour of his skin beneath his clothes. It occurs to her that out there on the bookternet, there may well be some young women who would kill – possibly kill *her* – to be in this exact position right now, breathing in the same air as Alex Maxwell, being able to name the elements that make up his particular scent. Sharing Jaffa cakes and the home-made flapjacks her grandma slipped her when she called in on the way to get her train. Never mind getting to work with him. In her googling, in her research of the many online pages bearing the suave black-and-white author picture where he rests his chin on his upward-facing palm and gazes thoughtfully into, presumably, his own glorious future, she has found evidence of past workshops where people have paid thousands of pounds to do just that: to sit not quite as close to him as she is now and absorb the wisdom that she is getting for free.

Because she *is* getting wisdom from him too. If it was up to her, she would, for example, merrily cut most of the descriptions and get straight to the action, to the meat of the relationships between the characters. When he explains his narrative choices, when he sticks to his guns as to why certain things belong where they do, when he insists that certain characters retain the backstory he has given them – or certain long descriptions have a purpose besides showcasing his brilliant prose – she has to admit that it all makes a lot of sense. He is thoughtful – the more considered yin to her sometimes hasty yang – and she knows that she can learn from that.

'A cup of tea would be great, thank you,' Alex says now.

'Milk, no sugar?'

'Exactly. Because—'

She resists the temptation to gently whack him on the back of the head. 'Don't say it,' she says instead.

He pouts, playfully she thinks (hopes!), clearly disappointed to have the wings of his terrible joke about sugar and sweetness clipped. 'Okay,' he says, relenting. 'Fair.'

The pre-boiling hum and bubble of the kettle fills the silence, and she lets it. She knows she has a tendency to talk, talk, talk, and she is gathering from Alex that he only speaks when there is something to say. That silence is his lifeblood. That a whole weekend with her talking non-stop might actually kill him. And, surprisingly, she finds that she definitely doesn't want to do that.

'How are you feeling?' she asks him, setting the cup of tea on a coaster to his left.

He looks a little frightened. Perhaps talk of feelings is a little much for a privately educated Englishman, even one who has spent time in America, where, if films and TV are any indication, everyone is forever discussing their emotions.

'What do you mean?' he asks.

She resists the urge to tease him by explaining what an emotion is.

'About the work we've done so far. Are you happy with it?'

He chuckles, two quick breaths through his nose. Jess finds this endearing. 'I don't know about *happy*,' he says. 'I'm feeling a little bruised.'

'Bruised in . . . a good way?'

Alex frowns. 'How can a bruise ever be good?'

'Well, you know. I went snowboarding in the Alps with my friend Lily last year, and it was harder than I thought it would be, and I spent the whole week on my backside, it felt like. And I came home covered in bruises. But every bruise was a reminder of the fun I'd had. Learning something new. Breathing in air so clean it tingles in your nostrils. The beautiful landscapes with all that bright white snow. The belly laughs and late-night chats I'd had with my friend. If I accidentally poked one of my bruises for a couple of weeks afterwards, it would hurt, but I'd also remember the good times, and it would make me smile.'

'I see,' Alex says, nodding. 'Well, this isn't like that.'

This is a little disappointing. Jess had hoped Alex would be enjoying himself at least a little bit. Enjoying the flapjacks, at least. But she senses anxiety beneath his words and centres herself, resolving to be patient, to let him articulate his feelings.

'I recognise we're doing good work,' he says. 'I love your suggestion of breaking up long passages of description with some snappy dialogue. I think you've made some great points, and I admit that the book will be stronger for the work we're doing. But that's not quite the same as, well . . . as snowboarding.'

'Fair enough.'

This is progress, after all. A whole lot of progress when she considers how he clearly felt about writing with her back at the beginning of this whole thing.

He takes a long sip of tea, and she senses there's more, that he's formulating a sentence with his face hidden in his mug.

'This isn't easy for me. But that doesn't mean I don't appreciate what you're doing, Jess.'

She loves the way he says her name, the S almost imperceptibly there, gentle, like the softest tickle on the inside of her wrist.

Alex clears his throat. 'I'm really impressed with what you're bringing to this discussion. And I . . .' He raises his head, makes eye contact. 'I'm sorry that I was so rude to you during that first meeting. I'm sorry that I doubted you.'

Jess presses her lips together, aware of the blush creeping up her chest.

'Second meeting, really,' she says, deflecting.

'What do you mean?' The smile passes over his lips so quickly that it would have been possible to miss it. But Jess doesn't.

'I thought we had a moment in the bookshop. Then you acted like you'd never seen me before, and I thought maybe I'd imagined it.'

'You didn't imagine it,' he says, his eyes still on hers. Her stomach flips over itself and, jolted, she has to look away, bury her own face in her own overly large mug of tea. 'We did have a moment.'

This feels like another moment – here, now – but Jess is paralysed. Without meaning to, she pictures herself walking over to his side of the table and leaning towards him, kissing his cheek. She pictures him turning his face to her, finding her mouth with his. She yanks her mind away from imagining him deepening the kiss, from thinking about what might happen next. She wriggles in her seat, with pleasure and also to try to drag her mind and the responses of her body away from these things. She takes another sip of the tea, hiding for as long as she can get away with, willing her blush to crawl back down her cheeks and her neck, down onto her chest, under her top.

When she can no longer get away with pretending there's any tea left in her mug, Jess puts it down. She forces herself to look at Alex. He is watching her, a smile playing at the edge of his lips, and she can't bear to look at him.

'Moments like that aren't very professional, I suppose,' she says eventually, when she feels like she can trust her voice not to wobble and betray her.

'No,' he says. 'But you know what they say about all work and no play . . .'

From the bottom of one of their bags, a phone rings. Neither of them makes a move to dig out their phone, to check who's ringing. But the outside world has intruded, and this moment, like the bookshop moment, is over before it has even begun.

After all, maybe it's Nathan, checking up on their

progress. They've barely been here a few hours; imagine having to tell him that they've got distracted, that maybe they'll need a bit more time . . . that, ahem, *other things* have got in the way. Or maybe it's Lily, who can read Jess like a book, who reads most of Jess's life like a romance novel. Jess would never hear the end of it if she was forced to admit to what is going on.

Besides, Alex is right. They *are* doing good work. It would be such a shame to knock that off course for the sake of a little fun. And how awkward would it be to criticise the sentence structure of a man whose bed you have just left – or whose bed you are still in?

They need to leave this cottage with a plan, with their heads held high, professional novelists worthy of the title. Although Jess is beginning to think that maybe they shouldn't be in a hurry to leave this cottage. That maybe being stuck here with Alex for a few more days than originally planned would not be the worst thing in the world. That maybe, despite the very reasonable points she is currently making to herself, it would be good if there was time for those, ahem, other things.

Chapter Eighteen

ALEX

Well. This is very inconvenient.

Alex has never been the best at reading signs, but the electricity between him and Jess is crackling so hard that he thinks the whole of Godalming must be able to see the sparks. A shower of shooting stars raining on the town, perhaps. Not to be dramatic about this, of course. Drama being, after all, not really his style.

To top it all off, she has made him the perfect cup of tea. He always says, *Really strong, just a tiny splash of milk,* and then everyone ignores him and thinks he can't possibly mean *that* little milk, but he did, and now they've put too much in, and the tea is ruined. But Jess just *knew*. She knew how to make it.

Which is fine, because he doesn't believe in signs.

But if he did, that would be a neon flashing one. Tea, like coffee, is very important in Alex's life.

He glances at his watch. It's too early to suggest dinner, a change of scenery, some fresh spring air to slap them both round the face and bring them to their senses. They haven't really done enough work yet to justify calling it a day. And the nagging ring at the bottom of one of their bags – Nathan, he'd be willing to bet: *Just checking in, no pressure but wondered how it's going* – brought him to his senses just in time. Just before he reached his hand out to put it over hers. To say some things that could not easily be taken back, that would hang in the air between them, screaming for resolution – the kind of resolution that can only take one form.

'There'll be time for play later,' Jess says, eventually, after what feels like an impossibly long silence, each of them, he suspects, weighing up the pros and cons of giving in to their animal instincts. He is glad someone has broken that silence, that someone has been sensible. He would have assumed it would be him, but in the moment, he lacked the willpower. He knows he is not currently boyfriend material; he knows he has a deadline for this novel in order to keep his advance, and he needs the advance, and he knows that there is no way he'll meet that deadline, never mind the micro deadline Nathan has set them both, if he allows himself the kind of distraction that comes with the beginning of whatever this would be – a fling, a relationship, a friendship with benefits beyond co-authorship of a critically acclaimed novel. But he is only human, with human desires, and it's been a while, and there's something about Jess and the way the occasional sunray lands on her hair, colouring it honey-toned, the way her layered eyes seem to promise depths of thought and mystery – something that makes him light up inside so that he wasn't quite able to hold his hand up and say *no, stop, let's not do this, at least not yet.*

He nods, agreeing, not questioning out loud what she means by *play* or what she means by *later*. And so they go back to the book: back to thrashing out the plan they hope to present to Nathan next week, back to restructuring the story, and arguing over plotlines and which characters should be amalgamated or disappear entirely. Jess, he has noticed, is careful to say encouraging things about particular turns of phrase or scenes that she thinks land well. He knows it's the compliment sandwich at work again; and yet, knowing this doesn't change the fact that every time she says something positive about the book, something inside him melts. He is a chocolate soufflé with a gooey middle, the kind that come in pairs of glass ramekins you save because you tell yourself you'll make a soufflé of your own one day and not just keep buying them at the supermarket.

And now that he is thinking about chocolate soufflés, Alex notices that he is genuinely hungry. Looking at the clock, he is surprised to see it is well into dinner time. They've survived on buttery flapjacks all afternoon and he hasn't noticed the hours ticking by. At home, he works in a room where a clock looks down at him at his desk, simultaneously mocking and motivating him. He is constantly checking it, monitoring his own progress, calculating and re-calculating his writing speed, even though he knows that repeatedly doing this is responsible for slowing him down considerably. But here, he hasn't thought about the time at all. Here, writing has been fun, energising. He remembers this feeling from his first book, when he wrote without knowledge of the publishing industry and its vagaries, when he wrote without the pressure of prior success and the reading public's expectation of his Next Great Novel. He wishes he could recover that pre-MFA joy: the joy of storytelling, of painting with words, of unbridled creativity. Now, there is too much baggage that he drags across the page along with his pen. But Jess has made him feel lighter again; it's as if he's had a transfusion of her passion, of her excitement. Her eyes dance and her hair bounces on her shoulder as she scribbles lists and circles bullet points. She has something of that beginner's joy he misses in himself, but it's something else, too – her innate zest for life itself is contagious. And attractive. Has he mentioned attractive?

He finds himself wanting to protect her, wanting nothing to happen to her that would tarnish this joy.

'You keep looking at the clock,' she says now. 'Am I boring you?'

But she asks this with a smile, knowing the answer.

'Sorry, sorry,' he says. His constant double apologising had been trained out of him in the US, but he's been back in London for long enough now that the habit is back in full force. 'I'm just thinking about dinner.'

'That's a good thought,' she says. 'We should probably save some of these flapjacks for tomorrow at least.'

Alex reaches into his bag for his phone. He's about to grab it to google restaurants in Godalming, but he thinks better of it. He doesn't want to see his missed calls, his social media notifications, his email.

'Let's walk into town,' he says. 'See what it has to offer.'

'The old-fashioned way? No Yelp, no Google?'

'No Yelp. No Google. We wander, see what takes our fancy.'

She looks ruefully at her own bag, wondering perhaps if it's socially acceptable for her to check her own phone.

'Deal,' she says, though she takes her bag with her when she goes to freshen up. He won't judge her for quickly scanning her messages, for not wanting to stay in their bubble, just the two of them and their novel. He'll be disappointed, but he won't judge her.

* * *

He has an urge to walk hand in hand with Jess through the town, but he manages to suppress it. They walk close to each other, though, and seem to bump shoulders more frequently than he usually does when walking side by side with someone. Which of them is responsible for that, he couldn't possibly say.

'This place feels very familiar,' Jess scrunches up her face when she's confused, a small vertical line appearing between her eyebrows, which by the time she is his age, in a few years' time, will no doubt have scored itself there permanently.

She's not wearing her glasses, so maybe everything looks familiar to her in a blurry kind of way. He can't work out what she needs these glasses for: sometimes she wears them to work on the book, and sometimes not. Sometimes she wears them out and about, but also sometimes not. 'It's getting dark,' he points out, steering clear of saying something that would betray how closely he is observing her, and filing it away as something to ask her about later. 'So it looks like most English towns right now.'

'You might be right,' she says, in a tone that suggests, *You're definitely not*. She's done this a few times today and he is learning to recognise it as one of her habits – perhaps conflict avoidance or lack of confidence or, as his sister Louisa might have said, just a lifelong skill born of living in a world where women have to placate irritable men who don't like being questioned.

'I mean,' he says, 'I might also be wrong. You might have been here before, for all I know. Or maybe seen it in a friend's photo.'

But then they turn down a street, and she starts laughing – a different laugh from the easy, joy-filled sound he so loved earlier. A harsher laugh.

'I can't believe it,' she says.

'What?'

'I've figured it out. You don't recognise these cute cobbled streets?'

'No.'

'It looks exactly like *The Holiday*.'

Ah yes. He's vaguely heard of that film.

'Please tell me you've seen *The Holiday*?'

Alex has not. He feels the best course of action here is to stay silent.

'You know – Cameron Diaz swaps houses with Kate Winslet and falls in love with Jude Law?'

'Right, right,' he says, sounding unconvinced even to his own ears. 'Of course.'

'I can't believe Nathan sent us to a film set.'

'I mean, technically, I think people really do live here.'

'Yes, but look at it.' The streets are picture perfect. She isn't wrong.

'He's sent us to the set of one of the most romantic films of all time, Alex.'

He tries not to dwell on the fact that it's the first time she's said his name. That he likes hearing it in her voice. He tries, instead, to concentrate on what she's saying – or rather, what she's *not* saying. What she's implying.

'I think this is just genuinely where he happens to have an Airbnb?'

'Oh yes, I know that. But, still. He could have booked us an all-day meeting room in the enormous building where he works. We could have had fancy mineral water and expensive biscuits all day and he could have checked up on us multiple times to make sure we were on track.'

'I think I like your grandmother's flapjacks better than mass-produced biscuits,' he says, trying to diffuse whatever tension has mysteriously appeared.

'Thank you,' she says, more gently now. 'I love it. I'm glad you do too. But don't get me sidetracked.'

To be fair to Alex, he is confused about where she is going with this. What it is exactly that is making Jess angry, and whether he, too, should be angry at Nathan. They have slowed and then stopped outside a pub which looks promising for dinner, and now that he's started thinking about the possibility of fish and chips, he's finding it hard to concentrate on much else. But Jess, still wound tight, is pacing now.

'So, we're mad at Nathan for sending us to a lovely cottage in a pretty town where one of your favourite movies was filmed?'

'No. We're mad at Nathan for setting us up to fall in love.' Instantly, her face is flushed. He suspects his is too. He certainly feels warm all of a sudden. 'I mean, not that that's what's happening here, obviously.'

'Oh, obviously,' he says. Should he feel hurt? He has whiplash. Screw it, he's going to ask. He has no self-control when he's hungry. 'Would it be so terrible if that *is* what he's done?'

Jess stops pacing. She opens her mouth to speak, then closes it again. There is no good answer to this question, and she seems to know it. 'I just don't like to be manipulated,' she says at last, deflated.

'Me neither,' he says. He stretches out his arm for her to take his hand, and she doesn't seem to hesitate to respond. Now that the words *falling in love* are out there, they might as well own it.

'Come on,' he says, drawing reassuring circles at the base of her thumb and gesturing to the pub with his free arm. 'Let's eat.'

Chapter Nineteen

JESS

It is possible she may have overreacted. Jess sees that now. But in her defence, she was starving, and not thinking straight. Now, with her stomach full of toad in the hole and her second glass of Merlot in her hand, she feels she should apologise. Although it's difficult to know how to do that without admitting some things she isn't ready to admit yet.

'Alex . . .' she says, at a suitable pause in the conversation. He has told her about his complicated family: four siblings whose parents divorced and each remarried partners who already had kids, then had two more of their own. He's the eldest of a tribe of biblical proportions.

'Don't worry about it,' he says, seemingly guessing what she's going to say before she's even formulated her sentence. 'You were hangry.'

'I know, but—'

'It's okay.'

'Okay,' she says, mirroring him. She'll leave it there for now, grateful that he's being so gracious. She didn't really want to have this conversation anyway. Not now, not with Alex. Maybe later, with Nathan. A part of her likes to imagine she'll have the guts and gumption to march into his office and demand to know what he was playing at, sending them to the centre of a romantic fairytale. A part of her, though, wonders if before this weekend is over, she'll be grateful; if she'll instead be planning a sheepish, loaded thank you to Nathan. A Fortnum & Mason hamper, maybe, with a cryptic-but-not-that-cryptic note.

'So tell me about your family,' he says.

'There's not a lot to tell compared to yours,' she replies. 'It's pretty much the opposite. I'm an only child.'

'Wow.' Alex looks impressed and vaguely surprised, as if confronted with a reality he's only read about in psychology textbooks. 'What's that like?'

'Mostly pretty lonely,' she says. 'I made my own fun, though. Wrote stories starring my friends and handed them out to them at break time. Played the saxophone. Set up a Monopoly board and had my imaginary friend play alternate turns. And I read a lot.'

Jess braces for the inevitable next question, the one whose answer tends to crease brows in sympathy.

'Just you and your parents, then?'

Alex speaks with something like awe. Truth be told, she'd have killed for a family like his. Noisy dinner times, brothers to wrestle with, sisters whose clothes she would steal. Multiple adults around at all times.

'Just me and my mum, actually.' She takes a deep breath to get the next part over with. 'My dad died when I was little. I don't remember him.'

There it is: the brow crease. 'I'm sorry to hear that.'

'It's okay, it really is.' She takes a deep breath, ready for her standard spiel, to get this over with as quickly as possible. She hates feeling like she has to comfort other people over her own loss and reassure them that she's fine and they don't need to waste energy worrying about her. 'My mum wasn't around much, either, so I spent a lot of time with my grandparents, and they're great. My mum had me in her twenties, so they were young grandparents, and they took me to the zoo and museums and all sorts.'

'Are they—'

'Still around, yes. It's the same grandma who made those flapjacks you enjoyed earlier. They live in Pimlico, just up the road from me now. I still see them a lot.'

When Lily moved out of the Brixton flat to get married, Jess couldn't bear to look for another random person to share a flat and a life with. She thanks the gods of Gumtree every day for delivering Lily to her the last time she did that, and she thinks it's unlikely that lightning could strike twice in that luckiest of ways. *Come and live in Pimlico*, Alan had said on the phone, and Jess had laughed because she knew what the rents in Pimlico were like, and her book influencer business was doing well – better than she could have hoped, in many ways – but not, like, *that* well. But then Val had added, *We'll help you with the money*, and the prospect of living alone suddenly didn't seem so bad if it included weekly comfort meals with two of her favourite people. She feels bad about the money, though. Every month, she thinks she's almost there, can almost pay the rent alone, but then the landlord will put up the rent or an affiliate platform will change the way they do payouts or a book festival will be late paying her for chairing a panel, and she'll have to put off the phone call she has been wanting to make for three years: *I'm okay now, don't worry about helping me out anymore.*

'That's cool,' Alex says. 'It sort of feels like how life used to be. Like maybe life should still be. People living close to their families, you know.' He tells her that his own parents – both sets of them: mum and stepdad, dad and stepmum – live in Tunbridge Wells, his siblings scattered throughout the UK, two of them still irritated that they had to come back from living in sunnier climes post-Brexit. He doesn't ask about her mum, perhaps fearing another brow-creasing moment, so she volunteers the information.

'My mum lives in Brighton,' she says. 'She loves the sea and the easy access to Gatwick Airport. She's always off on her adventures.' Did she roll her eyes as she said that? She does it almost unconsciously when she talks about her mum these days. Lily has often pointed it out, pulled her up on it.

'Brighton's cool,' Alex says, cautiously, like he can tell there's more to this whole thing. Perhaps she did roll her eyes; perhaps that's how he knew.

'It is.'

Jess, too, loves the sea, the sound of waves over pebbles, walks on the long promenade with the wind in her hair, the fresh sea water on the occasional hot day.

She doesn't get to go as often as she'd like. Her mum, even when she's there, is busy. Knitting groups, walking groups, Scrabble club. When Jess was a teenager, she worried that her mum would bring home a boyfriend one day. But it seems that these days she's too busy having fun to think about such things; maybe that was always true. Maybe, when Jess slept over at her grandparents' or they came over to babysit, her mum really *was* at book club or meeting with friends to go to the theatre, as she claimed. It was easier to believe that then, but maybe it was also true.

Jess is enjoying talking to Alex. He's a good listener, tilting his head slightly when she talks, looking at her intently, all of his attention on her. Asking good questions, like the one about her A Level Latin, which she deftly deflected, not wanting to go into the whole thing. Her dad was French, and part of her couldn't help wanting to connect with him. French itself felt too much, though, too fraught. Too emotionally dangerous. What if she wasn't any good at it? That would have been awkward and weird, like a denial of her birthright, a reminder of all she could have had: someone and something to grieve, when she's never actually felt any need or desire to grieve – even if the absence of her father has shaped a large part of her personality. The dad-shaped hole – half of her genetics – is a fire, raging, dangerous. She has to keep it at arm's length. Latin is that arm.

Alex shows the kind of thoughtfulness and emotional depth that she probably should have expected from someone who writes books like his, but she's still pleasantly surprised. It makes her want to tell him everything. About her mum, how Jess wishes she were more of a priority in her life. About her grandparents, how watching them get older and frailer breaks her heart and makes her worry about what life will be like without them; how she might need to be around a little more to care for them and for her cousin Ivy, whose dad is away a lot on business and whose mum has chronic fatigue and needs a lot of help. How, if she's honest, the thought of being tied down, of not being able to jet off to adventures at will, scares her a little. She wants to tell Alex about Lily, and how Jess knows she'll have to drum up enthusiasm when the day inevitably comes when Lily announces she's pregnant – when, really, she wants them both to be young forever, free to stay up all night talking and eat a little too much cheese at their local wine bar and sunbathe on Greek island beaches and slide down mountains on their bums after attempting snowboarding. Usually, she'd prefer not to think about any of that; she'd rather talk about books and how much she loves her job, her plans for future book clubs and podcast interviews. But with Alex, she feels like she wants to talk about life in all its messiness. It's a surprising feeling, especially after such a short time knowing him – like he's home, like he's a safe place.

But just as Jess is thinking this thought, she notices Alex's attention wane, his eye flickering over her shoulder. There's probably someone prettier than her on another table. She should have known this moment was too good to last or to be real at all, that the bubble she's been in with Alex would pop eventually. She had hoped it would take longer than a pub meal, but she probably should have known better.

'Sorry,' he says, breaking into her thoughts. 'I don't mean to keep looking over your shoulder.'

'But there's a really hot redhead over in the corner?' She meant this to come over as light-hearted, as a joke, but she hears a bitterness in her tone that is unattractive even to her.

'I'm not really into redheads, actually,' he says. Maybe he meant this light-heartedly too, but it comes across as surprisingly serious.

'A really hot brunette, then?'

'I like blondes, actually.' He makes eye contact as he says it and her stomach, traitor that it is, somersaults. 'But no. There *is* a woman over there, and she keeps looking at me in that *do I know you from somewhere* way.'

'One of your army of fans?'

Alex's cheeks instantly redden. Jess had been joking, but now that she thinks about it, it makes perfect sense that there would be an army of fans out there, with social media pages dedicated to his dimple, blog posts dreamily describing having met him at a book signing. Godalming is close enough to London for literary types to live there, and certainly to visit – literary types and exactly the sort of industry insiders who know enough about the It books of the moment to recognise not just book covers but authors' faces.

And then, suddenly, there she is, the brunette, materialising next to their table the way a waitress might to recite the day's specials. But alas, this is nowhere near as exciting.

'Excuse me,' she says. 'But I have to ask – I mean, you really look like Alex Maxwell. You know, the writer?'

'Ah yes,' he says, turning on his flashiest smile, the one with the dimple. 'I get that a lot.'

He's deflecting, maybe. But also, Jess wonders if he's prolonging the moment because he's enjoying himself.

The brunette's face stays frozen. She evidently can't decide if he is joking or trying to put her off the scent. If he wants to be left alone.

'So it's not you?'

There's a pause. Alex might be weighing up whether he wants to welcome in this interruption to their dinner, or whether he wants to send the brunette away as quickly as possible. Or maybe the pause is just for dramatic effect. It's difficult to tell.

'No, no,' he says. 'It is.'

For the second time this evening, Jess fights the urge to roll her eyes.

'Oh good,' the brunette giggles. 'Because that would have been embarrassing.'

Not unlike this moment, in fact. Jess can feel her body curling with the cringe of it all. And then it gets worse: the brunette produces a book from behind her back. Jess wants to ask whether she carries it around with her all the time in the hopes of bumping into him and getting it autographed. I mean, what are the chances?

'I thought I recognised you from when you spoke at Hay for your first book. Would you sign this for me?'

'I'd be honoured.' He feels in his pocket for a pen, but unlike Jess, who is always prepared, he doesn't have one.

'Here,' Jess says, fishing in her handbag then handing a biro to Alex. The brunette turns to her, seemingly becoming aware for the first time that he is not dining alone.

'Hello,' Jess says.

'Hi,' she says. 'Sorry. How rude of me.' She puts out her hand for Jess to shake it. 'I'm Cassandra.'

'Jessica,' Jess says, shaking her hand. When people have long names, it always spurs her on to deploy hers. In her peripheral vision, she sees Alex mouth it back – *Jessica* – as if it had never occurred to him that *Jess* might be short for anything.

'Cassandra,' Alex repeats now. 'That's a beautiful name. Should I make it out to you?'

'You're too nice,' she says, her hand on his forearm. 'Yes, please.'

'And are you a writer too?'

She gasps, her hand to her mouth. That same hand removed now, Jess notes, from Alex's arm. 'How did you know?'

'Sometimes you can just tell,' he says. *Oh please*, Jess wishes she could say. *I bet he asks everyone that.*

Keep writing, Alex scribbles, just above the signature that's more or less illegible apart from the two prominent Xs – the one in *Alex* and the one in *Maxwell*, interlocking in a way that's more artful than it has any right to be. After multiple thank yous, Cassandra leaves to go back to her table and, presumably, dig out her phone and tell the world what has just happened to her.

'You should ask for her number,' Jess says, teasing. Mostly.

'Stop it,' Alex says.

But she can tell he's enjoying himself.

Chapter Twenty

ALEX

If he's honest, Alex would have to say that he isn't sure how they each make it to their own beds that night without so much as a kiss. They linger in the kitchen, making unnecessary post-dinner tea. Jess teases him about Cassandra, seemingly as reluctant as he is to go their separate ways. But they get there, eventually. He lies awake for a while, thinking of her on the other side of the house, wondering what she wears to bed, whether she sleeps on her side or her back, if she always reads or journals before she falls asleep. He imagines she has a whole night-time routine, imagines her going through it – mildly distracted, he hopes, by thoughts of the day they've spent together, by thoughts, perhaps, of his own bedtime routine. Eventually, he falls asleep, dreams the kind of dreams he will never admit to in public.

When he wakes up, he throws on his trusty Durham University Boat Club sweatshirt and some socks and pads through to the kitchen. Jess is up already, swinging in the dark wooden rocking chair, sipping a tea and looking out of the window into the depressing British greyness, seemingly mesmerised by a squirrel jumping from branch to branch. Her mind is a mystery to him – and he is enjoying exploring it, though so far, he realises, he is only paddling in its shallowest edges.

'Morning,' she says, but she doesn't turn her head. It's as if she doesn't want to miss a second of the squirrel's dance.

'Morning. I take it you're a squirrel fan?'

'Of course,' she says, and this time she does turn to him, her smile lighting up her whole face, the whole room. 'How could you not be?'

'Indeed,' he says, despite his bafflement. He does not say, *Aren't they just rats with fluffy tails and good PR?* He does not say, *You know there are squirrels in London, too?* She is having what seems to be almost a sacred moment, with the squirrel, and he doesn't want to ruin it for her.

'I made a pot of tea,' she says. 'There's enough for you too.'

There's a crocheted tea cosy on the pot. He hasn't seen one of those in a long time. It strikes him as incongruous that Nathan would have one at all, let alone a spare one for this Airbnb. All these years being friends, and he didn't know Nathan was the type to have a tea cosy. Then again, he also wouldn't have had him pegged as a matchmaker. Surely that can't be what this whole co-authorship is about? Surely Jess has it wrong about Nathan sending the two of them to Godalming to – what were her words . . . her exact phrase – to *fall in love*?

'That's thoughtful of you,' he says. 'Thank you.'

He pours his tea and they sip, the silence punctuated only by their slurps. She is watching the squirrel; he is watching her watch it. It feels like something he could do for a long time. Her enjoyment is mesmerising, beautiful. *She* is mesmerising, beautiful.

Get yourself together, he tells himself. *You are here to do a task, not to fall in love.*

As if reading his thoughts, she drags her eyes away from the window.

'We should probably get to work.'

'We'll move the table,' he finds himself saying. 'So that you can watch the garden creatures at the same time.'

'I'd love that,' she says. 'You're not just a pretty face after all.'

He knows it's an expression, that people say this to each other jokingly, regardless of the state of their faces. But he takes it as a compliment nonetheless. She thinks he has a pretty face. That will do nicely.

'Neither are you,' he says.

She looks at him quizzically, perhaps wondering what has triggered this admission. Not knowing that her palpable joy is winsome, contagious. 'Thank you?'

* * *

They work all morning, following the groove they set yesterday. Outside, the clouds grow darker and then rain begins to drum on the windows. Page by page, Alex and Jess discuss the descriptions and the plot.

They brainstorm other ways the story can unfold, the characters that need a more substantial role. Alex is beginning to think he can trust Jess to write those missing pages, or at least to sketch them out and write a first draft they can then polish together. She's smarter than he ever gave her credit for. He tries not to let himself be distracted by how attractive he finds her mind at work. They skip lunch, fill up on the rapidly dwindling supply of flapjacks. And then, the rain slows and stops. The sun's weak efforts produce what seems to be a miracle: a rainbow. And apparently Jess can't take it anymore. She puts her pen down.

'I'm sorry,' she says, really just a clearing of the throat. 'But I have to go outside. It's just so pretty out there.'

'Of course,' Alex says. 'You've more than earned a break.'

She looks at him as if trying to figure out what is wrong with his sentence. Then she gets it. It's the pronoun he's used: the *you*.

'You're coming too, though, aren't you?' He doesn't want Jess to judge him. And he definitely doesn't want to disappoint her.

'It's not that,' he says, improvising. It's warm and cosy indoors. Outdoors, there'll be puddles, and the kind of damp that will chill him to the bone. 'It's footwear. I've only got my trainers with me, and they're not very waterproof.'

In his defence, he thought they'd spend their entire time indoors, huddled over a manuscript. But he should have thought about going out for dinner, should have thought more about needing some alone time, some fresh air. Should have thought, perhaps, if he hadn't been in denial, about romantic walks. After more rummaging, she finds some wellies for him. They are ridiculously big, but he doesn't want to draw attention to his embarrassingly small feet, to what the smallness of his feet might imply. He will slosh around in them and pray for blisters to form only after they're safely back in the comfort and warmth of the cottage.

'All right,' she says. 'Let's go.'

It takes them a few tries to yank the door open, but they make it out. And he has to admit, the rainbow is pretty. Jess's cheeks are flushed from the cold or from pleasure, or both, and she looks beautiful, too. 'See?' she says, pointing out a puddle where the rainbow is reflected. She reaches for his hand and squeezes it. 'Aren't you glad you came out?'

With her hand in his, it's hard to argue with that.

Chapter Twenty-One

JESS

Alex has been a good sport about going out for a walk, trying his best to pretend to enjoy it. Jess appreciates the effort. Still, he's clearly shivering now, and Jess has to admit the damp in the air is beginning to seep into her bones, too.

'Come on,' she says to Alex. 'You're getting chilly. Let's get you indoors.'

He has the decency to look disappointed. 'Are you sure?'

'I'm sure. You've done well. And I imagine you've got blisters by now from those too-big wellies.' She can't resist poking at his vanity.

'Oh no,' he says. 'These are fine.'

They are quite obviously not fine. She's seen him walking in them. But she won't argue.

'Come on,' she says again, squeezing his hand in hers to emphasise her point. "Let's get you warmed up.'

Alex wiggles his eyebrows. 'How do you suggest we do that?'

'I'll make us hot chocolate,' she says.

'Oh.' He pouts a little, like a disappointed little boy, though she can't imagine a little boy being disappointed about hot chocolate – not even Alex as a little boy.

'It's the good stuff,' she says. 'I brought Whittard's with me. Three different flavours. You get to pick.'

'Okay,' he says, his pouting forgotten. Justifiably, she thinks. A couple of months ago, she and Lily had spent hours of a rainy Saturday afternoon in the Covent Garden shop, sampling different flavours – white chocolate, chocolate orange, dark chocolate with a hint of cinnamon. It had been the closest Jess had come to a certain kind of pleasure in quite some time.

Jess turns the key in the lock and shoves the door with her free arm, but it doesn't budge.

Alex gives it a good go, too, and nothing shifts.

'Uh-oh,' she says. Her mind has already leapt ahead to the probable lack of locksmiths in Godalming past 6 p.m. on a Saturday, and to the equally probable lack of hotel rooms. Maybe they'll have to sleep outside. They really would have to be creative with getting warm then. She flushes at the thought, her body awakening to it, beginning to prime itself.

'Let's try together,' Alex says. Disappointingly, he does not seem quite as ready to give up as Jess is.

'Okay,' she says. Reluctantly, she unlocks her fingers from his, ready to use the strength in both her arms. She feels his hand there still, phantom fingers that belong with hers. She counts them in, and they both lean all of their weight against the heavy wooden door.

It gives instantly, like there was never a problem, like it was gaslighting them the whole time. They stumble forward; Jess almost falls. Alex, thankfully, grabs her arm, catching her. Warmth spreads through her, and she doesn't think it's just the central heating in the cottage that's responsible.

'You okay there?' he asks. Maybe he's noticed the sudden rise in temperature, too.

'Yes. Thank you,' she says. Landing flat on her face would not have been pleasant. It would have been painful, and also embarrassing. She's grateful he caught her. He probably doesn't need to still be holding on to her, but who is she to ask questions. His gentle touch sends a spark through her body, down into the pit of her stomach. His breath caresses her face. She closes her eyes, waits. It feels like a moment, like he is going to kiss her.

But he doesn't.

Instead, he clears his throat, and she opens her eyes to see that he's taken a step back, that he is closing the door.

'Teamwork makes the dream work,' he says, referencing, she supposes, the miracle of the open door. He rolls his eyes as he does so that she will know that he knows how cheesy it sounds.

'That's very American of you,' she says. What she doesn't say is that it's also true. The door opening: teamwork. More importantly, the novel writing: teamwork. Making *her* dream work. She has felt herself coming alive creatively as they've worked, as Alex has explained his thinking about novel structure and plot twists and character development, about anaphora and alliteration and the rhythm of sentences. Her long-held dream of being a writer, a novelist in her own right, feels within reach. She knows she has a lot to learn, still. That if even someone like Alex can struggle and get stuck, then she inevitably will, too. But her mind, like her body, feels alive and awake to possibility in ways it hasn't in a long time.

'Sorry,' he says, forcing an American twang. And then, back in his Southern English posh-boy accent, 'Americans aren't wrong about everything, though.'

'Such as?'

'Well,' he says. 'Teamwork really does make the dream work, does it not?'

'When it's a good team,' she says. 'Yes, I suppose it does.'

He searches out her eyes. 'A good team like us?'

'Maybe,' she says, her knees suddenly at risk of buckling. She forces herself to hold his gaze. *Kiss me*, she thinks. *Kiss me, kiss me, kiss me.* Lily's voice in her head responds, *Or you could kiss him.* 'I think we're doing okay,' she says.

'I think so too,' he says, his voice tender and full of kindness. And then, clearing his throat, his voice steadier, he adds: 'Now, about that hot chocolate . . .'

Chapter Twenty-Two

ALEX

Alex watches Jess measure out the milk in mugfuls, measure out the chocolate powder, light the gas, strike a match. He wants to help, but it doesn't seem to be a two-person job, and besides, he is kind of frozen to the spot. Ensorcelled, perhaps. He has fought so hard not to kiss her. Yesterday, when they were talking about their bookshop moment, and he could so easily have stood, walked over to her, and leaned down to meet her lips with his. Later, outside the pub, when she'd used the phrase *falling in love*, her righteous indignation somehow turning him on. And just now, by the door, when he'd had to count backwards from 100 and think of very unsexy things in order to tear himself away from her arm.

He has used up all his self-control.

All he can do now is stand very still and wait for the urge to pass.

But it's not going to pass, and if he's honest with himself, he knows it. *In vain have I struggled. It will not do.* Where is that from, again?

Jess stirs the milk with a wooden spoon. Chocolate tinged with orange mingles with the scent of apple shampoo. Despite the season, it makes him think of Christmas, of family and tradition, of the picture he has always had of himself with his own kids giddily unwrapping their presents. Now, in his mind, those children have honey blonde hair and a certain boisterous *joie de vivre* he somehow hadn't imagined before.

All of which, he realises, is ridiculous.

He hardly knows Jess. He didn't know she existed a few months ago. And now just is not the right time for a girlfriend. The *book* is the thing. Getting his anxiety under control is the *other* thing. His next girlfriend deserves better than his messed-up self.

He rehearses these arguments in his mind, as he has many times. But all the other times, Jess has not been standing in front of him, pink in her cheeks, gently humming an unrecognisable tune as she stirs what smells like a very pleasurable drink. Perhaps that's why, this time, it doesn't seem to be working. He studies the curve from her neck to her shoulder, the delicate gold chain around her neck, its clasp slipping further and further round.

And there it is, his excuse to touch her.

He moves towards her. She stops humming. He slides his finger under the gold chain at the back of her neck. Her skin – so soft. Her hair – so shiny.

She turns to him, eager, as if she has been waiting for him to do exactly this. As if to say, *What took you so long?* Her pupils are wide, and he reads determination in them, mirroring his own.

Later, they will argue about who leaned forwards first, who kissed whom.

But right now, it doesn't matter. All that matters in the moment is lips brushing together, tongues finding each other, teeth tingling as they awkwardly meet.

And heat, so much heat.

And then – 'Stop,' she says, pulling away. and his heart drops into the pit of his stomach until she tells him why. 'The chocolate is going to burn.'

'Let it,' he says, bumping her forehead with his, beckoning her in again.

'It's Whittard's chocolate,' she says, laughing against him. 'One does not let Whittard's chocolate burn.'

He groans (inwardly? Outwardly? Who can say?) but does not argue. She turns back to the stove, to the stirring. He slips his arms around her waist and she leans back into him. Emboldened, he kisses her shoulder, her neck.

She sighs against him. He thinks he might feel her trembling the tiniest bit.

And then at last, at long last, the hot chocolate is ready.

'You're going to have to let go of me so I can pour this,' she says softly, a smile in her voice. He reluctantly does, and he waits.

He waits interminably, it seems, though it is probably only ten seconds. She turns off the stove. Pours the hot chocolate from the saucepan into the mugs, sets them on the coffee table.

'Where were we?' he says, his arms around her again.

'Here,' she says, looping her own arms around his neck. Drawing him close, up against her. He holds his breath, vulnerable: in doing this, she is going to know how much he wants her. But if the moans in her throat as he kisses her are any indication, she wants him just as much.

'The hot chocolate,' she says, when they come up for air.

He has to laugh. 'You're obsessed with that stuff,' he says.

'Have a sip,' she says. 'You will be too.'

Reluctantly, he pulls away. Takes her hand, leads her to the sofa, picks up his mug. Inhales, as he has done so often at wine tastings. Then he takes a sip.

'Wow,' he says. 'That tastes—'

'Like an orgasm in a mug?' she says.

The word itself makes him groan.

'Don't,' he says. 'That's not fair.'

She looks at him, the picture of innocence. 'Not fair how?'

'Because . . .'

How to put this delicately? Romantically? Or at the very least, not smarmily?

'Because you're making me jealous of hot chocolate, which is an odd position to be in.'

She smiles. His favourite smile of hers – slightly crooked, mischievous. 'You've got chocolate on your bottom lip,' she says, and she leans in to lick it off. Slowly, teasingly. Electricity runs across his lip, then the other, and then his whole body lights up as in a game of Operation.

'Jess,' he says. 'You are killing me.'

'I'm sorry,' she says, but she doesn't sound sorry. 'Would you like me to stop?'

He shakes his head, but she pauses, looks longingly at her mug, as if torn between the taste of him and the taste of chocolate orange. Alex is going to track down Mr Whittard and murder him in cold blood.

She takes a sip, and then another.

There is no chocolate left on his lip for her to lick off.

'Maybe we should slow down,' she says. There's no teasing in her voice. She might mean it. She takes another long sip and makes the kind of all-body sound in response to the taste that he wishes he were responsible for.

'Jess . . .' he says. More to hear himself say her name than anything else.

It comes out like a moan.

'What if it gets awkward?' she asks.

'I think we're past that point,' he says. Hearing each other make the kind of sounds they have been making over the last little while feels as intimate as nakedness. Not that he'd say no to the actual nakedness. To see her body, her every curve, trace the outline of her waist—

Deep breaths, Alex.
Drink your chocolate.

Jess finishes hers with a satisfied slurp and puts the mug down. *Thunk*.

'Do you watch the Winter Olympics?' she asks, a swerve in the conversation so screechingly extreme that he wonders if he somehow hallucinated the last portion of the evening. Maybe the door came unstuck so violently that he stumbled, fell onto the ceramic floor, and gave himself a concussion? He scrambles to think of another explanation.

But Jess is looking at him expectantly, so he digs deep and finds an answer.

'I'm more of a Summer Olympics fan,' he says. 'Swimming and running, especially.'

'All right,' she says. 'So I take it you haven't heard of Tessa Virtue and Scott Moir?'

'It rings a vague bell,' he says. Which it doesn't, but these people are clearly important to Jess in some way, or she wouldn't bring them up at a time like this. He doesn't want to admit total ignorance.

'Canadian ice dancers,' she says. 'They won the gold medal in 2018 with this electric performance to the *Moulin Rouge!* soundtrack. And, oh my gosh, I have never seen anything sexier. It was incredible.'

He nods, earnestly, to show he is listening. And to speed up the story, so they can get back to previous activities.

'Supposedly, there's nothing romantic between them. But, honestly, the chemistry. It was electric.'

'I always thought electricity was more about physics than chemistry,' he says, because sometimes, he can't help self-sabotaging.

Jess narrows her eyes. 'Anyway,' she says. 'It had so much sexual tension. So much unresolved energy – like an unconsummated love affair.'

Such a quaint word, *unconsummated*. And yet it has an effect on him that is not at all quaint.

'I had an idea for a novel when I watched them. About ice dancers who are in love, but they decide, for the sake of their sport, their art, their chemistry – that they won't sleep together until they've won a gold medal.'

He is starting to see where she might be going with this. 'The magic is in the lack of consummation,' he says, defeated.

'Exactly.' She nods, her hair bouncing on her shoulders. 'You get it.'

He wishes he didn't.

He isn't sure how to respond.

The pause between them stretches and stretches.

'So you're thinking,' he says, processing, just making doubly sure he hasn't read this situation wrong, 'for the sake of this novel, we should also—'

'Leave things unconsummated.'

He nods, not *I agree* but *I understand*. He isn't sure he does, totally. Jess's sudden reluctance to, well, consummate, has come out of seemingly nowhere. Could it be that she is scared? Not of sex itself – he is pretty sure she is into that – but of the ramifications. The possibility of pain if whatever this is between them doesn't work out. Scared, maybe, of how vulnerable it feels to be so intimate. Either way, he won't push her.

'I might need a cold shower,' he says at last.

'You and me both,' Jess says, and he refrains from mentioning the obvious solution.

* * *

Jess comes out of the shower wrapped in just a towel, and he rushes in after her, not making eye contact. They have one more night in this cottage and that, Alex knows, is going to feel like eternity. *Damn you, Scott and Tessa*, he thinks, shaking his fist in what he assumes to be the vague direction of Canada.

He switches the shower to the coldest setting he can bear and tries to think about William Faulkner and James Joyce – writers he knows that he is supposed to deeply admire, to want to emulate, but that he finds unbearably pretentious, impenetrably obscure. Or, to put it in starker terms: boring. These are things he would not, of course, ever admit in interviews. But there are going to be other minefields when it comes to the interviews about this particular book. He is going to have to sit side by side with her, breathing in her apple shampoo, listening to her enthusiasm, maybe brushing her arm as they both reach for a glass of water – and somehow remain unaffected.

The apple shampoo has followed him here, to the side of the bath, and he can't help himself: he flicks it open, breathes it in. This will have to do for now.

And then he turns the shower temperature even lower.

* * *

When Alex comes out of the bathroom, having given himself a stern talking-to, Jess is in the living room in leggings and a hoodie, looking forlorn. His immediate, hopeful thought: perhaps she regrets putting a stop to things. Quite rightly, in his view.

But when she hears him behind her, she asks, 'Are you decent?' and this seems like an entirely different order of things.

'Decent as I ever will be,' he says, an attempt at a joke, which is nowhere close to landing.

'Okay.' She swivels her head round and says, 'So. You know how it's been raining quite a lot today?'

It is impossible to guess where this is going. 'Yeah?'

'I don't think the roof was properly equipped for that.'

He gives it a moment, ponders the possible implications. But he's still not quite getting it.

'Oh?' he says at last.

'There's a leak in the ceiling in my room,' she says. 'Right above my bed, as luck would have it.'

My bed. Very much not the point of her sentence, but his brain snags on it. Her bed.

He snaps out of it. 'Can we move your bed?'

'Maybe. But can I sleep through a constant drip?'

He probably could. With a house as full as his was growing up, you had to train yourself to sleep through everything and anything, or you didn't sleep. But she's the only child of a single mum, so he's guessing it's different for her.

'I don't know,' he says. 'I don't know your sleeping habits.'

It's an obnoxious thing to say, he knows, but he means it as a desperate kind of flirting. *I don't know your sleeping habits, but I know I'd like to.*

He does not have to look at her face to know it has not quite landed the way he intended it to.

'Well, I can't,' she says.

'Let's see the damage,' he says. He is trying not to let his brain go to where it has immediately gone. Before he suggests what he really wants to, he will offer to switch rooms with her. He can sleep through a drip. Probably. Or at least, he can sleep through it no worse than he will anyway. Noise doesn't keep him awake, but anxiety does. The thumping of his heart when he's thinking about her, in pyjamas just a few footsteps away – that does, too.

She stands up from the sofa and follows Alex into her room. The bed is tidily made; a pile of books sits on the bedside table: four of them. It's hard to guess when she imagined she'd have time to read those over a working weekend, but he's guessing she is one of those people who has to take multiple books everywhere because what she reads depends on her mood. Also, he imagines that she is someone who starts books, reads a few paragraphs, and gets sucked in, putting aside her current read, rather than just calmly proceeding through what she has already started. He has to admit he finds people like that hard to fathom. But that's a conversation he can have with her some other time. There are more pressing matters at hand.

Pretty much bang in the middle of her bed, water is accumulating into a bowl.

'Well,' he says. 'Clearly you can't sleep there.'

He looks up at the ceiling. There's an ominous patch of sagging plaster on the other side of the room, which threatens to start leaking any moment, too.

He points up at it. 'I don't think anyone's sleeping in here tonight, wherever we move the bed to.'

'Yeah,' she says.

'Hotel?' he says weakly. He wants her to know he is not jumping to the most appealing alternative.

'I've already checked.' His heart sinks. Anything to avoid sharing a bed with him, he guesses. 'They're all full around here tonight.'

'I'll take the sofa, if you like,' he says. 'You can have my bed.'

He's too tall for the slightly worn sofa, and they both know it. But if she sleeps there, she'll still be able to hear the drip. And it's freezing in the living room, anyway. Hardly an attractive prospect for either of them.

'This sofa is too short for you.'

He is out of non-obvious options now. He has reached the limits of the creativity he is willing to draw from, in order to keep a woman he is very much attracted to away from his bed.

'Well, then,' he says. 'I guess there's only one solution.'

She nods.

He extends his arm, and she takes his hand. He leads her – oh happy day – to his bedroom.

'There is just one problem, though,' he says. 'My bed is the smaller of the two doubles. There won't be much space between us.'

'I imagine that'll be okay,' she says, trying to make light of it. But she can't fool him. He heard her breath catching.

'We could move my mattress to the living room,' she says, her voice – he is almost sure – tinged with disappointment that she has thought of a way out of this predicament.

'Don't be silly,' he says. Not that she *is* being silly, not in the most practical sense. It's a plausible suggestion. It would do fine for him, if they weren't both so desperate to end up in the same bed, with a semi-plausible excuse.

But then he remembers his manners. He remembers the importance of enthusiastic consent, freely given. Stopping inches from his room, he takes her other hand too and looks into her eyes, making sure she knows he means it.

'We can do that, if you want. I'm happy to sleep on the mattress in the living room.'

Despite Alex's best efforts, his words come out with an edge of desperation.

'It's freezing in there,' she says. Grasping for excuses now, he hopes.

'I get hot at night,' he says, which is not at all true. Usually. Tonight, it might be. But, still, there are bound to be spare blankets in a cupboard somewhere.

'No,' she says, shaking her head for emphasis. 'I think the bed will be okay for both of us.'

If he can survive a chaste night with Jess in his bed, he is pretty sure he can survive anything.

Chapter Twenty-Three

JESS

Heat radiates from Alex as he lies in bed next to her, so close they are almost touching. Jess lies on her side, facing away from him. She pictures sheep jumping over a gate and counts them till she gets to a hundred. She counts her own breaths, forcing them to slow. She counts Alex's.

But her heart. Her heart refuses to slow.

She turns onto her back, stretches out her arm.

She finds Alex's hand, and she takes it.

Just to check.

That he is there. That he is awake. That he is not put off by having her in his bed.

He laces his fingers through hers, rubs circles at the base of her thumb.

'You're awake, then,' she whispers.

'Very much so.'

'Am I taking up too much space?'

'Jess, you can take as much space in my bed as you'd like to.'

His voice vibrates through the mattress and through her skin. Maybe that's where the tingly feeling is coming from.

'Glad to hear it,' she says.

Her hand is on fire. She wants that fire all over her, to have him touch every inch of her body.

'Are we going to be able to sleep?' she asks him.

'I doubt it,' he says.

'We probably need to sleep,' she says. 'To be at our creative best tomorrow.'

'For the sake of the book.'

'Exactly.' Theories about ice dancers and letting the tension build are all very well, but no good work can happen without sleep.

'The thing is . . .' Alex says. 'It's quite hard to sleep when I'm wondering what it would be like to—'

'You're right,' she says. 'It is hard.'

'Sounds like there's only one possible solution.' He squeezes her hand. 'If you're up for it?'

Jess would like to be self-controlled enough to think about it for a moment. To leave a dramatic pause, letting Alex's anticipation build alongside her own. But waiting suddenly feels like the most impossible thing in the world. She turns her body towards him, looks him full in the face. *This is the moment*, she thinks. *The moment when everything changes*. Not that she is prone to dramatics in any way.

She kisses him, long and hard. 'It's really the only solution,' she says, pausing to breathe, her hands in his hair. 'I don't see any other way out.'

'If you're sure?'

'I'm sure,' she says. She'll regret it tomorrow, probably. But right now, it feels like if they don't do this, she'll be eaten alive by desire. Like she'll be dead by morning. And better to be regretful than dead, surely.

Afterwards, Jess listens to her own breath slowing, in time with Alex's. She fights the urge to rest her head on his chest, to thread his fingers through hers. 'That's that done, then,' she says instead, wanting to lighten the mood after what feels like a heavy, portentous moment, but also to give herself a pep talk. To speak out loud that they have allowed themselves their one slip-up, and now that their curiosity has been assuaged, they need to get back to their plan, to their previous agreement.

'Now we can move on with our lives and our creativity and our book.'

'Yes,' he says, nodding earnestly. 'We don't need to wonder anymore what it would be like.'

'Whether there would be chemistry. Or electricity. Or whatever.'

'No. I mean, it's good to know for sure.'

'For science.'

'Exactly.'

And they can't unknow it now. Jess can't unknow the tender way Alex traced the freckles on her shoulder or the way he touched her, unsure at first, wanting to be certain that she liked what he was doing, that she wanted him to keep going. Or maybe like he was touching a precious object, running his finger over a vase to feel an ancient embossed pattern. Reading her like Braille, the lightest of touches teasing her until her breath quickened, shallower and shallower. She can't unknow how he repeated her name, as if in awe and disbelief at the privilege of being with her, or how he held her against his chest afterwards, until she fell into something like sleep.

Maybe it was enough to know. To have her curiosity satisfied. To be reassured that her instincts had not failed her – that there was something between them. Not so much a spark as an explosion of fireworks.

But also, maybe she was going to need to do it again.

'I think . . .' she says. 'I mean, I'm not a scientist. But I think that you're supposed to repeat experiments. To make doubly sure that something wasn't just a fluke, a random occurrence.'

'I'm not a scientist either,' he says. 'But that sounds really true to me.'

Before he has finished his sentence, his hands have found her again. This time, he's surer, hungrier, and she can feel that in herself, too.

'So now we know for sure,' he says later, much later. 'I guess we never need to do that again.'

'What a relief,' she says, laughing. Then he laughs too, because it's such a preposterous thing to say.

Chapter Twenty-Four

ALEX

If Alex had hoped that he and Jess, ahem, giving into their carnal desires would remove some of the distraction and restore focus – well, that hope was in vain. They do not, the next morning, bounce out of bed at the crack of dawn to begin work. They take their time getting up, get waylaid a couple of times along the way. The book that had seemed so all-consuming, almost a life-or-death issue, suddenly feels, at best, optional. It's only because of the thought of disappointing Nathan that, around 11 a.m., Alex reluctantly suggests that perhaps it's time to get dressed.

'Being not-dressed is so much more fun, though,' Jess rightly points out, a naughty glint in her eye.

'Stop it,' he says, wagging his finger at her. 'You're a bad influence on me.'

She catches his finger with her fist, and puts it in her mouth, sucking it slowly until he moans. Until he forgets all about the book, all about writing, all about why they're there, in the cottage, in the first place.

But eventually, hunger and the need for coffee get the better of him, and of Jess too. While she showers, Alex wanders to Gail's and picks up pastries, and sandwiches for lunch, and of course two flat whites. Eventually, they are both fully and disappointingly dressed and sitting at the table in the kitchen, their feet intertwined as they continue making their way through Jess's notes. When they make eye contact, his stomach lurches. When she talks, sometimes he is so focussed on her lips that he forgets to listen as carefully as he should to what she is saying. But somehow, they have a productive day. They have pages and pages of notes, and a revised outline to present to Nathan. Jess will write the scenes from the point of view of the newly fleshed-out female characters. He will work on trimming the excessively long descriptive passages and adding dialogue to break it up. She's written some light-hearted lines, some things to raise a smile in an otherwise fairly bleak narrative. Some light to balance the darkness. He'll read through the manuscript and find places where those lines could work.

'I guess we're done,' Jess says, not sounding as happy as he would have expected her to.

'You sound disappointed?'

'I'm not.'

But Alex is unconvinced.

'I think we've had a really productive couple of days,' she adds.

He can't help sniggering. She playfully kicks him under the table. 'You know what I mean.'

Alex wiggles his eyebrows. It's suggestive, but it's also, *Come on, you're not telling me the whole truth.*

'Then why don't you sound happier?' he asks her.

'I was secretly hoping we'd have an excuse to stay longer.'

Images from last night flash through Alex's mind. Her pale skin, lit by moonlight, through the window where the curtain wasn't shut quite as tightly as it probably should have been. Her widened pupils, then her tightly shut eyes as her pleasure built. He can't say he'd hate the idea of another night himself.

But, also. Another night, and his heart would be in danger. It is already. Already, he has found himself realigning his priorities, more interested in her crooked smile than in the perfect wording of his book's opening sentence. And while right now that feels fine – more than fine, it feels *good* – he knows that he will wake up tomorrow, or next week, or next year, and regret it. His career matters, and so does his reputation. And so, for that matter, does having Nathan's respect. Even if, as Jess suspects, he has sent them to Godalming with purposes beyond making a passable book into an excellent one; even if he wants to see Alex coupled up, Nathan is still his editor. And he's still the university friend who beat him to a first-class degree when Alex only just managed the very top of an upper second.

Besides, Alex has had years of practice at projecting a calm and confident demeanour. But if they get close, he knows that Jess will see that underneath it all, he's really just an anxious mess. And then, like Elodie, like others before and after her, she won't like him as much.

So, all in all, it's just as well that he has plans calling him back to London.

'I know,' he says. 'I can't deny I'd like that a lot. But I need to get back home – I'm on uncle duty tomorrow. Looking after my sister's toddler while she takes the baby for his six-week checkup.'

He sees the thought pass through her eyes, can read it as clearly as an embossed cover on a sprayed-edged paperback. She's thinking, probably, *I love toddlers! I could come too*. And he definitely can't let her do that. Can't let her look after a small child, gently lifting his small body to carry him away from whatever mischief he is heading for, while a part of her brain has already skipped ahead to the day when she and Alex will have one of their own. When you bring children into things, it gets instantly complicated. People get attached. And that is, at the very least, unwise. It's too soon. One night of passion does not make a relationship, much less the kind of commitment that demands introduction to his messy, raucous family. He's not ready for that, and he doubts she is, either.

'I love kids,' she says. 'Do you have lots of nieces and nephews?'

'Six, so far. One more on the way, that I know of.'

'Ah yes – of course. The big family. All the steps and halves.'

'Yes,' he says. 'Technically. But I don't keep track of all that. They're all family.'

The silence stretches. He knows she wants him to ask. But he pretends not to know that.

'What are your plans tomorrow?' he asks eventually.

'Catching up on sleep, for a start.' She makes meaningful eye contact, and he feels his neck redden.

'Very wise,' he says.

'And dinner with my friend Lily. But I'm otherwise free.'

'That sounds nice,' he says. His phone lights up next to him: saved by the bell, or at least by the silent notification. *Nathan*. And by the reminder, flashing up on his screen, that time is very much passing. 'I'll call him from the train. We should probably get going soon.'

It's not late, but by the time they've trekked back from Waterloo to their separate homes, it very much will be.

'I was thinking we could maybe get dinner?' He can tell she is trying for casual, but it doesn't quite land that way.

'Let's grab something on the way to the station,' he says. He's exhausted, suddenly. The sleepless night is catching up with him, and so are his emotions, all in a rush. The thought of sitting opposite Jess at dinner, trying his hardest not to mentally undress her, careful to be all that she deserves for him to be – all that he desperately wants to be for her: sorted, resilient, clever, funny . . . It feels like too much. The stakes are too high. On the train, he'll call Nathan back from the corridor. Then he'll take a few minutes to stare wordlessly into the darkness, get his breath back.

Chapter Twenty-Five

JESS

Alex feels suddenly distant, but Jess is probably imagining that. She was hoping to spend the train journey with her head on his shoulder, making plans with him for their next working session, which she hopes will be soon. She suspects that, otherwise, she will miss him in a way she has no business missing someone she only met a few weeks ago. But instead, he spends most of the journey in the corridor, on the phone to Nathan. She slides her headphones on and finds her Main Character Energy playlist, but looking out of the window at the English countryside doesn't quite hit the same when it's getting dark and all she can really see is her own slightly deflated reflection. And then, at last, his reflection too, when he finally slides into the seat next to her.

'What did you tell Nathan?'

His hand is on her leg, claiming her. *See*, she tells herself. *He likes you. You have nothing to worry about.*

'That we had a very productive time, and he'll be happy with what we've achieved. And also that his roof leaks and he should probably fix it. He asked if it interfered with our sleep. I said we figured it out.'

Jess covers her face with her hands. Nathan knows. Even with such vague information, there is no way he doesn't know.

Alex leans into her, his head now on her shoulder. 'We have nothing to be embarrassed about,' he whispers, his breath tickling her cheek. 'And if Nathan *did* send us there to fall in love, then, well . . . mission accomplished, wouldn't you say?'

'Please tell me you did not use those words on the phone to him.'

His silence is her answer.

But once she processes what he's just said, it's hard to be angry with him.

He's fallen in love with her.

This journey could not be more different than the journey just two days ago, before everything. They're sitting in a more or less empty train carriage. There's nobody across from them, nobody opposite. Jess doesn't have to worry about being 'that person', about them being 'that couple'.

'It's mutual,' she says. 'In case you were wondering.' She turns to kiss his cheek, then his mouth. It's an awkward angle and her neck will ache tomorrow, but she doesn't care. She can't quite believe she is snogging a hot man on a train. A famous author, no less. Her teenage self would be so proud of her. Lily will be, too – she can already hear her low whistle. *Good for you*, she'll say, switching the wine for prosecco to toast the success of Jess's writing retreat.

Now this, she thinks to herself in the meantime, self-congratulating . . . Noting once again Alex's skill with his lips, with his tongue, trying somewhat in vain to keep her body and her vocal chords under control. *This is Main Character Energy.*

The days drag interminably until Thursday, when Jess and Alex have agreed to meet again, to work on the book and, she suspects, their kissing techniques. Not that Alex needs to work on his. It's pretty much perfect as it is. Just thinking about it raises her body temperature a few degrees.

The book, however, is a different story. They've worked hard already and got a lot done, but the planning is just the beginning. The essential foundation, but not the visible house of words they are building. It's better, they've reluctantly agreed over WhatsApp, to spend some time apart, working separately. *Without distractions*, Alex had specified, as if it needed to be spelled out.

But now he's here, on her doorstep. She has spent the last day and a half not so much working on the book as doing an emergency deep clean, rearranging her furniture, buying flowers and artfully arranging them in vases, tinkering with her bookshelf so that the colour coordination is as visually pleasing as possible. It needed to be done anyway, for the sake of Instagram. Alex's impending visit is just an added motivation. At least, that's what she tells herself. And now he's standing in front of her. She'd somehow forgotten how much she fancied him.

'Hello,' she says, her voice wobbling between the syllables. Her knees are weak, like those of the teenager she once was, waiting in the sixth-form common room for the boy she liked to come in and play pool so she could watch him from the corner of the room. She hates being a cliché, and yet here we are.

'Hello,' he says. He leans over and kisses her cheek, in a swoonworthy and gentlemanly manner. Chaste and respectful. She probably should not be disappointed by this. Other people would no doubt find it delightful.

'Nice flat,' he says, almost too quickly – almost before he's had the chance to notice her freshly hoovered carpet, her newly dusted bookshelves. But she notes approvingly that he takes his shoes off out of respect of her clean floors, so maybe he's just a quick observer. He's wearing Mr Tickle socks. A gift, no doubt, from a beloved niece or nephew. Another very endearing thing.

She probably needs to breathe. Calm down a bit.

'Thanks,' she says. 'I love living here.'

Would she like a bigger flat, with more room for her books? Space to throw dinner parties? A spare room so her little cousin Ivy can come and stay from time to time, take the pressure off Val and Alan, give them more breathing space to put their feet up, maybe do some of that extended travelling they've been dreaming of for years? Of course. But none of that erases that this is home. That every day, still, after three years, she's delighted to live in Pimlico – a short walk from St James's Park, where each spring she lingers among the tulips and each summer she lazes on the grass, people-watching and trying not to drip chocolate ice-cream on her novel. The Tachbrook Street Market, where she's tried every kind of olive and ranked them in order of preference in one random Substack post that was linked to by London Centric, bringing her more new subscribers than a thoughtful review of the latest buzzy book ever has. And so close to the places that tourists fly thousands of miles to see: the Houses of Parliament a twenty-minute walk away; just beyond that, Whitehall and Trafalgar Square; or, across the river, the South Bank, where she loves to linger on sunny days, taking pictures of the ever-changing skyline of the capital or browsing through the book market under Waterloo Bridge.

And besides, when this book of theirs is a bestseller, maybe she'll be able to treat herself to a bigger flat. She can already picture the arguments with Alex, once they're together properly. Hampstead is so pleasant, there's no doubt about that: the beautiful Heath with its views of the City and its wild swimming in the Ladies' Pond, the pub up the hill with the best fish and chips she's ever had, the ever-present possibility – more thrilling than she'd like to admit – of bumping into any number of old white male writers of literary fiction. But it's not Pimlico, and it's not close enough to her beloved grandparents. She'll work on Alex bit by bit, have Val bake some more of her treats, till he realises that living near them is indispensable.

She is getting ahead of herself, she knows that. She's not even sure if they are officially an item, or just two writers who got a little distracted, when they were supposed to be working on a book, and had a bit of a fling. Then again, hadn't he said he'd fallen in love with her? That seems like more than a fling, or a distraction, or a way to pass the time in between chapter edits.

'I'd like to kiss you,' Alex says now, setting his bag down by the front door. 'But I'm afraid we won't get any work done if we start there.'

'Would that be such a bad thing?' She tries to keep it light, playful. Not begging and pleading, which is what she is doing in her head. It's been four days. Four interminable days.

He chuckles. 'Deadlines,' he says. 'The bane of my existence.'

'Fair enough,' she says, but she doesn't think it is.

* * *

Lily, of course, was thrilled when Jess texted her to tell her what had happened. She responded to Jess's WhatsApps with a longer and longer string of emojis, ranging from hearts to flowers to blushing faces and ending with all the party icons – streamers, balloons, champagne. She's never hidden that she wants Jess to have what she has with Gareth: they met at a Spanish evening class, their attraction growing stronger as the weeks went by. Jess would wait for Lily to return just after 10 p.m. every Tuesday night and they'd spend a delicious evening analysing every accidental brush of the hand as Lily and Gareth shared a textbook and every potential Freudian slip during conversational role play, until one night Lily texted Jess: *Don't wait up*. The stuff of romance novels; the stuff that convinced

Jess that meet-cutes really can happen; the stuff she dreams of for herself. Gareth has so far managed to be an exemplary romantic hero: flowers bought, cards written, thoughtful gifts purchased and delivered on important dates and sometimes *just because*. Jess had worried that she'd never think anybody would be good enough for Lily, but she's glad that Gareth has proved her wrong – even if part of her wishes he hadn't materialised and disrupted the life that she and Lily shared in the Brixton flat.

All in all, Jess should probably not be surprised when there's a knock on the door on that Thursday afternoon, just as she and Alex have sat down to a writing session in her flat. They both seem to be pretending that the plan has worked, that the weekend has got their attraction out of their system and now they can return to being professional. They've exchanged a polite kiss in Jess's doorway; she's made tea; they've got their notebooks and pens and laptops and manuscripts out. They've barely had time to say, *Now, where were we?* when they were interrupted by a knock.

'I was just passing,' Lily says, hugging Jess in the doorway. 'Thought I'd pop in for a cup of tea.'

'You were just passing Pimlico?' Jess is not fooled. 'On your way from West Dulwich to where, exactly?'

Lily's grin confirms Jess's suspicions. 'Nowhere in particular.'

'Uh-huh.'

Poking her head around the corner into the living room, Lily pretends to be surprised that Jess is not alone. 'Oh,' she says, nodding at Alex. 'Hello.'

Alex does a friendly little wave, a smile at the corner of his lips. He's apparently not any more fooled by this accidental drop-in than Jess is. Nonetheless, Lily makes a show of looking around at the flat – the table strewn with paper and highlighters, the stack of novels Jess has pulled out for reference – pretending to slowly piece the information together and figure it out.

'You must be the famous Alex Maxwell,' she says. 'Jess mentioned that the two of you were working together.'

Jess bites her lip hard to avoid sniggering. That certainly isn't *all* she's mentioned.

'I don't know about famous,' he says. The humility doesn't quite ring true, but Jess appreciates the effort in that direction.

'He got recognised in a pub in Godalming, of all places,' she points out. 'And if that's not fame, I don't know what is.'

'Well, to be fair,' he says, 'that's probably the most excitement they've had there in some time.'

'Since Cameron Diaz and Jude Law came to film, in fact.'

'*The Holiday*! I love that film.' Lily clasps her hands in a prayer pose beneath her chin. 'So romantic.'

Jess watches, amused, as a blush creeps up Alex's neck. He clears his throat. 'Yes, well.'

'Shall I put the kettle on?' Lily asks. She's clearly planning on staying for a while to suss out the situation.

'I'll do it,' Jess says. She's just fishing out the teabags when her phone buzzes in her pocket. She'd ignore just about anyone at this crucial moment – she trusts Lily, of course, mostly, but does she trust her not to playfully embarrass her in front of Alex, the way she imagines a sister might? She isn't 100 per cent sure, and it feels like it might be too much of a risk to take for the sake of a phone call.

But she checks, just in case, and when she sees *Mum* flashing up on her screen, it's a no-brainer. It's so rare that she calls. Poking her head around the kitchen door, she checks that Lily and Alex aren't sitting in awkward silence. In fact, Lily is throwing her head back, laughing. That is probably worrying in a different way, but at least Jess can assume that the two of them won't just stare at each other in awkward silence for as long as this call lasts, which, knowing Jess's mum, won't be very long at all.

'Hi, Mum,' she says, flicking the kettle on.

'How are you, love?'

How *is* she? That is an excellent question. Two of her favourite people are hanging out in the living room, their laughter filling the small flat. She's recently had the best sex of her life. And she has, basically, a book deal. Things are, in the main, looking great. It feels good to be able to say that – especially to her mum, who, much like her grandparents, has always been somewhat baffled by her chosen career, albeit ever-encouraging.

'Actually, things are going well at the moment,' she says, preparing to take a breath to say more, while at the same time wondering how much of it she should share. Her instinct is to talk about all of it, but so much of it feels precarious, and she feels protective of her new relationship-or-whatever-it-is with a hot, famous author. She feels, too, oddly protective of what she now thinks of as their book. She hadn't expected to have to decide how much to share just yet, so she stalls for time while her brain processes it. 'How are you?'

'Oh, good, good.' In the background, waves roll over pebbles. What sounds like a football is kicked. 'I'm having fun,' her mum says, which Jess has always assumed was code for, *I've got a new man*. But she's never asked further questions. She's always felt it's up to her mum to offer up the information, rather than have it dragged out of her. 'Off to Gibraltar tomorrow.'

'That sounds fun,' Jess says.

'I can't talk long,' her mum says, and why does Jess's stomach always sink when she says this? It's not as if a part of her doesn't expect it, every single time. 'I just wanted to see if you wanted anything brought back from Spain?'

The single Spanish thing Jess can think of in this moment is chorizo. But you can get some pretty good stuff round the corner these days, and there's only so much chorizo she can eat.

'I think I'm good,' she says. Lily's laughter rings out, and a thought occurs to Jess. 'Lily always likes a Spanish magazine, to keep up her skills.'

If Jess had met a man at Spanish evening class, she would have assumed that had been the whole purpose behind her going, that the gods of romance had sent her there not to learn a language but to meet a man. She would have immediately stopped going, relieved not to have to keep testing herself on obscure verb conjugations and on vocab she would, let's be real, never use. But Lily really *had* wanted to learn Spanish – so much so, that Jess has sometimes worried she would one day move to Andalusia or the Costa Blanca. She took a GCSE last summer and is considering an A Level. Gareth has lost interest, but that doesn't stop her soldiering on. Jess applauds her for that. Aside from all things books, Jess has dabbled in a million hobbies, never really sticking at them. She's been to a pottery class; she's tried wine tasting a couple of times; somewhere she's still got an Italian textbook. Every Christmas she proudly digs out the one decoration she taught herself to crochet – a snowman, copies of which she made for all of her friends that year – and wishes she'd kept at it, though she isn't sure how many lovingly home-made blankets the world really needs.

'No problemo,' her mum says on the other end of the phone. 'I'll pick a couple up at the airport for her. Must whizz, darling. Lots of love.'

And just like that, she's gone, leaving Jess with the usual mix of post-maternal-check-in, pit-in-her-stomach feelings. She's glad her mum calls regularly and seems to think of her often. But she also wishes she'd slow down long enough to really hear what's going on in Jess's life. There have been times when the subtext has been so obvious – when Jess needed a shoulder to cry on after a bad breakup, or in the aftermath of Lily moving out and the lonely silence that followed – but her mum has never taken the time to really hear it. Jess suspects, or maybe likes to think, that she'd be mortified if she knew that Jess needed her and she hadn't been there. She can hear her protests now, covering up her guilt: *But you said you were fine!* And, true, Jess hadn't decided if she was ready to tell her mum about Alex yet. Maybe she's glad she hasn't, in case it turns out to be nothing, though even just considering that possibility makes her feel sick. But it would have been nice to have the choice, that's all.

She sighs, then shakes her head to rid herself of these frustrating feelings. She wants to stay here, in her bubble of joy: a bubble where Alex and Lily are laughing together in her flat, probably about to mercilessly tease her over her lovingly made tea. A bubble where she and Alex are creating his next bestseller together and she is learning enough from him to write her own one day. It's a good place to be. Better, probably, than sun-drenched Gibraltar, no matter how plentiful the chorizo.

Chapter Twenty-Six

ALEX

Jess seems to have lost some of her sparkle when she comes back from the kitchen, tea in hand. Alex is instantly concerned – about her, and then about himself, about how quickly he is becoming attuned to the tiniest shift in her moods. He likes to think he is good at reading people, and the more he cares about them, the more effort he puts into it. This is precisely what is worrying him. He cares too much, probably. Too much, and too soon.

But also, it is kind of nice. To care like this about someone outside his family. To be getting to know Jess – her bright, electric, enthusiastic self. To be let in on her wider world – chatting to Lily has felt a little like reading a prequel to a favourite novel, the kind that zooms in on the backstory of a beloved character, so you can understand them better, be even more invested in what happens to them. Jess talks of Lily the way he does of his family; he knows she is important to her. He suspects, too, that Lily's approval of him could potentially make or break whatever this is between them. So he turned on his most charming, most witty self – the self that, to be fair, seems to naturally come out when he is with Jess. And it seems to be working. He'd kill to see the report card Lily will give him later on.

'What's new with you, anyway?' Jess asks Lily, handing over the tea when she comes back into the room.

Lily swats the question away with a hand wave. 'Oh, let's not talk about me,' she says brightly. A bit too brightly, maybe, Alex thinks, and by the looks of Jess's quizzically raised eyebrows, it seems he is right. But then Lily reaches into her handbag and pulls out a book. 'Although, I just finished this book on the way here, and let me tell you, it blew me away.'

Alex lets a gasp escape. It's the same book he was reading on the train to Godalming. He didn't think Jess had noticed, but the way her eyes are boring into the side of his face now suggests otherwise.

'So good, right?' Jess says, a sigh in her voice. 'I need to reread it. But, you know, so many books—'

'So little time,' Lily finishes for her.

This time, Jess turns to face him. Like him, she's no doubt relieved that they're on safe ground now – books.

'I think Alex has read that one,' she says. 'He was trying to hide it from me on the train, for some reason.' She nudges his foot with hers. 'Probably too proud to admit he was reading *romance*.'

'I was absorbed,' he lies. The book was making a valiant attempt at holding his attention, but with Jess that close, smelling that good, not even *Infinite Jest* would have stood a chance.

Lily swivels towards him. 'First romance novel?' she asks.

Damn her. He's going to have to watch out for this one. 'Maybe,' he says.

'Welcome to the party,' Lily says, throwing up her arms. 'Better to turn up late than not at all. Was it Jess's influence?'

Yes, it was, and also no, it wasn't. Eventually, he is sure that Jess would have pressed a book into his hands, and he would have been too weak-kneed and addled to say no to her about anything. Not to mention that he would have welcomed the opportunity to explore her world, to find out what makes her tick, what it is exactly that she loves and why. But this was Nathan's doing – his attempt to open Alex's mind, help him draw from other genres to lighten his own writing. Then again, working with Jess was part of that, too.

'Let's say *yes*,' he says.

'And?' Lily says. The weight of expectation feels crushing. There is only one correct answer here. Luckily, the right answer also happens to be the true one.

'Yeah, it's great,' he says. 'I really liked it.' He doesn't mention that when they got back from their weekend, he went straight to bed with the book to finish it. That if he hadn't been so busy – so distracted – all weekend, he would have been itching to do nothing but lie on the sofa, flicking page after page until he reached its satisfying resolution. Or that if he's really honest with himself, he's a little envious of the writing, of the ability of the author to evoke a depth of emotion in the pit of his stomach that he certainly hadn't expected.

'Well, well, well,' Jess says, letting him know with another gentle foot nudge that she is playfully teasing. 'Character growth. I like it.'

Lily laughs, then slurps her tea and makes a show of draining the dregs.

'I better be going,' she says. 'I don't want to hold you back from working your magic on this book.'

Internally, he breathes a sigh of relief. He had looked forward to being back in Jess's company, just the two of them. Working together, and who knows what else. Getting to know her. He's enjoying being in her flat, observing her in her natural habitat, letting his eyes wander over towards the books on her shelves, the pictures on her fridge of herself with various authors he recognises from bookish social media, the corner of the room where she sets up her Instagram flat lays – right by the window, where she has explained to him that it gets the best natural light. Once upon a time, he would have rolled his eyes at her rainbow bookshelves; he would have said that colour is a ridiculous way to organise novels. But he has to admit – it looks good. Plus, it is just about possible that Jess is changing him. Is that terrifying? Perhaps a little. But it's not unpleasant.

Meeting Lily is a valuable and important part of the Jess jigsaw puzzle, but he's glad she knows not to overstay her welcome. Apart from anything else, it speaks well of her and shows a degree of self-awareness he admires, even if he can't always emulate it himself. In turn, having a friend like Lily speaks well of Jess, too.

'Think I passed the test?' he asks Jess after the door has closed and he's counted seventeen seconds.

On the table, Jess's phone lights up.

I thought you might be exaggerating about how hot he is.

She blushes from her cheeks all the way up to her ears and then, disappointingly, puts her phone face down to protect herself against further incrimination. 'Looks like it,' she says, not quite meeting his eye.

He makes a show of checking his watch – a reminder that time is ebbing away. 'We should probably do some work.'

Jess looks disappointed. She was clearly hoping for further distraction. But she nods, and says, 'You're right.'

She's just out of his reach, sitting across the table from him so he can't kiss her without some uncomfortable leaning – and that's better for everyone; it's certainly better for the book deadline. When he writes at home, he puts his phone in another room, temptation out of sight and out of reach. Sitting just far enough from Jess is his best approximation of that in this situation.

He should not have used the phrase *falling in love* on the train. It's true, and they both know it, but the fact that he's said it implies some kind of commitment, some kind of intention on his part. And he's not there, not ready for that. His mind knows it. And yet neither his heart nor his body are inclined to agree, and he knows that Jess would be well within her rights to imagine that they are now a couple, or at least hurtling towards the stage where they can call themselves one. If he hadn't said *falling in love*, he'd be able to claim that they had got their mutual attraction out of their respective systems in Godalming and it was time to focus on the work in hand. But he *did* say *falling in love*, and now it feels as though he is leading her on. Which is the last thing he wants to do. It feels like a giant mess, one he should probably discuss with his therapist. But at the root of it all is the simple fact that he finds Jess very attractive and that he enjoys her company; if he felt able to entertain the thought of a relationship, it would be a no-brainer to be with her.

But as excuses go for slowing down, the deadline is all he's got.

'Remember your ice dancers?' he says, somewhat feebly. 'The tension being good for their art?'

He can't read her face. If he had to guess, he'd say that she is crestfallen but also touched that he's remembered her convoluted story, her initial reluctance to follow through on their feelings so that their passion and chemistry would feed into their writing instead. And also, perhaps, that he is out of the woods, that she won't be angry that he is slowing them down.

'Yeah,' she says. 'I wish I'd never mentioned that.'

'No, no. You were right. It's a good plan – to channel our energy into the task at hand. We can get to know each other. We can talk. That might be a healthier way into this anyway.'

He can't believe these words are coming out of his mouth – that he's the one suggesting talking first, when if he's honest, he'd be happy for that to come later. Maybe this, too, is character growth?

'You're right,' she says, nodding earnestly, perhaps trying to convince herself. 'Talking is probably healthier. We don't really know each other.'

He wouldn't have put it quite like that. Over the last few weeks, and especially the weekend away, he has felt them growing closer as they've analysed his book and compared it to other works of literature. He's always felt like books are a great way into someone's personality. There's a reason why book clubs are so popular, why people who attend the same one often find themselves becoming close, feeling they are kindred spirits. For a while, in DC, he'd found one of his own to join – a co-ed group, as they say over there, men and women together. He'd long been jealous of his sisters' and girlfriends' book clubs; he had never come across one that welcomed guys. The spirited discussions, the wine and the cheese, even the occasional weekend retreat – it had been delightful, and a great way of making friends and having discussions about the real stuff of life – the deeper questions, the things that keep him awake at night.

Under the table, Alex's feet find Jess's. He wants to communicate warmth and connection, make sure Jess does not feel this slowing down as a rejection. She smiles at him, a little sadly, and nods. 'We should get started on the book,' she says, and they find their rhythm again over the next couple of hours. In companiable silence, she reads his first drafts of new scenes; he reads hers. He is, frankly, impressed with what she has done. She has learned his style, his turns of phrase, the rhythm of his sentences, and written in his voice, but with additions of humour and light-heartedness. Exactly, he suspects, what Nathan was hoping for. Not for the first time, he is sorry he ever doubted her. In contrast, his first drafts are nothing to write home about. He is almost embarrassed about them.

'These are good,' he says, when he's finished reading and looks up to find she has too, and she is watching him. 'Really good.'

She bites her lip, maybe suppressing a smile. 'You think so?'

He searches out her eyes, makes sure she is locked into his. 'Yes.'

'I'm glad,' she says, and then, to break the tension, or hide a grin, or maybe go and do a secret celebratory dance, she offers him a tea and disappears back into the kitchen. Which reminds him of earlier, when she came back sad after speaking briefly on the phone.

'Were you okay earlier?' he asks when she's back in the room with a couple of mugs. 'When you left the room to take a phone call? You didn't seem quite yourself when you came back.'

'Oh, that. Yeah.'

He waits, giving her space to say more, if she wants to. He hopes that she does.

'Just my mum calling. She's always off doing something fun. Never has very long to talk on the phone or to really ask how I'm doing. I wanted to tell her about us – well, about our book – but I didn't get a chance.'

Inside, Alex is cheering the fact that Jess is proud of their book, but he tries to focus on what it is she is not saying, what's between the lines. The unsaid thing that, as is the case with so many unsaid things, holds a key to who Jess is, what life has moulded her to be.

'Has your mum always been like this?'

Jess bites her lip. 'Yeah, pretty much. She left me with my grandparents a lot when I was little, to go and have adventures.'

'What kind of adventures?'

'She didn't always tell me, and I didn't always ask. Travels, nights out with friends. Things like that.'

'That must have been hard.'

She shrugs and seems to swallow forcefully. 'Not really,' she says. 'I love my grandparents, and they were cool – always took me to fun places, played Scrabble with me, made me delicious meals. And my mum was always happy when she came back, and really glad to see me. She'd have gifts, hug me like she never wanted to let me go again.'

It sounds like love, but it also sounds like guilt.

What had Jess said about the plane crash in the book?

Just because they all survive doesn't mean they don't have issues.

'Still,' he says. 'Being left behind is hard.'

'Yeah,' she says, her eyes dropping to the table, and then into her mug when she takes a sip of tea – a sip that seems longer than necessary, perhaps trying to compose herself, half-hidden away.

'But I guess your mum was left behind too. When your dad—'

'Yeah. That's why I never minded, not really.'

He wants to say, *But you did mind, and you buried it*. He wants to say, too, that she was the child in the relationship, that she deserved to come first. But they're not there yet, in their friendship or situationship or relationship. He can tell that she's not there in her emotional journey. The way she'd denied that her mum leaving her was hard – that in itself spoke volumes. *The first step is naming and acknowledging our emotions*. That's what his therapist says, twiddling his greying moustache like a cartoon villain. Alex isn't very good at it yet, but he's learning.

Still, it makes sense now. Jess's escapism into the fun and guaranteed happy endings of romance novels, into the laughter of romantic comedies. It's not that she's unrealistic about the world, or that she's never experienced pain and thinks the world is candy-coloured, all rainbows and puppy dogs. It's the opposite: she knows all too well that it isn't, and that's precisely why she needs that escapism. Her chin is trembling, and he is glad she has shared this with him, but also sorry that he brought up this pain. He feels protective of her, sad for her and for her younger self. Not for the first time, he feels chastised, too, for the judgement he had rushed to when they first met. He reaches out for her hand, strokes her palm with his thumb.

'Thank you,' she says, meeting his eyes. And then, 'Where were we?'

Moving on quickly – her survival instinct. He follows her lead and turns to the next page in the book. One day, they will deal with this together. But this is not that day. Not yet.

Lily: I thought you might be exaggerating about how hot he is.

Jess: He saw that, you know.

Lily: Sorry not sorry

Jess: Humph

Lily: Well, did it lead to – you know, anything?

Jess: No. He pretended not to notice and I pretended not to notice he was pretending not to have noticed.

Lily: Seems much more complicated than it needs to be

Jess: The building tension helps us do our best work. That's the theory, anyway

Lily: Whose theory?

Jess: Mine, originally. And believe me, I am regretting that.

Chapter Twenty-Seven

JESS

It floors Jess that Alex has so quickly been able to put his finger on something that has long bothered her. Of course, it makes sense for Jess's mum to escape her life and her grief, to run off and have fun as much as she can. That's what Jess does, too: she doesn't dwell on hard things. Instead, she reads books, hangs out with Lily, watches something fun on Netflix, plans her next holiday. She knows, at some level, that buried deep in her gut are things that will need to be dealt with sometime. She can't read books about grief or sit very long in anyone else's pain. She's there for her friends, but being there means taking them out to eat good food and drink good wine, or at least plentiful wine, to book holidays for them and buy them thoughtful gifts for self-care. (*Never underestimate the power of luxury bubble bath*, she has written on many a card.) She feels herself tense up when they want to talk, and now, even when she wishes she could be that friend, she knows they no longer expect it from her. She knows, at some level, that Lily and Gareth are trying for a baby – why else would you move to West Dulwich in your late twenties, favouring a quiet inner suburb with a village feel, good schools, and a bookshop with weekly story times, over the bustle of Balham, the lively chaos of Clapham, or even just proximity to a Tube so you can easily get in and out of central London to brunch, to happy hours, to galleries and cinemas and theatres?

Jess suspects, though, that the trying maybe isn't going as planned. But she hasn't asked about it, and Lily hasn't offered up any information. It's a tricky subject, and Jess doesn't want to pry. And also, she's never understood this longing to settle, to tie yourself down to nights in at home and school catchment areas and child-friendly holidays at pre-defined times of the year, when there are so many adventures to be had outside those arbitrary parameters. Part of her hopes that one day she *will* understand it, will want it herself – and this *wanting to want it* is new and, Jess has to admit, a little surprising. But really, the main reason why she and Lily have never talked about this might be that they both know Jess isn't good at sadness and pain – managing her own or anyone else's. Escape is all she knows, and she learned that from her mum.

She doesn't want to cry in front of Alex – she hates crying anyway, in any context – so it's important to keep going with this book. Besides, as he keeps reminding her, they have a deadline. The quicker they finish the book, the quicker they can resume other activities.

Somehow, they get through the rest of the afternoon without any tricky talk. They keep it thoroughly professional. Maybe the weekend in Godalming really was just about getting it out of their systems. Maybe it was too soon to use phrases like *falling in love*. She's done this before, let's be real – thought she was in love with someone she barely knew. Most recently, with a publicist she kept crossing paths with at author events, the imagined reciprocity of her feelings probably helped along by multiple glasses of mediocre warm white wine in paper cups at the back of bookshops.

But she isn't imagining the chemistry between her and Alex, the way his eyes keep flicking to her face and then away, as if he's afraid of getting burned by the sight of her. She catches herself doing the same thing, too. Sparks fly off his fingers when they reach for the same Post-It notes, the same index cards, the same biro or highlighter.

'This is a lot of index cards,' Alex says, when they've written the outline of each scene on one and spread them all out in front of them so that they fill the whole table. He's not wrong: there are ninety-three of them. Jess knows, because as they've been standing there, surveying, she's counted them.

'I guess it's an epic book, in more ways than one.'
'It really is.'
'We have to be prepared that Nathan might want to cut some of it,' he says.

Jess shudders. She has spent so long thinking so intensely about these characters. She could no more cut them than she could kill them off in the fictional plane crash. The B-list actor who was afraid of flying anyway and will now never go near another plane. The middle-aged lapsed Christian woman who prayed that everybody would survive as the plane went down and is more surprised than anyone else when it seems to have worked. The couple who broke up in the line to check in, now bonded by trauma and a realisation that maybe, given how precarious life is, it doesn't matter precisely how somebody loads a dishwasher.

Jess can see them all, clear as day, before her – just as real as anybody else in her life. In her mind, she has cast some of her favourite actors in the movie that plays when she thinks of the plot of the book. She has written character sketches, given them each Myers Briggs personality types, even though Alex rolled his eyes at the idea of any kind of categorisation. Which is ridiculous, as he's the clearest example of an INFJ she's ever met: idealistic, sensitive, definitely a perfectionist. She's learned to translate each personality type into a fictional character of a TV series he likes – *The West Wing*, *The Simpsons*, *Friends*. (Has he watched anything made in the last twenty years? Doubtful.) She uses those to make her point, to argue that Character A would never behave in a particular way, or that Character B would never have that criticism of Character C. Alex doesn't like the reductionism of that, either, but he tolerates the notion of a personality type better when it's linked to a character he is attached to.

Jess is particularly fond of the characters she's created, or fleshed out from nothing or from the merest shadow that had previously existed in Alex's manuscript. The lapsed Christian, for example, whose only role in the previous draft had been to monotonously repeat a prayer until the other passengers wanted to, and then did, scream at her. Now she has a fully realised backstory, a reason she slipped away from faith, a path back to God. The possibility of losing any of that to Nathan's red pen (or, more likely, his delete button) feels unthinkable.

'Maybe he'll cut your descriptions,' she says. Teasing, but also hoping that this will be the way it goes. Descriptions, she can live with being cut. If she's totally honest, she skims them, at best, when she reads.

'I doubt that,' Alex says, all earnestness. Not taking it as the joke it's intended as. 'My readers love those.'

'*My readers*,' she repeats. There's something odd about that phrase. *My readers*, like they belong to him, like they're on his team. The way a political party might say *our voters*, as if they don't need to do anything to keep those voters, as if their allegiance is a foregone conclusion.

'My fans, if you prefer.'

'Wow.' She's not sure how else to react. But she looks at him, and he's grinning. He knows how ridiculous this sounds. His fans. His devoted groupies. But then she remembers Cassandra – perhaps not so ridiculous.

'What?' he says, bumping her hip with his. 'You don't believe I have fans?'

'I believe it,' she says, half of her body on fire. 'I've seen it in action, remember?'

'Ah, yes.'

Digging into his pocket, he finds his iPhone, unlocks it, opens his Instagram direct messages, then wordlessly passes the device over to Jess. In his inbox, there is line after line of the beginnings of adoring messages, hardly any of them with bot-like pictures or usernames. It's impressive, honestly. Idly, she taps on one of them:

> Hi Alex! Big fan of your novels. I see a lot of my own family in the way you write about siblings – it's been really cathartic, actually. I gave your last book to my sister for her birthday and we ended up having a long overdue chat about our childhood and our parents – I honestly think it healed some things in our family. And of course it's also a great read. So thank you! Looking forward to the next novel.

If all of them are like this, it's no wonder he comes across initially as having an inflated ego. Isn't that the dream for a writer? Entertaining people but also changing their lives in some positive way?

She taps on another.

> Love your novels. When's the next one?

And another.

> Can't wait for your next book!

She sees, now, the urgency, the pressure. To get another book out. To satisfy the hungry masses. It's impossible, she knows, to fully do so – a ravenous reader can get through a book in a day, and that same book might take an author three years to write. But most reasonable readers know this. And that's why they've waited, some of them for years, before politely enquiring. Or nagging. Or harassing.

'Wow,' she says again, bumping his body back the way he did with hers. 'We'd better get them this book quickly. Seems like some of them are pretty desperate.'

'I told you,' he says, his dimple popping. 'Fans. Lots of fans.'

'I never doubted it,' she says.

She's about to hand the phone back to him when a notification lights up the screen. *You have been tagged in a post.* Reflexively, she taps it.

'Hey,' he says. 'That could be personal.'

'That's why you should never hand over your phone to another person.'

'Fair.'

They see it at the same time: the tagged picture of the two of them on the most popular publishing gossip account, reposted from @bookish_cassandra. It's a little blurry, but it's unmistakeably Alex and Jess, walking hand in hand. The caption reads: *Well, I guess now we know why Alex Maxwell is too busy to write another book.*

'Busted,' Jess says, suppressing a snigger.

'But I'm not too busy to write another book,' he says. 'I *am* writing another book. That picture happened *because* I'm writing another book.'

'That's your first takeaway from this situation?' Jess is a little miffed. A photo of the two of them, and his first reaction is only about himself.

'Sorry, sorry, no. Of course not.' He smiles apologetically. Jess can't stay even a little bit angry when a dimple like that is on show.

'I'm glad it's a nice picture of us.'

Moving the phone closer to her face, Jess inspects the

image. He's not wrong. It is a nice picture. The first one of the two of them. The one that maybe they'll show their grandchildren someday. Not that she's getting ahead of herself in any way.

'Yeah,' she says. 'It is.'

Reluctantly, she hands the phone back. 'What do you think this means?'

'In what sense?'

'Like, what happens now?'

'We're not Brad and Jen,' he says, another not-exactly-bang-on pop culture reference, but she gets the picture. 'I don't think this blows up and the paparazzi starts chasing us to our deaths in a Parisian tunnel.'

'Dark.'

'Sorry.'

'Also,' she points out, 'a mixed metaphor.'

'You've got me. I'm even more sorry.'

Jess's stomach does an involuntary flip at the phrase *you've got me*.

'But maybe Nathan will get wind of it.'

'Nathan will be delighted. He's been trying to find me a girlfriend for the last five years.'

Five years? That, perhaps, explains his keenness to ditch what she thinks of as the ice-dancing rule. It perhaps also explains Nathan's keenness to get them working together, though she isn't sure how he could possibly have known that she and Alex would have this insane level of chemistry together. And she's determined to prove that she's not just good for Alex's love life, but that she's a great partner creatively, too. And a great author in her own right.

But also: a girlfriend? Is that what she is?

'So we're putting labels on it now?' She bumps him gently with her shoulder.

'Maybe not just yet,' he says, and her heart sinks. But he puts his arm around her, and she relaxes into him. He kisses the top of her head.

She stands, leaning into Alex, for what might be five seconds or might be five years. She tries not to think about the implications of what he's just said. Part of her is tempted to kiss him, but part of her thinks he doesn't deserve it, not after these mixed messages.

He shuffles against her, and she knows the moment is over. They pull apart and pretend to study the index cards laid out in front of them. Or at least *she* is pretending. Perhaps *he* really is studying them.

'Anyway,' he says after a while. 'This is the publicity that Nathan wanted, right? Weren't you supposed to *tease our collab* with Instagram posts?'

That had been the plan. But also, what she had with Alex felt too new, too precious, too murky and hard to describe to risk putting a name on it or exposing it to the world. She wants to keep it close to her heart for now.

Her phone lights up on the table.

> @allthemanybooks has tagged you in a comment.

Before she taps, she already knows what's coming.

> This you, @Jessandherbookobsession?

She'd met Allie of the All the Many Books blog at London Book Fair one year, in the queue for a talk by Taylor Jenkins Reid. They'd followed each other for a long time, exchanging book recommendations and mutual eye rolls on the ever-cycling social media discourse – *Are audiobooks reading? Is a three-star rating good or bad? Why is selling advance review copies such a terrible thing to do?* Jess used to earnestly join in – some of her responses, in fact, had gone viral and helped raise her follower count into the six digits a couple of years ago – but now she can't scroll past the threads fast enough. Instead, to scratch the itch, she'd DM Allie: *Do these people think they are the first person to ever have that thought?* And Allie would respond with similar snark.

She'd thought they were friends, but tagging her like this, so publicly, doesn't really seem like something a friend would do.

She stuffs the phone in her pocket. Out of sight, out of mind: if she does that, the problem goes away. At least for now; at least until she next opens her phone and the tags and DMs have bred like proverbial rabbits. The bookfluencer world in the UK is not all that big. The number of accounts with more than 100,000 followers is surprisingly small. Over the years, Jess has had her fair share of slightly passive-aggressive comments, or DMs that state admiration but smack of envy. She knows many others would love the paid partnerships with publishers, the limited-edition tote bags, the exclusive author events Jess is invited to. Like many fandoms, Bookstagram is kind and gentle on the surface and gives off a we're-all-in-it-together kind of vibe. But, just like with any fandom, there's competition and jealousy. More than the free stuff – possibly even more than the opportunities to rub shoulders with the author of the moment – everybody wants to be The Chosen One, the Big Name Fan, and many people would shock themselves with how eagerly they would tread on others to get there.

And, let's face it: everybody loves gossip. Everybody loves drama. Including Jess, usually. It would only be karma if she was at the receiving end of it for once; she knows that, but it still doesn't feel good. She can see it already: the speculation she only has a book deal because of whom she's dating. The assertions – true, as it turns out, but still – that her follower count was what got her a book deal, and that isn't fair when there are so many writers out there who are just as talented, maybe more talented, but don't have the *platform* and so get overlooked. She can already see the opinion piece in *The Bookseller*: *When will we start valuing talent over influence? How the publishing industry lost the plot . . .*

'I'm not sure our collab needs teasing,' she says. 'Your next book is going to fly off the shelves with or without a co-author's name on the cover. But first we need to write it.' She shakes her head to free herself of these uncomfortable thoughts. 'Let's get back to work.'

'Okay,' he says. Relieved, no doubt, to be off the hook on the girlfriend thing for now.

Chapter Twenty-Eight

ALEX

It goes on like that for a while: a couple of times a week, Alex and Jess meet up at her flat, or at his, or in a coffee shop – his preferred option, far from a bed, far from temptation. In between, they work on their own pages, their own characters. They swap pages and then edit them. Alex spends a few days with each set of parents. His stepmum wants to know about his next book; his brother asks about his love life; his dad scratches behind his ear and just wants to check Alex is okay and doesn't need any financial help. To all these things, he answers evasively, and not in a subtle way: *Look at the time* or *Nice weather for the time of year*, he jokes, and they leave him alone, continue to tiptoe around the contours of his life. Imagine if they knew about his therapist, he thinks. Let alone Jess, or the book: this book that he is beginning to believe could be the Next Big Thing in his career, maybe even also the Next Big Thing on the British book scene. He knows he shouldn't get his hopes up, but it's a challenge. He's not proud of this, but he misses the good old days when he was a literary darling: the people he got to hang out with, the events he got invited to, the thunderous applause of the crowd in a Hay Festival marquee. He is daring to believe that he could have some, if not all, of it back, and the thought of sharing the limelight with Jess is a surprisingly pleasant one.

And through all of this, he tries, really hard and very unsuccessfully, not to think about Jess during every waking hour: her laughter, her intensity, her quick humour. He tries not to think about the disappointment on her face when he teased the word *girlfriend* and then ripped it away from her. *It's for your own good*, he wishes he could tell her. *You deserve better than me.* He's brought this up in therapy. His therapist asked, 'Don't you think that's up to her to decide?' But he is protecting her by not giving her the option. Once he is sorted, once he is on the right dose of medication, once he feels like he's on an even keel and ready to be a worthy boyfriend – then, he'll seek her out. And maybe he'll have missed the boat by then, maybe she'll have found someone else. But it's a risk he's willing to take. She deserves to be happy, to be with someone stable. And if he messes this up, he'll never forgive himself – for hurting her, for causing emotional turmoil, for ruining a fruitful creative partnership.

In the meantime, he's enjoying getting to know her as a friend – a friend with an always-surprising wardrobe and a never-ending supply of different glasses. Or even a friend with benefits, if those benefits include apple-scented hair and the thrill of being near someone who admires him despite not having been easily won over by his name and his sales figures. She's told him about her family; he's told her about his.

'You know,' she says to him one day, as he drapes his summer jacket over the back of his chair in their favourite coffee shop. 'I keep expecting you to have a technicolour coat.'

He looks at her blankly. Not because he doesn't know the reference, but because she doesn't seem to see the irony: she's wearing her own multi-coloured clothing, a playsuit with asymmetric patterns that almost hurts his eyes to look at.

'Like Joseph,' she clarifies.

Ah. This is a common mistake. 'Joseph wasn't the oldest. He was the favourite. There's a difference.' And doesn't he know it. If anyone among his siblings was going to have a coat of many colours, it would be David, the baby of the interminable family. He who, in the eyes of just about all of them, can do no wrong.

She scrunches up her face.

'So who's the oldest in the Joseph story?'

'Reuben. The boringly responsible one, who stops his brothers from killing Joseph and decides for some reason that throwing him into a cistern is the way forward.'

She looks at him intensely. 'Is that how you see yourself? Boringly responsible?'

He would have thought this was obvious. 'Yes.' He twirls his pencil, deciding how much to tell her. 'Remember how you ribbed me once for going to America to do an MFA when there are perfectly good courses here?'

She nods.

'It was my own act of rebellion. I wanted to write, and I didn't want to keep getting interrupted by my family needing something from me. The older of my siblings were always calling in babysitting favours, and my younger ones always needed driving around or helping with homework. When you have a family as big as mine, there's always someone having an emergency, and there's only so much your parents can handle on top of busy, responsible jobs and new families and marriages they're determined to make a success of, the second time around. So nine times out of ten, I was the one who dealt with that emergency. And I was happy to, you know? I love my family. Until suddenly I wasn't. I wanted time to myself. I wanted to be able to get into the creative zone and not worry about getting yanked out of it by a desperate text from one of my siblings asking for advice or whatever. So I left. Hardest thing I've ever done. None of them understood, because of course I didn't give them the real reason. My sister Jen did some research and presented Norwich to me as an option. I was gutted that Iowa rejected me. Thankfully, American University saved me by giving me a scholarship, and that was as good an excuse as any. And I think DC was a lot more fun than a middle-of-nowhere city would have been, anyway. The fly-over states, they call that part of the country. I guess there's a reason for that.'

He takes a breath. Phew. He hadn't meant to be so honest all at once, to tell her all of that. He feels vulnerable now. He closes his eyes and waits for Jess's response.

'Well,' she says. 'That explains a lot.'

'Like what, exactly?'

'You. Being the way you are.'

He isn't sure if this is a compliment, but it feels dangerous to ask.

'Okay,' he says uncertainly. Now that he's been so open, so frighteningly vulnerable, he feels emboldened to ask the same of Jess. He'd like her to open up, if she wants to. He won't push. He'll just nudge the door ajar.

He runs a hand through his hair, aware as he's doing it that his therapist has picked up on this anxious gesture of his. 'What about you, Jess? What do you think explains you?'

She bites her lower lip and exhales slowly. He doesn't know, of course, what's going through her head. But if he had to guess, he'd say she's wondering whether to deflect. Back to him, or back to something lighter, something more fun. But to her credit, she does neither of those things.

'I suppose,' she says, her voice likely as light as she can make it in this moment. 'A therapist would probably say that my never knowing my dad explains a lot about me.'

He lets the moment land, lets her hear her own words. And then he asks, gently, 'And do you think that's true?'

She shakes her head. 'I honestly don't think about it that much. My childhood was just normal to me.'

Of course you don't think about it that much, Alex wants to say. *You escape, rather than facing up to difficult feelings. Into books and romance and adventure. Nothing too difficult, nothing too sad.* But he doesn't go there. Not yet. There'll be a time for that, probably. He wants to lead her there gently.

'Do you think,' he begins instead, aware that he might be poking a bruise, 'that it might be a good idea if you did?'

Jess visibly flinches; her sharp intake of breath is audible. He wonders if he's gone too far; he curses himself inwardly when he can see in her face that she'd like nothing more than to run away.

'Too many feelings,' she says, her voice on the edge of trembling.

'Easier to put them in a tightly shut-up box and never open it?'

She nods. But Alex is learning in therapy that it isn't, in fact, easier. It might seem it at the time, but you might not have any control over when the box springs open, its contents leaking all over your life and your relationships. He considers whether to say any of this and opts for a middle ground instead, a creaking open of that box.

'Is there anything you know about your dad that you'd be willing to share with me?'

He watches as her face changes, moving through a variety of expressions to reflect no doubt, a multitude of emotions. Even her eyes seem to cycle through different combinations of colours, but he is probably imagining that.

She settles on something at last. 'He was French,' she says. 'My mum met him on her year abroad in Nîmes.'

This is a start. He can work with this. Then something occurs to him. 'Jess . . . Martin?'

'It's not really Martin,' she admits. 'It's pronounced the French way. It rhymes with *vin*.'

'*Martin*,' he says, taking care with the nasal vowel at the end. He thinks, briefly, of Hyacinth Bucket and her insistence on the *Bouquet* pronunciation. But now isn't the time to bring it up – it feels like the wrong moment to gear-shift into humour. Not to mention that she would probably tease him for being an old man with a working knowledge of Nineties culture, even if that was technically before his time. 'That's beautiful.'

But then it's her turn to gear-shift. 'Yeah, I find that guttural French *r* to be the height of beauty.'

He knows her well enough by now, though, to know what she is doing: deflecting from difficult emotions. 'Do you speak French?' he asks, knowing the answer before he's even formulated the question.

She shakes her head. 'Latin's as close as I got.'

'*Post hoc ergo propter hoc.*' *After it, therefore because of it*. A phrase known and beloved by fans of *The West Wing* the world over, for too long and complicated a reason to bring into this conversation. He is testing her, gently – will she rise to the challenge, respond with a quote from this favourite TV show, or stare at him blankly instead?

She pushes her glasses up her nose, counters with her own random Latin expression. '*In vino veritas.*'

'*Veni, vidi, vici,*' he says, and then they're both out of stock Latin. *I came; I saw; I conquered*. And it feels oddly apt, this phrase. It feels as if he has, in some way, conquered – won – by getting Jess to talk about her dad, to crack open that box a tiny bit. They are friends with benefits, after all, and those benefits should include being able to talk to each other about the hard stuff. Even though, if he's perfectly honest, he finds it as terrifying as she does.

Chapter Twenty-Nine

JESS

When Lily opens the door, Jess almost falls into her arms as if she were the love interest in an old-fashioned romantic film. Truth is, she's desperate for a hug. Hugs steady her, and she needs steadying. The thing with Alex, it's starting to feel like a roller coaster. The unspokenness of what it is they are to each other, and then his questions about her dad – questions she's never cracked open before with anyone, let alone any quasi-boyfriends. She's always loved roller coasters, but the thing is, if you stay on them long enough, you end up feeling a bit sick. Not to mention dizzy and disorientated. And like the ground is shaking under you.

Jess knows she isn't making up her chemistry with Alex. You can't make up what they had in Godalming, and there's something soft in his voice when he talks to her that tells her how he feels about her. But this reluctance to commit, to call a spade a spade – it's odd, and she doesn't like it.

'Are you sure he's not just being, you know, male?' Lily asks her when she's got to the bottom of why Jess is hugging her a little longer and more desperately than usual. 'They can be like that. Non-committal. They think playing hard to get is going to make us work harder for their affection, somehow.'

'Did Gareth do that with you?'

Lily looks at the ground. 'No.' She's always been aware of how easy her love story with Gareth has looked from the outside, though when Jess hints at this, she gets defensive, says things like, *All relationships take work* and *Nobody's perfect, not even Gareth*. She moves off the subject now, back to Jess and Alex. 'Honestly, Jess. I've seen the way he looks at you. He's smart, he's funny, he's got a killer dimple. Don't give up on this one.'

'Who said anything about giving up?'

'Just – I know what you're like. You get all excited about a guy, and then things get tough, or he wants to talk about stuff that isn't as fun, and you move on to another crush.'

Now it's Jess's turn to feel defensive. But the truth is, she knows Lily's right. This is the great thing and also the worst thing about having been best friends for years. There's no hiding; there's no convincing Lily that she is anyone other than who she is. And in Jess's case, that's flighty, pain avoidant, easily distracted. Except when it comes to books – the passion she's stuck with the longest. But maybe that's because each book is different, its own journey with its own setting and story and characters, each one lasting a comparatively short amount of time. Reading is, in many ways, the perfect hobby – the perfect career – for people always looking for adventures.

'It feels like this isn't like the other times,' Jess says, and this isn't a lie.

'That sounds familiar.' Lily is smiling. They both know this is always what Jess says.

'No, but I really do mean it.'

'That sounds familiar, too.'

Lily isn't wrong. Maybe Alex isn't any different from the many crushes she's dabbled in her entire adult life. She broke up with her first boyfriend at school for no specific reason – just because she stopped being excited about him. The poor guy was crushed, and Jess felt terrible, but less terrible once she'd moved on to another boyfriend. The pattern had pretty much repeated itself all the way through her uni years, until the most recent drought, which had lasted a while. She was sick of the merry-go-round. She wanted to find someone she could commit to, someone who would keep her on her toes. Someone with whom life would feel like an adventure, so she wouldn't feel she was giving up on adventure when she settled down with them.

Jess was pretty sure she'd found that person this time. Alex's brain, his creativity – they are a source of endless fascination to her. She knows that when two or more bookworms are gathered, they are never short of conversation: whether it's a spirited disagreement on the personal ranking of Emily Henry novels, or a passionate defence of their favourite independent bookshop, or discussions on the relative merits of prologues and epilogues – there's always something to talk about. And the problem with a lot of Jess's previous boyfriends was that they just hadn't been that interested in all of that.

When she met Alex, she'd thought his strong views on romance as a genre were the biggest imaginable turn-off, but actually, the biggest imaginable turn-off is having no strong views at all, especially on matters having to do with books. Convincing him to love the genre will be a challenge – the kind of challenge she loves – although, thanks to Nathan's choice of reading recommendations, perhaps an easier challenge than she'd anticipated.

'Just . . .' Lily says, brow wrinkled in concern. 'I say this with love. But I'm concerned you won't give this one enough of a chance.'

'There's nothing I'd like more than to give him a chance. But it feels like he's not giving me a chance to give *him* a chance, you know?'

Lily grabs the gin from the cupboard. She doesn't ask if Jess would like any; she knows the answer. Besides, this is an emergency situation; the gin is medicinal.

'Speaking of shots,' she says, putting a glass in front of Jess. 'You're sure he's not just leaving things on hold till the book is done?'

'No,' Jess says. 'I'm not sure he isn't. But I'm also not sure that he *is*. It feels like there's something he's not telling me.' She hadn't even realised this till the words were out of her mouth – but yes, that's exactly what it feels like.

'Like a wife in the attic?'

'He doesn't have an attic.'

'But if he did, and there was a wife in there, do you think you would know about it?'

Jess pauses, thinking. Alex has definitely been vulnerable and transparent in some ways, for sure. But maybe those ways are a cover. Maybe he's told her just enough so that he doesn't have to tell her everything?

'It's possible that I wouldn't,' she concedes.

'Well, then. Maybe you could start there. Push on some conversational doors. See where they lead.'

The idea of making Alex uncomfortable – of, frankly, making things uncomfortable for them both – while they are in this forced-proximity situation, while the book is still being worked on, being worked out, seems extremely questionable. Jess squirms and grimaces.

'I'm telling you, Jess,' Lily says. 'I've got a good feeling about this one. This relationship is worth fighting for.'

The word *fighting* doesn't exactly make Jess feel any less squirmy. Relationships should be about joy and fun, especially at the beginning. Surely?

'You always end up having to fight for your relationship at some stage. And maybe you do it now, then the rest of it is relatively struggle-free. Or maybe it isn't, and you've learned the hard things about communication and openness now, and they'll stand you in good stead later.'

The thing with having a married friend is that sometimes it feels like Lily is light years ahead of her in terms of emotional maturity and general wisdom. Like she's an adultier adult. Like she knows some secrets of the universe that Jess doesn't. If it was anyone other than Lily, or if theirs was a different kind of friendship, maybe it would come across as smug and unlikeable. But Jess knows that Lily's wisdom is hard won, that she is sharing it to help her and not to show off.

Still. Words like *fight*, words like *struggle* – they make Jess wonder. If anyone is worth putting herself through that, it's definitely Alex. But still. 'I don't know, Lily. Maybe being single is easier.'

'Well, I don't think that's true,' Lily says. 'I think being single and being in a relationship both have their challenges in different ways. But even if that was true – let me ask you this. Is something being hard a good enough reason not to do it?'

She might as well repeat what she said when Jess was deciding whether to write the book with Alex. *It's not like you to shy away from a challenge.* It was true then, and it's true now. And maybe the boys she used to get bored with weren't as much of a challenge. Maybe it's a good sign that making it work with Alex might take more work.

She smiles. 'Obviously not. You know I love a challenge.'

'Exactly,' Lily says. 'That's the spirit.'

Never able to resist a good 'speaking of . . .' segue, Lily pours them both more gin, topped up with tonic this time. Food is supposed to happen at some stage this evening, but there's no evidence of that yet. Still, that's what Deliveroo is for. For now, gin. And gossip.

'So what do you think his secret is?' she asks. 'If it's not a wife in the attic?'

'A secret baby?' Jess pulls a face. 'That has to be one of the worst tropes in all of romance.'

Lily nods vigorously. 'Agreed. A secret stash of money, then?'

'Nah, it can't be that. He's made it clear that he needs this book deal as much to stay afloat as he does for his ego. Besides, he's got a huge family, so even if there was a massive inheritance, it would be divided between a lot of kids.'

'Ah. Secret pen name as a writer of erotic fiction?'

They dissolve into giggles, and it feels good. Everything has been a bit intense lately – all these big feelings about Alex, all this hard work around the book. Imagining Alex blushing away at his typewriter (it would have to be a typewriter) takes the edge off all of that. And so, if she's honest, does the gin.

Chapter Thirty

ALEX

Sipping his flat white in the coffee shop while he waits for Jess, Alex ponders the progress they have made together. The book is gradually taking shape, like a misshapen lump of clay being remoulded into something that's both beautiful and useful. Alex feels connected to his characters in ways he hasn't for a while – not since his first novel, when they had seemed to come alive and talk to him in ways that he knows make no sense to people who don't write, who haven't experienced this phenomenon first-hand. Of course, it's always possible that he's confusing his sense of connection with his characters with connection with Jess. She, too, talks about the characters as if they're real, with fondness and affection for them. Maybe this is part of the reason why she had wanted them all to survive – she has become attached to them. That is always a dangerous thing as a writer. A good plot often relies on catastrophes and difficult situations for the characters to show their mettle, for them to grow and change and learn. You have to be willing to turn the pressure up, to throw your characters into tricky quandaries, to have them experience pain and jeopardy. He has tried to explain this to Jess, as gently and unpatronisingly as he knows how. But he caught her wincing, and then caught himself not wanting to hurt characters because of how much they mean to *her*. Just as she's become too attached to their characters, he's become too attached to her. All of which is a little terrifying.

'Hey.'

Jess is sliding into the seat opposite him, flat white in hand. He hadn't noticed her come in – hadn't noticed that he has been sitting with his notebook open and his pen poised above it in the air for goodness knows how long. He's shaken out of his thoughts by the sight of her, by how pretty she looks today, with her hair down and the burnt orange jumper which seems to bring out the colour in her face and the green in her eyes.

Yes. He's definitely too attached.

'Hi,' he says, his voice cracking a little. A throwback to his inability to speak to his teenage crushes. His cheeks burn.

'You seem very deep in thought.'

It's charitable of her not to point out the strikingly deep red he has probably just turned.

'Yes,' he says.

'Penny for them.'

'Ah, sorry. I don't take cash.'

'Contactless? No problem.'

She holds out her phone as if about to pay. It's silly, but it makes him laugh, and he loves how satisfied she looks to have provoked this reaction. But then she says, 'No, but seriously. Tell me.'

'Fine.' He sighs. She isn't going to like this. 'I was just thinking that we need to push a bit harder on tragedy. Amp up the stakes, make the characters face some hard things.'

'They've just been in a plane crash,' she says. 'You don't think that's enough trauma?'

'The more trauma the better,' he says, and there's that wince again, followed immediately by the pinch in his own heart.

'I was thinking the opposite,' she says. 'I was thinking that maybe what this narrative needs is for us to lean a little harder on the romance.'

He's been expecting this. He's surprised it hasn't come sooner. They've explored plot lines with marriages in trouble, with feuding friends reconciling, with one passenger thinking about his long-ago lost love as he plunged, he assumed, to his death. It's bad enough that they've had to pair up a couple of passengers. So obvious. A little cinematic, and not in a good way – in an angling-for-a-film-deal kind of way. And now Jess seems to be suggesting that she wants to dig deeper into their story. Surely, she's not going to suggest a third-act breakup and a grand gesture at the end? He knows, though, that in pairing him with Jess in the first place, this is exactly the kind of thing Nathan had in mind. Alex takes a deep breath in, then a slow breath out, aware of Jess watching him intently as he does so.

'Okay,' he says eventually.

'Okay?'

'In exchange for some additional trauma.'

Her turn, now, to breathe in deeply; his turn to

watch her as various emotions cross her face: fear, thoughtfulness, resignation. Something like the stages of grief.

'Deal,' she says. 'It's only fair. We can at least try.'

He hadn't expected her to agree so readily.

'We're really only at the drafting stage,' she says. 'Who knows what Nathan will cut. We might as well throw everything at the wall and see what sticks.'

Ah. This explains it. Jess is clearly aware that Nathan won't cut the romance. She might, however, think he'll cut some of the near death, the injury, the heartbreak. But Alex knows he won't. Trauma is, after all, where Alex shines – 'intricate examination of the psychology of suffering' is a phrase that has been used in reviews of his novels. 'Insightful empathy,' another. This is what his fans come to him for. Romance – not so much. But maybe Nathan is right: maybe romance will bring Jess's fans along for the ride. Maybe this book will be his most successful yet, the one that entices a whole new audience. The key will be to tread delicately, so as not to alienate his original readers.

But Alex also knows the pain of editing. The pain that Jess feels when a character is plunged into hot water is the pain he feels when a carefully drawn character is removed or an intricately plotted storyline is cut. Editing is a logistical nightmare for a thoughtfully written book, the kind where each part of the plot links together, each character's storyline propelling the others'. Removing planks is intellectual Jenga, requiring just as much care. If you edit out the wrong thing, the whole structure crumbles, even when that thing does not appear to be foundational. Weaving in new plotlines isn't without its risks or its difficulties. So it's best if once they're in, they're in for good.

'I'm fairly certain the added trauma will stick,' he says. It will have to.

'We'll see.' She's smirking; she knows that in some sense she has won. And their old rivalry – the chemistry of that competitiveness – is back. He relishes this. It seems less dangerous than other kinds of chemistry, and almost, though not quite, as enjoyable. It's going to be a good session, he can tell already – brainstorming new angles for the plot, maybe zooming in on characters who until now had only been in the background.

In his pocket, his phone vibrates. Should he ignore it? He should probably ignore it. Allow the creative buzz he can feel bubbling in the pit of his stomach to take over the afternoon, enjoy the creative process with Jess. But when – aside from those addle-brained days in Godalming – has he ever been able to ignore a ringing phone? It could be someone from his family. Someone might need him.

Jess is looking at him, waiting for him to continue their verbal sparring. Expectant. And he very much wants to be able to concentrate on that. But he knows he can't concentrate until he has picked up his phone and at least *checked* it's nothing urgent.

'Hold that thought,' he says to her, and reaches into his pocket. His heart sinks when he sees the name: Francesca. Sister number three. 'I'm sorry,' he tells Jess. 'I have to take this.' He doesn't focus on her face; he doesn't want to see the disappointment there, doesn't want to see her wish he would give her his full attention, when that's all he wants to do himself. He stands up from the table, paces a little until he finds a spot in a recessed corner.

'Hello,' he says into the phone, and has to stop himself from adding, *What do you want?* But once Francesca starts speaking, he softens. He loves all his siblings; he can't say no to any of them. They all know this. Do they take advantage? Maybe. But is he glad they do? Also maybe.

'Hey,' she says. 'How's my favourite big brother?'

'I'm fine, thank you,' he says, evenly. Instead of, *I'm a little annoyed that you've interrupted this moment, actually.* 'You?'

'Oh, you know.' She laughs, but he can tell it's forced, an attempt at bringing light-heartedness into a stressful moment. And he knows there are a lot of stressful moments in Francesca's life, that she barely has time to breathe, let alone eat or shower, with three under-fives at home. She's logged dozens, if not hundreds, of hours at A&E for asthma attacks and various injuries sustained through overly rambunctious play. 'Never a dull moment around here.'

'I'm guessing you'd saw off your right arm for a dull moment.'

Another laugh, this one even hollower. 'Any chance you're free to babysit on Saturday? It's our anniversary, and Steve wants us to go out.'

He notes the phrasing of this – *Steve wants us to* – and imagines that the last thing Francesca feels like doing on Saturday is squeeze her still-tender body into a pre-pregnancy dress, put on some uncomfortable heels, and apply some make-up in-between pumping milk for that evening's bottle and soothing her eldest, promising him that Mummy and Daddy will be back before he knows it and Uncle Alex will take good care of him in the meantime. She has obviously decided to pick her battles, though, and to do whatever is necessary to ensure her marriage doesn't splutter and die, suffocated by nappies, Calpol and unending piles of laundry. And if she can do that in her sleep-deprived state, of course he can help out for a few chaotic hours. Francesca knows this, and Alex knows she knows it.

Plus, he can't think of a single reason to say no. What else would he be doing? Writing? Brainstorming with Jess? He spends three-quarters of his time doing one or the other of those as it is. And although he doesn't love the chaos of small children, he loves his nieces and nephews, and he loves his sister.

'I'm sure that can be arranged,' he says.

'Thank you.' He hears palpable relief in her voice. The stakes for this dinner might have been higher than he'd realised.

Back at the table, he apologises profusely for the interruption, catching Jess's gaze and holding it. Trying to communicate, *Let's get back to where we were, banter-wise.*

'Everything okay?' she asks, her frown communicating concern and readying itself for empathy.

'Yes,' he says. 'Just been called up for emergency babysitting, that's all.'

'That happens a lot, doesn't it?'

'Three separate sets of families nearby. I'm the ever-reliable brother. Plus, I'm happy to do it.'

Happy-ish would be more accurate. He has found himself bristling lately. He dislikes this about himself. He likes being reliable; it's an expression of love.

'Okay,' she says. She takes a sip of her flat white – a performative sip, surely, as she must have finished it by now. A pause, he guesses, for dramatic effect, or to give him a chance to re-evaluate what he's just said.

'What does that mean?'

'Nothing.'

If there's one thing Alex has learned in his short time on this earth, it's that when a woman says *nothing*, that is almost never what she means. He chews on the inside of his cheek, considering whether to pursue this any further.

'Come on,' he says at last. 'Tell me what you're thinking.'

She takes a deep breath, as if preparing for something intense. He braces for impact.

'It just seems like your family maybe takes you for granted a little bit.'

He leaps to their defence, as he always does – as a loyal brother should. 'I don't get that sense.'

'When was the last time someone in your family did something for you?'

'Oh, they do all the time.'

In that moment, though, he's unable to think of a specific example. His sister Jen planned his last book launch, but that was more than four years ago at this point. And he used to get invitations to dinner all the time, but he can't remember when that last happened without it being linked in some way to babysitting or another favour. He opens his mouth again, hoping something will come out, but it doesn't. He closes his mouth again.

'When you were in the US, they just had to cope, right? Figure things out without you?'

'There were fewer nieces and nephews then. Life was easier.'

'Oh, so before nieces and nephews, they never asked you for anything?'

She is backing him into a corner, and he isn't sure why. Where is she going with this? He wishes he hadn't opened up to her about the frustrations of family. About being the Reuben, the boringly reliable older brother.

'I worry about you,' she says. Her voice is gentle, her brow furrowed with compassion, but the words don't land gently. 'I worry that you let your family take advantage of you too much.'

'Yeah, well.' His voice is louder than he intends. 'At least I *have* a relationship with my family.'

The instant the words are out of his mouth, all he wants to do is take them back. Jess winces, bites her lip. He is mortified, devastated. Here he is, having done the very thing he was trying to avoid by not getting too close: hurt her.

'I'm sorry,' he says, but it's too late. Her eyes are filling. 'I didn't mean it.'

'I think you did,' she says.

He wishes she were wrong. A high-pitched sound rings in his ear: the sound of panic. What to do, what to do? How to make this better? He doesn't know. He's ruined everything. He has to go.

'I have to go,' he says, gathering up his things. Maybe she'll think the emergency babysitting is now. Let her think that. He'll figure it out later. For now, he needs to get out of here, before he forgets how to breathe.

Chapter Thirty-One

JESS

What on earth just happened? Jess can't quite figure it out. One minute they were talking, then he erupted, like a bubbling volcano that had been waiting for a slight shift in the earth. She doesn't know him well enough to have noticed the bubbling, she supposes. She also clearly doesn't know him well enough to know how hurtful he is capable of being, how he is able to wield her own fears and hurts against her. Besides which, he is wrong: she *does* have a relationship with her family. Maybe it looks different from other families, but it still counts. She loves her grandparents; they've always been there for her. She tries not to think about their age, about the fact that they won't be around forever.

And yeah, sure, she hates being an only child. Always has done. Sometimes, growing up, she'd wake up panicking at her grandparents' house, thinking maybe this was the time her mum wouldn't come back for her, that she'd be having too much fun to remember she had a daughter and a life in London. Or, worse, that she'd remember, but choose the fun over the daughter and the life in London. At those times, she wished she could nudge a sibling awake and share the anxiety with them. Lily always tells her that it's not like that between sisters, that half the time she and Anna ignored each other or fought, and that if Anna had woken her up in the middle of the night, she probably would have told her to shut up and just go back to sleep, but even that seems preferable to and more companiable than the dark and the loneliness. She can't imagine a sibling being cold-hearted enough to ignore her as she quietly sobbed into her pillow. When the iPad came out, she begged her mother for one, and her mother, at some level wracked with guilt, complied. Problem solved: in the middle of the night, she didn't have to cry anymore. Instead, she could download episodes of her favourite shows and laugh quietly into her pillow. The downside was that she didn't always feel great the next day at school – but she probably wouldn't have felt great if she'd been up crying half the night, either.

But now, Alex has made her face the pain she's been running from her whole life. Keep moving, keep working, and when she's not working, she's having fun – snowboarding with Lily, planning a weekend retreat with her book club, binge-watching *Parks and Recreation*. Writing had seemed like another fun activity, another fun challenge, but Alex has ruined that, too. Writing now seems to be a place of vulnerability, where the areas that feel tender are poked at and prodded.

And why? Because she cares about him; because she was trying to get him to see that he deserves to be looked after, too.

Maybe all along she was just projecting onto him. Being looked after is what *she* has wanted out of life. Maybe it's wrong of her to assume that it's what Alex wants or needs.

She's been holding it together as she packs up her notebook, her pen. But this coffee shop feels suddenly claustrophobic; Jess needs to get out of here. Walking along briskly while thinking about all of this, she bites her lip to stave off tears, but here they come anyway. Luckily, this is London, and nobody notices – or if they do, they have the decency to look away.

* * *

When Jess gets off the Tube at Pimlico station, her feet take her not to her own flat but to her grandparents'. Perhaps it's an old instinct from childhood: she'd go to her grandma with her tears when she wanted to talk and she was home alone, or when she knew her mum would try to cheer her up rather than wade through any difficult emotions with her.

Her grandmother, as she always has, takes one look at Jess's mascara-streaked face and envelops her in a hug. Not that she wouldn't hug Jess if she hadn't been crying; hugs are Grandma Val's default love language. But this is an extra warm, extra tight hug, of the kind that has always made Jess feel better – always made her feel *understood* and accepted.

'Put the kettle on, Alan,' she calls in the vague direction of the kitchen as Jess pulls back to wipe her tears. 'And bring me some tissues, would you, love?'

With her hand on her shoulder, Grandma Val leads Jess into the living room. 'So,' she says. 'Tell me.'

Jess takes a deep breath and ponders how far back to go, how much to explain.

'Remember the good-looking writer I was forced to work with?'

'The one who wasn't your type?'

Jess winces slightly. She hopes it's not visible. 'Yeah. That one.'

'Turns out he is your type after all?' Val might be good at deploying strategic silence and letting the other person talk, but she also can't resist a *told you so*.

'I'm not sure,' she says. 'I keep changing my mind. But today it feels like I was right in the first place.'

Jess paints a quick picture, which it turns out isn't as complicated to explain as she thought it might have been: she and Alex have been getting close, but every time one or the other of them touches on a difficult topic, it all goes belly up. And the last thing Alex said to her had been pretty unforgivable, and even though she'd have been well within her rights to get up and go, *he* was the one who'd added insult to injury and done that.

'Sounds like he didn't know how to make it right and he was mortified at himself, and so he left rather than face the hurt he'd caused.'

'That's pretty much it.'

'Hmm.' The silence this time is not so much for Jess to fill as for Grandma Val to think things through. 'Do you mind me asking what the unforgivable thing he said was?'

Jess isn't sure she can repeat it without crying again. She wipes her eyes and blows her nose with the tissues Grandpa Alan has procured, buying some time and readying herself for the inevitable next onslaught of tears. She's very good at distracting herself so that she doesn't cry; but when she starts, it is usually inconvenient, and she can't stop.

'He said, *at least I* have *a relationship with my family.*'

'Ah. Implying you didn't?'

'Yeah.' Jess swallows hard. 'I mean, he was lashing out. I'd been gently trying to challenge him on his own family because they tend to take him for granted. He's the one who looks after everyone else, you know? But it's still very harsh.'

'Well, first of all, love. Yes. It's harsh. It's also not true. What is this, right now, if it's not a relationship with family?'

Jess blows her nose again. 'Exactly,' she says. She feels vindicated as well as loved: a powerful combination.

'But why do you think it hurt so much?'

This question feels like a punch to the gut. Now that the metaphorical box under her bed has been kicked open, she's been asking herself the same thing and come to some painful conclusions. Obviously, it's true that her relationship with her mother isn't healthy and never has been. But also, by not engaging with memories of her dad, she's been denying herself whatever relationship with him is available to her, too.

'Because of Mum, I guess. Because of the ways she . . . is. And also because of Dad. Because I've never properly grieved him. I've always avoided thinking about him. But like, maybe I need to.'

'Maybe you do,' Grandma Val says, kindness in her eyes, extending her arms from the sofa where she sits. Jess joins her there, nestles her head on her shoulder. 'Maybe you need to get in touch with aspects of who he was.'

'You mean, learn some French?'

Jess can feel Val's smile in the way her breath shifts. '*Je pense oui?*' she says, in the world's worst accent. And for some reason, this tips Jess from tears into hysterical laughter. It spreads to Grandma Val, until both of them are shaking and holding their stomachs.

'Who needs therapy,' Jess says, when she finally catches her breath, 'when you've got this?'

Chapter Thirty-Two

ALEX

Alex isn't sure where he's going when he gets up and leaves, but the autopilot leads him there anyway. He's now made a total fool of himself and hurt Jess, when he was desperately trying to avoid doing that, and there's only one person who can help him make sense of it all.

'Nathan's on a call,' his secretary tells Alex. 'I'll let him know you're here.'

Alex sits, but that instantly feels wrong, and he stands again. He paces a little in the small hallway. Counts forty-one steps. Nathan's secretary looks at him over the top of her glasses.

'Can I get you anything?' she asks. 'Maybe a glass of Scotch?'

Despite himself, Alex smiles. 'Sorry, sorry. I'll sit.'

She smiles tightly back at him.

'But maybe a tea.'

He doesn't need a tea. But he does need something to do with his hands, and that seems like a good solution. Although the secretary doesn't look thrilled when he takes longer than necessary stirring in the sugar he neither wants nor needs. Sweet enough – yeah, right.

'I'm sure Mr Thomas will be ready for you soon,' she says. Perhaps trying to convince herself that she only needs to be patient with Alex for a little while longer.

'Sorry,' he says again. He sips his tea; he bounces his leg. And at last, Nathan pokes his head out of the door to his office.

'Alex,' he says. 'This is a nice surprise. I was just about to pop out for lunch. Want to join me?'

He sees his own gratitude reflected in Nathan's secretary's face. Walking to Pret feels like something his limbs need. Being cooped up in an office probably wouldn't do him any good.

'So,' Nathan says, holding the door for Alex. 'I'm guessing this isn't just a friendly catch-up.'

Alex gets straight to the point. 'I've messed up.'

'Jess?' Nathan does not sound surprised. Resigned is probably more like it. Ready for another round of this seemingly interminable drama.

'Yes.'

'Tell me.'

Outside in the sunshine, Alex feels unexpectedly exposed. 'We were – you know. Getting close. Which, I assume, was part of your plan.'

He catches the hint of a smirk playing across Nathan's lips. 'I can neither confirm nor deny the accusation without the presence of a lawyer.'

'I thought as much.'

But Nathan clearly has no interest in lingering on the part of the story where he might be to blame. 'So what did you do?'

'I said a mean thing. And then instead of apologising, or staying to talk it through, or even giving her a chance to walk away, I'm the one who walked away.'

'Wow. Impressive.'

'I know.'

Alex is saved from further judgement by their arrival at Pret and Nathan's scanning of the shelves. 'This Pret is always running out of hoisin duck wraps,' he says.

'I'm sorry for your loss,' Alex says, with only a little sarcasm. He's not a monster, after all. He understands the struggle of the out-of-stock favourite lunch just like anybody else.

'Thank you. I appreciate your sympathy at this difficult time.'

Hoisin duck wrap notwithstanding, they eventually find a satisfactory set of lunch items, and, miracle of miracles, an empty table.

'So what was the mean thing you said?'

Alex feels his shoulders slump as he recounts the story. 'She said I shouldn't let my family take advantage of me so much. That I should let *them* do things for me sometimes. And I said, yeah, well, at least I *have* a relationship with my family.'

'Ah.'

'And then I made a pathetic attempt at an apology and left before I could see her cry.'

'So, basically, you took out your pain on her?'

'My pain?'

Nathan bites into his Caesar salad wrap and lets the words hang in the air while he chews.

'Yes,' he says eventually. 'Your pain.'

Alex looks at him, waits for him to elaborate.

'Well,' Nathan says, when it's been long enough that it's become clear Alex isn't going to read between the lines himself. 'It's true, isn't it? Your family *do* take advantage of you. They *do* expect you to drop everything for them the minute you need them. I seem to remember you moved to America to get away from that.'

Deep in his gut, Alex recognises the same instinct, the same anger bubbling up, that caused him to lash out at Jess. He bites the inside of his cheek so he doesn't say or do anything as destructive as he did with her.

'Why do you think that is?' Nathan asks him.

Alex shrugs, a little boy being lectured by a headmaster.

'Do you think maybe you've trained them to do that? By always being so ready to drop everything, always being on call for them?'

'That's just being a responsible brother.'

'Yes, but it's also letting them take advantage of you. That's what Jess was getting at. And it's not the first time your loyalty to your family has clashed with your loyalty to a girl, is it? What about Elodie?'

Alex thinks back to that phone call from his sister, the one that interrupted him as he was about to say *I love you* for the first time. To what felt like a rip through his torso as he was faced with the need to choose between letting down his sister Louisa and disappointing his girlfriend.

Nathan waits for Alex to make eye contact. 'You've seen *Love Actually*, haven't you?'

'All my girlfriends have forced me to.'

'The scene with Laura Linney and that Karl guy. Did that ever resonate?'

Alex is hopeless with names, with pop culture. 'Remind me?'

'The woman with the brother who's always calling. And she's got this huge crush on this colleague of hers, and something is finally about to happen, and then the brother calls. And the colleague, Karl, is nice about it at first. But in the end, it breaks them up, because she doesn't have the appropriate boundaries.'

'I see.'

It's not subtle, what Nathan is getting at. And he's also not wrong. But Alex doesn't quite see what can be done about it. He's been avoiding the subject of his family with his therapist. So much so that he has asked him: *What exactly are you not telling me here?* Alex had shrugged, the small boy in front of the headmaster there, too.

Alex had expected a little more sympathy from Nathan. A little more practical advice on how to reconcile with Jess. But on the other hand, it's not rocket science. It's pretty obvious that he needs to apologise. He just isn't sure what happens after that. Or how to solve this seemingly intractable problem – too many people needing him at once. But Nathan is looking at his watch now, and Alex knows what's coming.

'Sorry, Alex. I have a meeting in ten.'

'No worries. Thanks for listening.'

Not that Nathan has listened, not that much. He's done most of the talking, most of the interrogating.

But he has cut through to the heart of the matter, and maybe that's what Alex needed for now. He takes out his phone, opens WhatsApp, and types.

> Jess, I'm so sorry. I should never have said what I said, and I should never have walked out rather than talk to you about it. I hope you can forgive me.

A little overly formal for a WhatsApp message, maybe, but GIFs and emoji don't seem like they would really be up to the task. He presses send and watches one grey tick appear, then another next to it. They both turn to blue: she's read the message. But there are no appearing dots below. She isn't typing back. She probably needs a moment. Several moments. Alex sincerely hopes it isn't more than that.

Chapter Thirty-Three

JESS

If Alex thinks a WhatsApp message is all it's going to take, then she was clearly crazy to ever contemplate liking him. Considering the empathy and emotional intelligence on display in his novels, she really had expected better from him. Maybe all of that was Nathan's doing, during the editing phase. But no – she knows better. She's worked with Alex; she knows that he understands people at an intuitive level. They've talked about characters and subplots and emotional arcs. So if it's not lack of empathy or lack of emotional intelligence – if it's not cluelessness – then the only possible conclusion is that he deliberately meant to hurt her. Jess can't fathom why, but it's the only thing that makes sense. She wasn't being unkind. She was only looking out for his best interests.

Maybe she should just walk away now. She's probably done enough work on the book to earn the contracted payment and a cover credit as a co-author. Enough, too, to earn her the right to have her own book published someday – one that will be much less fraught to write, just her and her laptop in a bustling café, building characters she loves and not having to negotiate her way out of convoluted descriptions of aeroplane landing gear. She hopes so, at least. Because much as she's trying to ignore it, there's a knot in her stomach, and she doesn't enjoy this feeling. It's time to go back to doing the things that bring her joy. She'll travel! She'll learn to knit! She'll take a cocktail-mixing class. There'll be time in her life and space in her brain for those things again. And, also, for the work she has fallen behind on. It's only a matter of time before somebody slides into her DMs to complain that her newsletters are now fortnightly, and they're paying for weekly, so what gives?

She turns the idea of being done with Alex – with this whole thing – over and over in her mind, and when she's had enough of doing that, she emails Nathan. This will require delicacy, so she can't say what she really wants to, which is: *I can't do this anymore*. She has mentally spent the money; she has promised her grandparents a cruise. She can't renege on that. Instead, she asks if he can do coffee.

From: Nathan Thomas
To: Jess Martin
Subject: Coffee

Hi Jess,

Nice to hear from you. To coffee: gladly. But just to clarify – I assume this isn't just a social call?

Nathan

From: Jess Martin
To: Nathan Thomas
Subject: Coffee

You assume correctly.

All best,
Jess

So now, here they are, back at the same coffee shop where she and Alex had their first disastrous work meeting. The one she is beginning to wish had never taken place. At the time, it had seemed life-changing, in the best of ways. A dream come true: her name on a book. Maybe her way into writing her own books. And for the briefest of seconds, before she realised his arrogance, the hope that she might be doing all this with someone the romcom gods had deliberately sent her way via a bookshop meet-cute. This is where, perhaps, her constant escapism into fiction and fun has served her poorly. She has clearly not been prepared for the harsh realities of life. She sees that now.

'Can I get you a pastry with your coffee?' Nathan asks, all smoothness. Wanting, no doubt, to improve her mood with some sugar, to literally sweeten her up. But the fact she's seen through it doesn't mean she's immune to the charms of a pain au chocolat.

'Yes please,' she says. 'That would be nice, actually. Something with chocolate?'

When he returns, with pastries for both of them, he leans forward, attentive.

'So,' he says. 'Tell me. What's Alex done now?'

The directness of it, the way he has guessed so easily, makes her smile. 'So we're not pretending you don't know what this is about?'

'I've known him for a long time,' Nathan says. 'I know how impossible he can be.'

'So you threw me under the bus to get his book done, then?'

This, admittedly, probably isn't how she should speak to her editor. But something about Nathan puts her at ease; she feels she can be honest with him.

He smiles, a little crookedly. Seemingly not at all offended. 'Something like that.'

Something about the way he says this reminds her of her previous suspicions. 'Just for the book, or was there an ulterior motive beyond that?'

'Just for the book, at first. But after that . . . there might have been an ulterior motive.'

'I see.'

This isn't exactly a shock. Should she go there – ask him about it? Chide him gently? She'd probably need something stronger than coffee if she was going to do that.

But then he goes there for her. 'The ulterior motive hasn't worked out, I take it?'

'It did,' she says, looking away, thoughts of what they had done in Nathan's Godalming house feeling surprisingly fresh and tender. 'And then it didn't.'

'Ah.'

'You mentioned he can be impossible, so . . . Yes. That.'

'I see.'

He doesn't ask for specifics, which makes Jess wonder if he already knows; if Alex has already told him what happened.

'So basically,' she says quickly, in an effort to move on from this particular topic, 'I was wondering if we have done enough on the book together. We've worked really hard, and I think the draft is in really good shape. And maybe, given – everything – I can leave Alex to finish off our work. Maybe I've taken it as far as I can go. You know, without murdering him.' She's going for a joke, a lightening of the mood, but it doesn't quite land that way. Sometimes Jess wishes it were acceptable to put *lol* or *haha* on the end of a spoken sentence the way people do with texts. She takes a deep breath and says the next part really quickly, the part that matters most to her. 'And I hope I've proved my worth as a writer and my potential for future projects.'

Nathan nods, almost imperceptibly. She'll take it.

'What does Alex think?' he asks.

'I haven't asked him.' She leaves out the part where they're not speaking; it feels juvenile and immature, and unnecessary for Nathan to know about. 'I was hoping maybe *you* could,' she adds.

She forces herself to meet Nathan's gaze. He seems to be weighing up the pros and cons. Maybe he's wondering if he should punish her for giving up so close to the finishing line – punish her by making her speak to Alex again, rather than walking away forever, which is what she'd really like to do. At least for now; at least until the book is published and they have to grin and bear each other's company for the sake of book events and publicity photos. By then, she imagines she will be less angry. All of what's happened will be water which has long ago flowed under the proverbial bridge.

'Okay,' Nathan says, obviously deciding that Jess has suffered enough. 'I'll talk to him.'

Chapter Thirty-Four

ALEX

'Right,' Alex's counsellor says when he's heard the whole story of Jess, ending with the WhatsApp message she still hasn't replied to and the email he got from Nathan this morning, asking if he felt like their writing partnership had accomplished what it needed to. He twiddles his grey moustache and leaves his customary silence, waiting, probably, for Alex to piece together all the clues and come up with a theory. But if Alex were capable of doing that, he probably wouldn't be in therapy in the first place. 'So why do you think you reacted so strongly to her suggestion that you put better boundaries in place with your family?'

That word again. *Boundaries*. Therapy-speak for not being there for people when they need you.

'I don't know,' he says.

'How did you feel when she said it?'

He thinks back to the punch in his stomach, to the adrenaline surge. His breathing accelerates. 'I suppose anger is probably how I'd describe it.'

The therapist crosses and uncrosses his legs, nods vigorously. 'Right. But anger is a secondary emotion –

it's usually a sign of other emotions under it. Hurt, or sadness, or a feeling of betrayal, for example. Was it any of that?'

Alex rubs the back of his neck and considers this. 'I'm not sure.'

'How does it feel when I suggest that you should put boundaries in place with your family?'

Tedious. It feels tedious.

'Baffling. Because I don't know where to start. Or, really, what boundaries actually are.'

'Hold that thought, we'll get back to that. When you said you felt angry, do you think your anger was really aimed at Jess, or were you misdirecting it?'

Alex closes his eyes and tries to locate the anger, the way he sometimes tries to locate the source of a tension headache. Usually, he is unsuccessful at both.

'Because...' the therapist prompts. 'It seems she spoke really gently, and not unkindly, and that your response was maybe out of proportion to what she'd said. Which suggests that your anger was there, bubbling under the surface, and just needed a small trigger to come to the fore. You lashed out. Which suggests that Jess wasn't the cause at all. Are you angry with your family?'

The answer comes to him straight away: *yes*. But he checks himself, because that seems odd. He loves his big, messy family. He can't think of anything any of them have directly done to make him angry. His parents were – are – loving, as were, and are, his stepparents. And even now, they come to his launches; they buy his books and review them on the websites that matter. They pick up the phone when he calls them.

He laughs with them, plays board games with them, cuddles his nieces and nephews. He doesn't feel uneasy around them.

'Why would I be angry with them?'

The moustache twiddle again. 'You tell me.'

He wants to shout. *No. You tell me! You're the one being paid because you know the answers!* He pictures himself slamming down a fist and yelling this. But that would likely be more misdirected anger.

'How did it feel to always be the responsible one? The one who looked after everybody else?'

Alex swallows around the lump in his throat. 'I like looking after everyone.'

'Yes, I can see that. But let me ask you something else. Who was looking after *you*?'

The question lands like a thump in his gut.

'I wasn't, like, neglected or anything,' he says, but he hears his own voice catching.

'So your parents recognised your anxiety and took you to the doctor, got you a prescription and some therapy?'

Alex isn't sure he likes the smug way in which the therapist has said this, with the triumph of a person solving the day's Wordle in two lines. Nonetheless, there's only one possible answer to his question.

'No. That's something you and I worked out together a few months ago.'

'Right. So is your anxiety a recent thing?'

He thinks back to his afternoons with the school nurse, a hot water bottle on his stomach while he waited for one parent or another to come and pick him up. To his avoidance of walking on the cracks in the pavements because the last thing he needed was bad luck. To the times he stayed up way too late finishing off homework because he wanted it to be perfect. To the time he couldn't stop crying after getting 99 per cent on a maths exam, because he couldn't figure out where that missing 1 per cent could possibly have come from.

'No,' he admits. 'It is not a recent thing.'

'But your parents didn't notice it when you were growing up.'

'It's possible they noticed it. It just wasn't talked about as much back then.'

'And how does that make you feel?'

Ah. The dreaded question again. It feels like going round and round in circles. Alex shrugs. He can hardly blame his parents for British culture, and he doesn't want to blame them for how busy they were with their marriages and careers and divorces and re-marriages and new babies. But inside him, he feels the bubbling up of that rage again. He was just a little boy, crying out to be noticed and looked after, and instead it fell to him to look after others.

'I suppose,' he admits reluctantly, 'it makes me feel sad for the child I was.'

'Now we're getting somewhere,' says the therapist, twiddling that moustache again.

By the end of the session, Alex has come to the conclusion that he needs to explain all of this to Jess. He doesn't exactly relish the thought of being so vulnerable with her, knowing full well that he used her own vulnerability against her, and she could well be tempted to do the same back – though he hopes she isn't as petty as that. She seemed to really like him – judging by their Godalming weekend, to really like him *a lot* – but he can't stop picturing the wounded look on her face when he twisted that knife in. She doesn't strike him as the vindictive type, but he wouldn't have said that about himself, either – and yet he was apparently more than capable of lashing out in pain, so why shouldn't she be?

The problem – or at least *a* problem – is that she's not replying to his messages. He doesn't want to be that guy, someone who wears her down with insistent texting. He knows he needs to leave her the space to come to him when she's good and ready. But he wonders, too, if she'll ever be ready, since she has no way of knowing that his lashing out wasn't really about her at all. He worries about her being tied down to help her grandparents but, really, those worries are a projection – the person he is actually worried about is his own younger self.

What he really needs is a woman's advice. Lily would be good to talk to, but he isn't sure how to find her – doesn't even know her surname. Maybe with some judicious Facebook stalking, he could figure it out? On the other hand, he runs the risk of Lily telling Jess, which is where, surely, her loyalty would lie. But then, it comes to him – Jess's advice, his therapist's advice: think of a way someone in your family can help *you* with something. And he needs a woman for this. He calls Louisa. After all, she owes him one. She owes him several, in fact.

'Sounds to me like you need to buy some flowers,' she tells him after hearing the whole sorry tale. Well, perhaps not the whole tale. Now doesn't seem like the time to go into why he and Jess were arguing in the first place.

'Buying flowers is a little clichéd, isn't it?'

He can almost hear Louisa's shrug through the phone. 'It's clichéd for a reason. It works.'

There's silence on both ends of the phone for a moment.

'Hey, Alex?'

'Yes.'

'Thanks for coming to me for advice. It's nice to do a little role reversal.'

Alex can hear the next conversation with his therapist already: *And why does it surprise you so much that other people might enjoy helping you the way you enjoy helping them?* He knows the answer, too. It's because they never have. And they never have because he's never asked.

'I might come to you for advice more from now on. If that's okay.'

'I would love that.' There's so much warmth in Louisa's voice. Has it always been there? 'Especially if it ends with you being successfully coupled up. I know we'd all love to see that.'

The irony of Louisa being the one to say this is not lost on Alex.

'Thanks, Lou. Now, one more thing: do I take the flowers to her house, or send them with a letter of apology?'

'Take them to her house, but write the letter anyway, in case she doesn't want to talk. That way she can at least *read* your apology once you've gone. Letters have a way of percolating and thawing rage.'

'Sounds like you're speaking from experience.'

'I am.'

'Well, thank you. That sounds like a genius idea.'

'It's always worked on me,' she says. 'Now stop procrastinating and go and buy those flowers. Love you. Bye.'

Alex had always assumed that the 'love you' Louisa said before ending a call was a payback for whatever favour she was asking for on the call. But there's no favour here. No doubt his therapist would say, *You deserve to be loved even when you're not doing something for someone.*

Whatever. He'll take it.

Chapter Thirty-Five

JESS

Jess has decided it's fine. She hasn't heard back from Nathan, and she hasn't heard from Alex since the WhatsApp she ignored, so she's just going to assume that it's fine. Her work is done; she's off the hook. She can go back to her previous life of interviewing bookshop owners, reviewing books, taking nice pictures, and revelling in the endorphin rush of social media likes and free novels landing with a thud on her doormat on a regular basis. And it feels good! She's missed it. It's work, but it's not like traipsing through treacle, not the way that writing sometimes feels.

She puts on her feel-good playlist, tears open the latest packages, and organises the books on her shelf of proofs, in publication-date order, as always. It feels good to be back to her routine, back to what she knows, her muscle memory remembering what to do. She's just opened her spreadsheet to log them – publisher, genre, date forthcoming – when her buzzer goes. She feels a crease in her own forehead form as she tries to think who could be at the door. Normally, she'd assume the postman, but he's already been today – her newly reorganised shelf is evidence of that. As far as she remembers, she hasn't ordered anything from Vinted in at least six days, so it can't be that, either.

Reluctantly, she stands up from her chair and makes her way to the door. When she opens it, her stomach sinks. But part of her has to admit that she already knew who it was going to be.

'Hello,' says a person camouflaged behind the prettiest bouquet of flowers she has ever seen. A voice she recognises all too well.

It's physically impossible for her to slam the door in Alex's face. Firstly, because his foot is partly on the threshold, and while it might give her satisfaction to stub his toe, she might also break it that way, and she doesn't fancy being sued. Plus, as annoyed as she is with Alex, it seems like a broken foot might not be a proportionate response to some ill-advised words.

But also, these are some beautiful flowers, and it would be churlish to refuse them. If nothing else, they'll make for a pretty background for the bookstagram photos she's about to take.

'These are lovely,' she says.

'Glad you like them.'

Alex hands them over. She can't resist burying her face in them and smelling them.

'I suppose you better come in,' she says. A smile on her face to soften the words. She wants him to know, though, that it's going to take more than a multi-coloured bunch of daisies and gerberas to make up for what he said and how he behaved.

'You're too kind.' A smile on his face, too. Not the dimpled kind. The barely-there kind.

'I know.' Jess pushes her glasses up her nose while she considers what to do next. 'And let me extend that kindness by making you a drink. Tea?'

'That would be great.'

This may be a mistake, she realises. Tea can take up to half an hour to drink. An hour, if you really want to drag it out and don't mind the lukewarmness of it. Does she really want him here for half an hour? Or longer? On the other hand, if he does annoy her, then kicking him out when his tea is only half-drunk would be a punishment that fits the crime. Less harsh than breaking his foot. Also, less suable.

'You sure you don't want sugar?'

'Very funny,' he says.

'Thank you.'

In the kitchen, she takes a moment to compose herself – to breathe in slowly, hold it, breathe out. That little trick she learned during the pandemic. She's been caught off guard by seeing him with no warning. She hasn't planned what to say. But maybe that's why he showed up unannounced – so she wouldn't be forearmed. On the other hand, it might also be because if he *had* tried to warn her, she would have told him to get lost.

She roots around for a vase. The flowers need water, but mostly, she wants to extend this suspended pause, this moment before she has to decide how to respond to whatever Alex has to say. She already knows that she can't trust her body not to respond to him. Can she trust her mind?

When she can no longer justify faffing around and killing time, she sets his tea down in front of him. And one for herself, too. There is, after all, nothing better to steady her nerves. Tea is even better than taking deep breaths and holding them. She picks her mug up and holds it with both hands, the way she does in winter to warm them up. She feels like at this moment she needs the comfort of warmth. It steadies her.

She forces herself to look at Alex, and waits. He's the one who's turned up, after all – the one who started this whole thing. Besides, she doesn't feel like making this easy for him by asking leading questions or apologising first, in an effort to clear the air and make things feel less awkward. Let him feel the awkwardness. It was his doing, after all.

Despite all of these very rational thoughts, Jess is tempted to fill the silence, when it starts to stretch interminably. But Alex clears his throat and starts to speak.

'I feel I owe you an explanation, as well as an apology.'

'Okay,' she says uncertainly. Forces herself, again, to wait.

'Well, on the apology front, I hope the flowers speak for themselves. But just in case they don't – I want you to know how sorry I am for saying what I did. You've been vulnerable with me and spoken about how you wish things were different with your mum, and I used that to hurt you, which is pretty much unforgivable.'

There's a lump in Jess's throat, and she is determined not to cry. She nods, and swallows hard.

'I know you were also being kind, and trying to help me have a healthier relationship with my family. And I know that came from a good place. But the thing is, I've been working on things from my past with my therapist, and I've been really angry at my family, as different things have come up. So, that anger . . . Well, I misdirected it, and you bore the brunt of it. The anger was just there, waiting to be triggered, and you inadvertently tripped a switch.'

A week ago, she might have probed further. She might have asked what exactly he was angry about, helped him work through it. But she has her own anger issues now. The flowers have softened her, and the tea is warming her through – or maybe that's just the effect of his dark eyes on hers. But still, she doesn't quite feel like engaging in conversation that might bring up difficult emotions. It feels like a cost he has not quite earned. And anyway, she doesn't want to risk poking the beast again.

'Okay,' she says again, instead.

Alex runs a hand through his hair and takes a sip of his tea. Uncertain, perhaps. Or waiting for a more thorough response. He looks down into his cup, then back at her. She forces herself to look at him. Part of her wants to stay angry, but she is having to really fight for that. It would be so easy to just let his chocolate-brown eyes melt her.

'I can't do this without you,' he says.

'This?' She wants to probe a little. If he just needs her for her editing skills, he can jog on. She's done more than enough to make this next book a success. She owes him nothing beyond that. 'Writing, or—'

'Writing, yes. But also, maybe, life.'

This would admittedly be a lot more romantic without the *maybe*. But despite herself, her heart softens a little bit. Despite herself, she puts her mug down and reaches for his hand, interlaces her fingers with his.

'You're a smooth talker,' she says.

'It's true, though.'

'Okay,' she says again. And then, curiosity having got the better of her, despite the risks, she adds, 'Can I ask you something?'

'Of course. Anything.'

'You said you were angry with your family. What is it that you're angry about?'

'I thought you were going to ask about something more romantic than that.'

'All in good time.' Jess doesn't know what she even means by that, but it feels like the thing to say, to reassure him, as if her hands threaded through his weren't enough.

'Well, I realised that I was always so busy looking after them that I never let anyone look after me. I never asked them for help. And I was a really anxious little boy, but there was so much going on in the family that nobody really noticed. And I know kids' mental health was talked about less then, and all that. But I can't help thinking that if my anxiety had been treated properly back then, I'd have been a better adjusted kid and better adjusted adult. I'd have learned how to manage my anxiety and not let it rule and run so much of my life.'

This explains a lot. 'Thank you for telling me that,' she says. Her mind is already racing with all the things she wants to do: read a book on anxiety, find some novels with characters with anxiety, throw herself down some rabbit holes on Reddit. She wants to understand Alex better, to be able to help him with this. Even though she'd rather avoid thinking about hard things, if she makes it into a project, she can convince herself she's having fun. 'You're forgiven.'

His shoulders visibly relax. 'Thank you.'

She's wondering whether to walk around to him, to lean down and kiss him, when her phone lights up on the table, interrupting her thoughts. *Mum*.

'Take it,' Alex says. 'I don't mind.'

'Thanks.'

It's as if her mum has a sixth sense. This is twice now that she's called while Alex has been at her flat. Her mum has always loved gossip – from earliest childhood, Jess remembers copies of *Paris Match* strewn around the house. *Just brushing up my French,* she would say, when Jess looked up from her homework to find her mum lounging with a glass of wine and a magazine – never mind that *Paris Match* was mostly pictures and there wasn't a pen or notebook in sight, let alone a dictionary. And now, it's as if her mum can sense the presence of a hot man in Jess's flat and can't bear to be left out, wants to know *everything*. Or as much of *everything* as she can glean in a two-minute phone call on her way to the airport, at least.

'Hi, Mum,' she says.

'Just a quickie, love. Calling to see if you want anything from duty free? Are you running low on perfume? I'm just at the airport and they've got a special deal on that one you like, Woman by Ralph Lauren?'

It was three Christmases ago that she'd asked for that particular perfume. Jess doesn't have a signature scent – she likes to play around, try different things. These days, she's quite into Armani Sì – she likes how it smells, but also the name, Yes, the idea of embracing life. But still, it's sweet that her mum remembers. And she's not running low, but she knows her mum loves to treat her. Or that treats are a way of assuaging her guilt for not being around as much as Jess would have liked. Would still like now. But whatever: either way, Jess gets a treat.

'Yes, actually, Mum, that would be great. Thanks.'

Behind her, Jess can hear the bustle of an airport shop. 'On your way back from Spain?'

'Off to Tenerife,' she says. Jess can't keep up. Does this make her a bad daughter? Or does it just make her mother an unhealthily frequent traveller? Opposite her, Alex is draining the dregs of his tea. And then he starts coughing.

'Oh, sorry, love. Have you got someone with you there? I didn't mean to interrupt anything.'

'It's just Alex,' she says, and Alex can't be choking to death, because he has the wherewithal, between coughs, to raise his eyebrows at her, as if to say, *Just?* 'I told you about him, remember? We're writing a book together.'

Alex is still coughing. Jess tries to communicate with her eyes, *Are you okay? Do you need a glass of water?* But that turns out to be too much to communicate with eyes alone. Her mum takes a breath, preparing, no doubt, to pelt her with *Paris Match*-worthy questions.

'I should probably go, though,' Jess says. 'Just check he's not dying.'

'Fair enough.' Her mum sounds disappointed, and a part of Jess feels guilty, though a part of her feels vindicated. *This is what it feels like*, she wants to say, *when you want to keep talking but the other person has somewhere more interesting to be*.

'Love you,' she says, feeling oddly self-conscious about saying *love* in front of Alex. 'Bye.'

And then she's by his side in a flash, slapping his back. It's not a romantic kind of touching; there are no sparks, metaphorical or otherwise. But there's something oddly intimate about tending to him in the ordinary details of life, and that is enough to get the butterflies in the pit of her stomach dancing.

'I'm all right,' he says, between slaps. 'But maybe some water?'

She rushes off to the kitchen.

'Those tea dregs always get me,' she says as she hands over the glass of water and takes the seat next to him. 'The bits of limescale at the bottom . . .' One of the less delightful aspects of London life.

'I take it you don't filter your water?'

'Not for tea.'

'You should,' he says. 'It tastes better. Also, it prevents needless choking-related deaths.'

'I'll bear that in mind.'

It feels like the end of a conversation, rather than an easy segue to something else, and maybe that's why silence falls between them, heavier and heavier as Alex looks at her deeply, as if drinking her in.

'Can I ask you a question?'

'Anything.'

'What's the deal with the glasses?'

Jess can't help but burst out laughing. She'd thought it would be deeper than this. More . . . Well, more romantic. 'What do you mean?'

'I can't work out what you need them for. There doesn't seem to be any consistency in when you wear them. Sometimes it's for computer work, and sometimes it's for being out and about, and sometimes you go for long stretches without wearing them at all.'

'They're not prescription. I just wear them when I feel like it.'

'Ah.' He is silent for an unsettlingly long time, processing this. 'What's the point, though?'

Back when she met him, Jess would have assumed this was judgement of some kind. Alex's way of saying she was unserious or immature. But now she realises that he is only wanting to understand her better, that he gets that her mind works differently from his and this is something to be explored and embraced.

'The point is fashion, Alex. The point is that it's fun and I like the way they look.'

'I like them too,' he says, smiling.

Gently, he removes them from her face. Respectfully, he folds them and places them on the table. Tenderly, he traces the side of her face with one finger, and then at last, he leans in, close enough that his breath tickles when he speaks.

'I love your mind,' he says softly. 'I love the joy you take in things.'

He doesn't give her a chance to respond. If he did, she would say, *I love how deeply you think about things. I used to think being serious was about being boring, but now I realise it means you have substance and depth, and I want to get to know those depths*. But he is kissing her before she gets anywhere close to formulating those thoughts in anything like a coherent way, and then, with his warm lips on hers, coherence seems like it might take a backseat to all other considerations for a while.

As they come up for air, slightly dishevelled, Jess's phone lights up again, this time with a WhatsApp notification.

> So when do I get to meet this 'Alex'?

'My mum wants to meet you,' she tells him. She's not sure why she shares this straight away, without thinking through the ramifications. Maybe to test his loyalty. Maybe to emphasise that yes, in fact, she *does* have a relationship with her mum, thank you very much. The sting might have been taken out of his words now that he's explained why he was lashing out – now that they seem to have moved on to other things – but that doesn't mean she's forgotten them entirely.

He wiggles his eyebrows. 'Doesn't everybody?'

It makes Jess smile, but it feels like a deflection, and she isn't going to let him get away with it quite that easily.

'Nice try. So what do you say? Day out in Brighton sometime?'

Chapter Thirty-Six

ALEX

As it turns out, they don't have to go to Brighton, which is just as well, because this way, Alex doesn't have to admit how much he dislikes the beach. From everything he has learned about Jess, he suspects she won't approve of this. The way she speaks of the seaside with nothing but joy – the sound of the waves over the pebbles, the smell of suncream, even the squawking of seagulls – is at odds with how he's always felt about it. Pesky, persistent sand which finds its way into every crevice of your shoe, even on a rocky beach like Brighton's. Children running around with no regard for anything or anyone but their own fun. Ice cream which always seems like it's a good idea until it's stickily dripping down your wrist and inner arm. Fish and chips, too – admittedly delicious, but impractical to eat in any other place than at a dining-room table with a plate and a proper knife and fork. Alex suspects that if Jess were to write a list of desirable qualities in a suitor, 'loving the beach' would be near the top – or perhaps not even on it, under the assumption that it was a given that everyone loves the beach, just as she would never write 'has a pulse' and 'breathes' on such a list.

One day, he will have to come clean. But this, thankfully, is not that day.

Jess's mum comes up to London every year for the Wildlife Photographer of the Year exhibition at the Natural History Museum, and they arrange to meet up for dinner in South Kensington.

'My mum studied French at uni,' Jess explains to him, and of course Alex remembers that's how she met Jess's French dad. 'So any chance she gets, she likes to eat French food. Show off her accent a little bit. Bask in some nostalgia.' Jess mentions all of this off-handedly, glancing past the topic of her dad without landing on it, and Alex takes his cue from her. This clearly isn't the time to open up that particular can of emotional worms, especially not once Jess's mum joins them.

'I see,' he says, leaving it at that.

He isn't sure what to expect of Jess's mother. Jess hasn't shown him a photo, and he hasn't spotted any in her flat, although it's possible that they are on display in her bedroom, an inner sanctum he has not yet been invited into. Alex has stalked Jess on Facebook, even scrolled quite far back, and didn't come across anything. He's curious to see what her mum is like, and if she is flighty and easily distracted, the way he imagined Jess to be before he really knew her.

Jess's mum, as it turns out, is more glamorous than Alex expected: her blonde hair in the same kind of messy bun that Jess seems to instinctively prefer, her nails immaculately painted a cherry-bright shade of red, perfectly matched to her high-fashion branded handbag. As for Jess herself, she looks more stylish in yellow dungarees than anyone has the right to, especially yellow dungarees that are patterned with bees.

To Alex's slight horror, her mum holds out her arms for a hug. *No, thank you*, he wants to say, but he ignores his churning stomach and obliges. She smells of bergamot and citrus, a pleasant scent that brings back memories of his own mother, younger and carefree, before the arguments with his dad started, or at least before Alex was aware of them.

'I'm Ellen,' she says into his hair before she lets him go. 'It's great to meet you.'

'You too,' Alex says. 'I've heard so much about you.' Which isn't true, of course. Mostly, what he's heard about is her absence, even if Jess brushes it off as no big deal.

'All good, I hope,' she responds, standing back and appraising him with not a hint of subtlety.

'Of course.'

He can't help noticing that Ellen doesn't say she's heard a lot about him, too. This could be for one of several reasons: maybe she hasn't let any calls with Jess be long enough to find out about him. Or maybe she *does* know about him, but she's trying to protect Jess. Or maybe what *she's* heard is not, in fact, all good, and she can't bring herself to lie about it. But he is practised at this kind of social situation. He'll squash down his anxieties and make polite chit-chat. It's not his favourite thing, but he has learned to be good at it. With a family the size of his, there are a lot of in-laws to get to know; and in his more successful days as an author, there were a lot of book launches to attend – warm white wine sipped from plastic cups in too-hot bookshops while making polite conversation calculated to raise a smile and not offend anyone. He learned, then, to observe or remember a detail about the person he is talking to, using it to flatter slightly and as a way into the required small talk.

And here, the menu they pick up at the crêperie table, with words like *galette* and *ratatouille*, provides him with the perfect way in.

'Jess mentioned you speak beautiful French.' Jess hasn't, of course; but that's not really the point.

Ellen beams, pink in her cheeks, batting away the compliment with her right hand. 'I enjoy it,' she says. Is it possible she picked the *ratatouille* just to have a chance to show off her accent? Let's just say it's not impossible.

'This one was never interested, were you, love?'

Jess shrugs. She's told Alex that she has a vague memory of watching *Pierre Le Facteur* on old DVDs and of her mum reading Mr Men books in French to her, but that's about it. It was probably never realistic for an English woman living in England to bring up her English daughter to speak French, especially when being a single parent likely presented plenty of its own challenges, without attempting to live life in what remained essentially a second language. But in this moment, he wonders if there is something more to it – a lightly spoken criticism belying deeper frustration, just as Jess's shrug was shorthand for a multitude of emotions.

'*Quel dommage*,' he responds, trying not to sound smug about his own more-than-passable accent.

'There's a lot of verbs,' Jess says. 'I'd never have the patience for all those – what do you call them again?'

'Conjugations?' he supplies.

'Conjugations, yes. I should know that.' She shakes her head, as if willing her brain to cooperate. Her A level Latin brain, which surely knows all about conjugations and parts of speech and all the other awkward grammar. Her brain which, in this moment, is perhaps vying for supremacy with her bruised heart.

'Nonsense,' says Ellen. 'You're perfectly capable.'

Something pleading in Jess's eyes instructs Alex to move on.

'I think I'll have the *ratatouille* too,' he says, leaning into the guttural *r*, showing off a little perhaps. And it has the desired effect: Ellen's eyes crinkle around the edges, and she touches Alex's forearm as she tells him he's made a good choice. Opposite, Jess rolls her eyes good-naturedly – the kind of eyeroll Alex recognises from noisy family Christmases when Susannah is cheating at Monopoly again: the eyeroll that says, *Your ridiculousness makes me somehow even more fond of you.*

Despite the initial foray into discussion of the French language, which so clearly made Jess uncomfortable, this is all going very well. Over savoury *galettes* – smoked salmon and spinach for Jess, ingredients both easy to pronounce and written in English on the menu – Ellen asks insightful questions about the writing process, and how editing works, and the dynamics of co-authoring. By the time they are onto their desserts – Nutella and strawberries; bananas and chocolate; apples and cinnamon – they are also onto their second glasses of wine, conversation and laughter flowing more freely, which is maybe why Ellen feels free to ask a question he probably should have prepared for.

'So am I right in assuming that the two of you are more than just writing partners?'

The blood in Alex's veins turns into ice. He knows this is not rational. Although he hasn't told anyone apart from Nathan and Louisa about his increasing closeness to Jess, it's not a *secret*, as such. But still, there's something about family knowing – his family, her family – that makes all of this real in a way that he isn't sure he is ready for.

He takes another gulp of wine to steady his nerves. His feet find Jess's under the table. He hopes that they communicate several things to her: *Ignore how pale I probably am; I definitely like you*. And also, *Over to you, to answer this question*. And finally, *Please get me out of this conversation*.

'A little bit more than that, yes,' Jess says. Her cheeks are pink, and he's pretty sure it's not just the wine.

'Well, I very much approve,' Ellen says, making what seems like meaningful eye contact with her daughter and touching Alex's forearm again, and then moving on to talk about her latest holiday. His charming French has clearly done the trick, and just like that, it's official. And yet, what it is that is actually official is a little unclear. Are they boyfriend and girlfriend? And what is it about those words that makes him feel like a gangly, acne-ridden teenager, sweaty-palmed at the idea of speaking to the girl sitting next to him in A Level English? Are they *partners*? Such a clinical word, so achievement-driven, reminiscent of unromantic things like law and business. *Seeing each other*? Yes, that. Seeing each other regularly to write and sometimes to do other things too. Although it's been a while since the other things, and he certainly doesn't want to think about them in the presence of Jess's mother. And her seal of approval – clearly meant to reassure; clearly, in most contexts, a green light to proceed with those other things – makes his chest tight, his blood cold. It's just a dinner, he tells himself. It's just crêpes.

He practises the grounding technique his counsellor has shown him. Three things he can see: a father cutting up a crêpe into tiny pieces for his daughter; a group of tourists waiting for a table; a butterfly on the window just past where they are sitting. Three things he can hear: a baby whimpering in its pushchair; a mangled pronunciation of French words two tables away; and, regrettably, the buzzing of his own ears. Three things he can feel: the tang of apple on his tongue. The warm metal of the fork in his left hand. Jess's foot brushing his, entirely non-threateningly.

But, despite all of this, his chest remains tight and he remains terrified. It's all he can do to stay in his seat, to keep making pleasant conversation, while he has the bizarre sensation of being outside his body, watching himself be trapped.

Chapter Thirty-Seven

JESS

Jess is grabbing her phone on the way out of the door to head to Alex's for a writing session when it lights up with a call from her grandparents. They know she prefers texts; they only call when they're flustered, or desperate. Her heart sinks. Much as she'd like to think they'll both live forever, she knows that it's unlikely; one day the phone will ring and it will be for the very worst of reasons. Her knees buckle, and she leans against the wall.

'Hello?'

'Hi, sweetheart. Nothing to worry about.' Jess has explained that this caveat is necessary at the beginning of phone calls to get her heart rate back down to an acceptable rate. 'But your grandpa's had a bit of a fall, and he's okay, but the doctor wants to just give him a bit of a checkup. The thing is, we've got Ivy with us today, and we're not sure—'

Jess doesn't hesitate. She'll have to cancel or re-arrange with Alex, but it's a no-brainer. 'I'll come and get her, and she can hang out with me for a while.'

'Are you sure?'

Jess can hear the relief in her nana's voice, a weight lifted from her shoulders.

'Of course. I'm glad you caught me while I'm still at home. I'll come over now.'

She fires off a quick text to Alex. *I'm really sorry, but it turns out I'm emergency babysitting my little cousin. Any chance you could come over here for our session today?*

She'd been looking forward to going to Alex's flat. She'd wanted to thank him – with words, and then in other ways – for being so warm and kind with her mum. He'd been the exemplary boyfriend, despite the B word not actually being used. Really, she couldn't have asked for it to have gone better. *A lovely boy*, Ellen had texted later. *You've done well for yourself, Jess.* The stamp of approval from her mother had meant almost as much as Alex being up for the dinner meeting in the first place: it seems that whatever reservations he may have had about commitment, he has got over them now.

But they've got time, she supposes, for all that. Right now, her grandparents need her; and isn't that exactly why she agreed to this writing lark in the first place – to travel less for work, to be more available, to put some money aside in case they need her, as well as to treat them to a cruise and to anything else they've been wanting to do but have had to forgo for Ivy's sake. They've spent so much of their lives caring for others – for her, for her little cousin, for people in their church who've needed a lift to the shops, or a hand with the garden, or a few home-cooked meals delivered after the birth of a baby or the grief of losing a loved one. Someone needs to look after them, and it's definitely her turn.

No problem, Alex texts. *I'll be there in an hour or so, if that's okay?*

That gives Jess time to collect Ivy and sit her down in front of *Bluey* or whatever else is on YouTube, while she quickly does a little bit of tidying. Alex coming to her house regularly has meant that the flat has been in better shape than previously, but this level of tidiness requires constant maintenance, and there's always something more fun, more important, or more worthy of Jess's attention. And she may have pivoted to writing, but that doesn't mean she can neglect her Instagram or her TikTok or her Substack. She's behind on all of those, never mind the state of her email – publicists *just* checking if she got their last message, *just* following up about the book, *just* letting her know about the opportunity to interview some exciting debut author. She's barely had time to catch up with Lily lately, or stay on top of her favourite Netflix shows or the latest series of *Would I Lie to You?* or *Only Connect*.

Given all of that, tidiness is low on the priority list, except when Alex is coming over. She knows from the state of his flat, his always carefully combed hair and tucked-in shirt and immaculate grammar, that tidiness matters to him. And she might as well get used to not leaving her stuff lying around, because if they ever share a home, he probably won't find it endearing that she leaves a half-read book on every surface, a graveyard of used tea mugs on her bedside table, and a bag of recycling next to the door because she can't quite be bothered to go outside every time she finishes rinsing out a yoghurt pot.

'My friend Alex is coming over in a little bit,' she tells Ivy as they walk across Vauxhall Bridge Road hand in hand, the zebra crossing beeping in the background. 'We're going to do some writing together. But I've got some colouring books and some dot-to-dot puzzles for you so you can sit at the table with us if you like.'

'Okay,' she says. 'Maybe I can do some writing too.'

'Maybe.'

Jess is just getting out the felt tips and puzzle books when the doorbell rings. Ivy follows her to the door. 'You're a boy,' she says to Alex, by way of greeting, her brow furrowed as if with wisdom beyond her years.

'Yes, I am,' he says. 'It's nice to meet you, Ivy.'

'I've got a friend called Alex,' Ivy explains. 'But she's a girl.'

'Ah, yes,' Alex says, seemingly not in the least flustered. 'She's probably called Alexandra. But I'm Alexander. The boy version. Does that make sense?'

Ivy nods more gravely than the situation seems to demand.

'Shall we let him come in, Ivy?'

Biting her lip, she nods again and moves to the side, letting Alex through. There's something earnest about this little girl that Jess is particularly drawn to. She's all thought and intensity, in the most endearing of ways.

On the living-room table, where Alex and Jess usually work, there's not a lot of space left. The puzzles and colouring books sit in the middle, surrounded by felt-tip pens. Next to them: a chess set.

This is new.

'I didn't know you played chess,' Jess says.

Another earnest nod. 'We have a club at school. And do you want to know a secret?'

'Always.'

Ivy leans into Jess's ear and whispers loudly enough for anyone so much as passing the flat to hear.

'I'm the best player.'

'Wow, that's cool.'

Alex plays along, pretending not to have heard. 'Are you good at it?' he asks.

'Yes.'

Jess envies this ability to state facts as they are. Ivy hasn't learned to be self-conscious yet, to worry that it doesn't do to be too confident, or too open about your achievements. Jess hopes that Ivy never learns this. That she gets to go through life with self-assurance, stating her strengths openly. Is that too much to wish for this far into the twenty-first century? Jess hopes not.

'Want to show me how good you are?' Alex asks. 'We can play, if you like.'

'Aren't you and Jess supposed to be writing, though?'

Alex looks at Jess for permission.

'It can wait,' she says. She feels guilty about making Ivy mostly sit quietly and look after herself while she and Alex work. Jess loved staying at her grandparents' as a child, but she also remembers a feeling of being shunted around from grown-up to grown-up, trying to find her footing and different things to keep her busy in different homes. It's how she discovered books, and probably why she's always loved them. *A uniquely portable magic*, Stephen King called them once, and for Jess they were that, but also something else: a uniquely portable home. Something she could easily put in her pocket on her way to her grandparents', and it didn't really matter where she was, because where she *actually* was – the only place that mattered – was between the pages of her book, in Narnia or Amsterdam or a bygone London. The continuity of that was comforting, and it was why she especially loved long series whose stories unfolded in one place: a particular boarding school, a magical land, outer space.

It assuages Jess's guilt to allow Ivy and Alex to play chess together for a while. Besides, how good can Ivy possibly be? She's seven. The game won't last long.

'The King's Pawn opening,' Alex says, scratching his chin in a thoughtful-grandpa kind of way that makes Jess smile. 'I see. You're not going to get me with the four-move checkmate, I'm afraid.'

Ivy wrinkles her nose. 'Oh.'

Chess isn't one of the many hobbies Jess has dabbled in over the years. Whenever anyone has tried to explain it to her, her eyes have glazed over. She can tell, objectively, that it's an elegant game. She *wants to* want to learn. But she doesn't actually *want to* learn.

She can, however, admire the concentration of two supposedly wildly mismatched players biting their lips and puffing out air as they concentrate; Ivy is holding her own against Alex, who has not taken the easy way out and let her win within minutes, even when he surely must have had the opportunity to. She admires this about him: this treating Ivy like an equal, with the respect she deserves. Since Jess doesn't understand chess, she can't possibly know how good Alex is, or whether he's faking being terrible when in fact he was a world champion in a past life. In her head, she runs through the synopses of his novels: no main character who is a chess grandmaster, so perhaps that's a clue that it's not something he excels at in any noteworthy way.

Ivy and Alex seem to be settled in for the duration, each one taking turns to groan at the other's brilliant moves. They've entered their alternate universe, one that Jess is not a part of. So she pulls out her laptop and works on adding affiliate links to her latest Substack post – something mindless she can do while still half-watching Ivy holding her own, and Alex unpatronisingly praising her. It's inevitable, and she hates the cliché, but it goes through her head nonetheless: *What a great dad he'd make.*

Chapter Thirty-Eight

ALEX

'Ivy seemed to take to you,' Jess says, after her grandma has popped in to pick her up and reassure Jess that the doctor has pronounced that her grandpa is fine, that his fall was unlikely to be related to cognitive decline.

'She's very sweet.'

There's certainly no denying that. It's not immediately obvious that Ivy is related to Jess, even with the wavy blonde hair and the dusting of freckles, but he felt instantly attached to her in an uncle/niece kind of way. He has learned through his life that family is what and who you make it, and little Ivy could easily be part of his. He is pleased with himself for letting her win in a way that wasn't obvious to her, so that she still got to be proud. She deserves to be; she's genuinely talented for a seven-year-old.

But it freaks him out how easily he has got attached, how quickly his brain seems to have accepted Jess's family as his family too. When Ellen had asked what they were to each other, he hadn't known what to say, had let Jess do the talking. Jess's response indicated that she didn't know either. And now, he feels a little nauseous, a little like he unknowingly wandered onto a roller coaster which doesn't appear to have an obvious end point. He wasn't ready – isn't ready – for commitment. He wants to get off and wait for the dizziness to fade. He's a mess, still, and he doesn't want to get into a relationship till he's sorted himself out.

'I'm hoping to spend a bit more time with her, actually,' Jess says. Her tone is the tone of someone who is trying to sound casual but is actually saying something that matters a great deal to her.

'Oh?'

'My grandparents aren't getting any younger. They've spent a lot of time looking after family – looking after me! And it's time they were able to travel the world a little, you know? Maybe my grandpa's fall really was nothing. But maybe one day he'll hurt himself, or my grandma will, and then they'll have mobility issues, and . . . well, they deserve to have some fun before it gets harder. But Ivy stays with them a lot, and so that would mean I'd need to step in.'

His chest feels tight, suddenly. But he fights to ignore it. 'What's the story with Ivy's parents?'

'Her dad travels a lot for work, and her mum – my cousin – has chronic fatigue and she needs a lot of rest. Which isn't always possible with a seven-year-old around. She also worries about her daughter seeing her so unwell. Which I totally get.'

Alex bites the inside of his cheek. 'That makes sense.'

Because of course it does, whether you look at it logically or even emotionally. But just like at the restaurant with Jess's mother, Alex feels trapped, breathless. He counts backwards from ten, but his heart rate still feels elevated, so he tries counting backwards from 100 in threes. Better, much better. More distracting.

But now he is aware that Jess is looking at him weirdly. Is he sweating? He might be.

'Are you okay?'

'Yeah. No. I mean, I think I need to go home.'

Her brow furrows, and he sees it – the family resemblance with Ivy, when she had crinkled her own brow in response to finding out he is a boy despite being called Alex.

'Can I get you some water at least?'

'Yeah. That would be good.' He forces himself to make eye contact as he adds, 'Thank you.' He downs the glass and escapes out of Jess's flat as fast as he can.

Chapter Thirty-Nine

JESS

Jess can't believe he's done it again – walked out in the middle of a difficult moment, rather than addressing whatever the issue is that needs addressing. Maybe he genuinely didn't feel well. He was pale, sweating. Maybe she should go after him, check he is okay, not slumped in the middle of the street somewhere, gasping for breath.

It's hard to know, though, what her responsibility should be, what she is to him. What they are to each other, really. It's never been explicitly defined, even during the dinner with her mum, which had seemed to be a massive step forward. She paces her tiny living room, grabs her keys, then runs down the stairs to her front door, round the corner, a few steps up the road. She spots Alex ahead of her, in his red shirt, his head bobbing as he turns into Pimlico Tube station. Good – he's made it that far. He's not slumped in the middle of the street after all. And even if she starts running now, she'll likely not catch up to him before he gets on a Tube. It's the first time she's felt outraged at how frequently the Victoria Line trains arrive. Who would have thought that could be an inconvenience?

Honestly, give me strength some days, she types into WhatsApp. She double-checks she's sending it to Lily and not anyone else. Since the email incident last year, she always double-checks.

> Alex?

> How did you guess?

> Call me psychic.

Dots appear, disappear, reappear. *Gareth is away this weekend, if you want to come over for dinner?*

Jess's shoulders relax. She feels herself taking a long exhale. *That would be great, actually.* She could choose to be annoyed at the implication: *I have time to see you because my husband's away*. But she takes a deep breath and swallows the comment, because that would be unfair. Lily has never been that kind of friend.

Jess gets through the week the only way she knows how – by ignoring every difficult emotion and squashing down every painful thought. She plays her feel-good 90s playlists, rewatches *Derry Girls*, and buys way too many flat-lay props on Etsy. She scrolls through forthcoming courses at City Lit and finds a French taster course, feeling inordinately proud of herself. It's a one-off, with no ongoing commitment, so it feels less scary. And on Friday, she spends too much money on a bottle of red wine and takes herself off to Lily's.

'Fancy,' Lily says, when she hands the bottle over.

'This is not just wine,' Jess says, wiggling her eyebrows. 'This is M&S wine.'

Lily rolls her eyes. 'That ad campaign needs to die a death.'

It's unlike Lily to be so grumpy, even in jest.

'You okay?'

She nods earnestly – almost a bit too earnestly. But they've got wine – that famous breaker-down of resistance. Eventually, if Lily wants to, she'll talk.

'Okay,' Jess says.

'I thought we could get takeaway,' Lily says. Brightly, cheerfully, in a *this-will-be-a-treat* voice. The biggest treat, though, is Lily's cooking, and not just Magic Pasta. But takeaway is always good. So many options.

'Sounds great,' Jess says, matching Lily's forced jollity with some of her own. Though it isn't forced, not really. 'Italian? Indian? Chinese? Oooh . . . Wagamama?'

'We're not having Wagamama,' Lily says. 'We're not students anymore.'

'You don't have to be a student to enjoy their fried duck gyoza, though.'

'Still. Veto.'

There's a great Indian takeaway around the corner, and they settle for tikka masala and butter chicken, because the classics are classics for a reason.

But first, while they wait, wine.

'So,' Lily says, in a voice that, if Jess were overthinking, she might call *resigned*. 'Tell me about the latest Alex nonsense.'

'I had to emergency-babysit Ivy when we were supposed to be writing. She came over, and they played chess, and Alex let her win but in a not-obvious way so that she still got to be pleased with herself, and it was all going so well. And then he went pale and sweaty and left. So weird.'

'Huh. Weird. Sudden onset of Covid, maybe?'

'Yikes.'

'Sorry.' She grins: not *that* sorry. 'But seriously: he could have felt ill. These things can come on suddenly.'

'I think he would have said so if that was what was happening.'

'Unless it was something embarrassing. Like diarrhoea?'

'I feel like getting on the Tube with diarrhoea coming on is probably not the best strategy.'

'Fair enough.' Lily taps her chin with her finger. 'Do you think it could be the intrusion of real life?'

'What do you mean?'

'Well, up until now, it's been the two of you, in your bubble. The two of you, and the book . . . and yeah, occasional interruptions by people like me wanting to check his intentions are honourable. But things like grandparents falling and cousins needing a babysitter – that makes things real. It's the stuff of real life, of real relationships.'

'Commitment.'

'Exactly. The things that aren't always romantic or fun.'

Jess swallows hard and reaches for her wine glass.

Lily pours more for each of them. 'So I'm guessing he freaked out at the idea of taking on responsibility – not just for you, but for your grandparents, for Ivy, for people in your life. It's a big step, and maybe he doesn't feel ready for it. I mean, that's my guess. I obviously don't know for sure.'

'So he hasn't been over here for counselling?'

'This is not just counselling. This is Lily counselling. But no.'

Jess forces her laugh a little at this lame joke. The wine is going down easily. She pours another glass without asking; what's the point in having M&S wine if you're not going to drink it? And wine never tastes as good with curry as she hopes it will. They might as well enjoy it while they wait.

'So what do I do now?'

'Well.' Lily takes a long slurp of wine. 'First, I guess you have to decide if this relationship is worth fighting for. How much do you like him, exactly? Or do you just like the idea of him?'

In that bookshop all that time ago, Jess would have had to admit that she liked the idea of him more than anything else. His fingers brushing hers, his Darcy-like hand clench, the gentle flirting and meet-cute of it all. If she'd known he was a writer, she would probably have liked the idea of him even more. But then when she met him again half an hour later and he was rude and dismissive and condescending, she didn't like the idea of him at all. If you'd told her she'd be in love with him in a matter of weeks, she would have dismissed it as ridiculous. *What*, she would have said, *do you think I'm completely lacking in self-respect?* And yet, here she was, in love. And now – well, now it's become very inconvenient that she likes him so much, when he messes with her head on a regular basis. The idea of him is less than appealing, and then she sees him, and she's all weak knees, butterflied stomach, and wobbly legs. So this is a confusing question.

'The idea of him is inconvenient in a lot of ways,' she says eventually. 'So I think I'd have to say that it's him I like, and not the idea.'

'Right. So this is worth fighting for?'

'I think so,' Jess says. 'If this ends happily.'

'Well, you can't know that. That's the rub. You can't ever know if something ends happily. You have to hold your nose and jump off the diving board and hope the water is there to catch you and you're not just going to land in an empty concrete pool and snap your neck.'

'That's not exactly reassuring.'

'I know.'

'But, wait . . .' It's possible that the wine is blurring Jess's thinking. 'In this analogy, wouldn't you look first to check there is water in the pool?'

'Right. You would. You do your due diligence. You list pros and cons. You think about whether this particular pool is one that looks worth the risk. And then you jump.'

'But I guess you still have to trust that you haven't hallucinated the water.'

'Exactly.' Lily nods. 'You can only be so sure. Especially with relationships. People are complicated.'

Jess takes another sip, pondering this. 'So if I decide he is worth it, and I'm going to jump – what then? What does jumping mean?'

'It means not being afraid to address the difficult stuff. To have the tough conversations.'

Jess shudders. 'I don't like the sound of that.'

'I know you don't. But life isn't all puppies and rainbows. To make a relationship last, you have to be willing to address the difficult stuff, not stick your head in the sand and cover it up with fun stuff.'

'Sticking my head in the sand has always served me well, though.' Jess means it light-heartedly, as a kind of joke. But Lily doesn't take it that way.

'Has it, though?'

Jess is saved from having to consider this question by the proverbial doorbell: the Indian takeaway has arrived in a turquoise cool bag on the back of somebody's bike. And Indian takeaways are another thing that have always served her well. There is certainly no doubting that.

Plates, serving spoons, cutlery: it now seems foolish that Jess and Lily didn't have all this ready long before the arrival of the food. It's not as if they didn't have long enough: they've had plenty of time to down a couple of glasses of red wine each. Jess isn't sure how long that is, exactly. Her head is spinning a little.

They dollop food onto plates – a little of each dish, as is their tradition – and Jess tears the sweet-smelling peshwari naan into two roughly equal halves. She hopes Lily doesn't notice when she takes the slightly-more-than-equal half for herself. Maybe her Alex trials are enough of an excuse to do so.

They have done all of this wordlessly; maybe Lily is still waiting for an answer, and she is letting the silence linger so that Jess will eventually squirm enough to admit that, actually, avoiding all unpleasantness and leaning into fun hasn't always worked great. In her first year of uni, it led to a few questionable one-night stands and a lot of hangovers – never made easier by impending essay crises. These days, it means she's wasted her time on more than one questionable Netflix series and more than a thousand two-and-a-half-star reads. Anything to escape, even if the escape itself isn't that great.

'But you and Gareth are happy,' Jess says.

'You're not going to answer my question, are you?'

'What question?'

'Jess.'

Lily knows her too well for this kind of crap. Still, it's always worth a try. Her avoidance urge is powerful.

'Now you're not answering mine.'

Lily puts a forkful of tikka masala in her mouth and chews, making Jess endure silence the way Jess had made Lily put up with hers. It makes her itch, like an open bracket in a Word document which someone has forgotten to close.

'We are happy, yes,' she says eventually. 'Broadly speaking. But there are hard patches, and there are things we have to address. This last year . . .' There's a catch in her voice. 'It's actually been really hard. We've been trying to get pregnant, and . . . Well.'

'Oh, Lily. I didn't know.'

'I didn't tell you, so how would you?'

Jess puts her plate down and joins Lily on the sofa, her hand on her arm. 'I'm so sorry.'

'It's okay.'

'But it's not. It sounds really rough. You can tell me these things, you know.'

Lily nods, hard. So hard that it's not quite convincing.

'Oh, I know. But you like things to be fun. And when you're having a romance crisis, well . . . It never seems like the right time to tell you.'

Lily's point earlier comes back to Jess. Perhaps pushing away the hard stuff *hasn't* always served her well. It hasn't served people around her well, either, because it's stopped them coming to her, knowing she's uncomfortable with any kind of pain, hers or theirs. It's stopped her being as good a friend as she could be. As good a friend as Lily deserves.

'I'm sorry,' Jess says. She feels guilty about taking the bigger share of the peshwari naan now. Frustration over a man doesn't quite compare with what Lily has no doubt been through. Has she done IVF? Has she had miscarriages? Is it even okay to ask? Jess doesn't know. And every instinct she has is to offer to do something fun to take Lily's mind off it. She doesn't know how else to be a good friend.

'It's okay,' Lily says, even though it's not, not really. 'I'm telling you this mostly because I guess what I'm saying is that even in a happy relationship, hard stuff happens. Things you can predict, things you can't. And so, if you're going to be with Alex, you need to figure out how to deal with the hard stuff. Sounds like you're both conflict-avoidant. He physically runs away every time something difficult comes up. And you just squash it down. And in the long run, that doesn't make for a very healthy relationship.'

Jess tears of a piece of naan and savours it while she thinks. 'I guess you're right.'

'I'm definitely right.'

'This is not just advice,' Jess says. 'This is M&S advice.'

Lily rolls her eyes. 'Drink your wine,' she says.

Chapter Forty

ALEX

'And what's going through your head when you walk away in the middle of a conversation like that?'

Alex's therapist asks him this question in almost an offhand way, so casually that he makes it seem like a minor thing.

'Panic, mostly,' he says.

'Blank panic?'

'Yes.'

Just thinking back to the moment when he left Jess's flat brings him right back there: his palms are clammy; his heart is thumping. He wills it to stop, but it won't.

'Did you try the grounding technique?'

'The thing with the senses?'

'Yes.'

'No. In the moment, I forgot. I told you. Blank panic.'

'Okay. We need to figure out a way to have you remember to do that in the middle of these moments, so that you can stay and work them through.'

'What if I don't want to stay and work them through?' He hears himself asking this in a small voice. The voice, almost, of a child.

'Well, that's a bigger problem.'
'Why?'
'You tell *me* why.'

This is the part where Alex always wants to roll his eyes. He's paying a not insubstantial sum to an expert to fix him. If the answer was deep within himself all along, isn't this a giant waste of time and money?

He shrugs.

His therapist waits. The clock ticks, each tick a not insubstantial portion of that not insubstantial sum. If Alex wasn't writing this book, he wouldn't be able to afford any of these ticks. But then, if Alex wasn't writing this book, maybe he wouldn't *need* to afford any of them.

'Let's assume I don't know,' he says eventually, when a respectable number of ticks have gone by. Fifty-one, to be precise.

'If you keep walking away in the middle of conflict, how will that conflict get resolved?'

'It . . . won't?'

'Bingo.'

Another silence. Another opportunity for Alex to, presumably, look deep within himself. And this time, he does find something there.

'Unresolved conflict is a source of anxiety.'

'Exactly.'

'And we're trying to reduce anxiety in my life, so that means being able to deal with sources of stress, like conflict.'

'Yes. Also, it makes for better relationships.'

'Ah.'

He can't fault this argument. Walking away when things get tough has not pleased Jess, and he can't say he blames her. It's a new thing, this anxiety that makes him unable to think straight. Before he'd uncovered it all in therapy – when he was just internalising it with stomach aches and sweaty palms – it was easier to manage. But now, it's like a scab he's started to scratch, and it's bleeding, and Jess is somehow getting caught in the crosshairs. Maybe having therapy wasn't such a good idea after all. Expensive *and* dangerous seems like an unhelpful combination.

Still, he's here now. He might as well get his money's worth.

'So can you help me figure out why I was so anxious?'

'Why do *you* think you were so anxious?'

Alex looks around for a pillow to scream into. Sadly, there isn't one. He digs a nail into a palm instead, and that seems to help.

'I don't know. I was enjoying hanging out with Ivy. I like kids. I love being an uncle, and I feel like I'm good at it. I let her win at chess and she didn't even realise that I had. Not to brag, but that's a special kind of skill.'

'But you didn't know you were signing up to look after a child when you went into this relationship.'

Alex's breath catches. Yes, this is it. The bait and switch.

'And you're not ready for that kind of commitment?'

That doesn't feel like it's what it is. Once he's in with Jess, he'll be all in. He's always wanted children of his own. Some nights, and some days too, he's even dreamed of it, dreamed of a baby with Jess's freckles and honey blonde hair. 'I don't think that's what it is.'

'Well, tell me this. How did it feel when Jess dropped your writing session so she could look after Ivy?'

'She didn't drop it.' It feels important to point this out. He is defensive of her. 'It was just delayed. And then, admittedly, I walked out, so it didn't happen. But that wasn't her fault.'

'But if she had cancelled it, would you have been angry?'

He looks down at his fists. He hadn't realised he was clenching them. 'Yes.'

'Why?'

'I suppose because I'm realising how often people put me second. And I know that if we commit to each other and have kids, I'll be second a lot. But it's the beginning of our relationship, and I'm just working through all this, so it feels, I don't know, raw?'

'Good,' says the therapist, pushing his glasses up his nose. 'Good. That's good.'

'It doesn't feel good, though.'

'It's good that you're recognising all of this. Also, let me ask you something else: is there a part of you that worries that Jess is putting *herself* second?'

'Bingo,' he says. Not a word he has ever used in his life, at least not like this. His fists unclench; a weight lifts from his shoulders. Even just understanding this about himself helps. 'I love her,' he says – and probably the first time he says this should not be to someone whom he is paying to hear it, but oh well. 'And so I feel defensive of her, I suppose. And worried that she'll be taken advantage of and have to give more than she's prepared to.'

'Good,' the therapist says again, and Alex does his best to suppress his irritation in the midst of this small cathartic victory. 'So what do you think you need to do next?'

The answer is so obvious that it makes Alex want to roll his eyes. 'Talk to her, I'm guessing?'

His therapist takes a breath.

'Please don't say *bingo* too,' Alex says, and the therapist chuckles.

'Okay,' he says, and does a thumbs-up sign instead. Which might be worse.

* * *

It's all very well saying that he needs to speak to Jess, but that requires her being willing to talk to him. Alex has already done the showing-up-with-flowers trick, and while he doesn't put it past himself to need to do that again sometime, it seems a little too soon since the last time. A little unoriginal, which in turn smacks of insincerity.

Besides, it feels like this moment needs something bigger than just flowers. Honestly, he is starting to feel ashamed of his inability to deal with the hard stuff of life, to stay and work through things. He knows from his childhood, from his parents' failed and then successful marriages, that relationships are hard and they require work. He's been exploring the nuances of that in his books for a decade at this point, and successfully so, if his critics are to be believed; and he has certainly always been inclined to believe them.

He takes out his phone and scrolls to Jess's name, but a text seems so pathetic, and it didn't impress her last time. An email, maybe? But that's so . . . formal. So unromantic. They don't have the greatest of histories with email, either. And yet, if he could express himself in writing, it would definitely help his cause – help him to say exactly what he needs to, without stammering or stuttering or getting the nuance wrong and unwittingly digging himself into a hole or making everything worse than it already is. Maybe he'll put something in the book? Dedicating a book to someone is always a nice touch, something that tends to move people. But you can't dedicate a novel to your co-author; that's just weird. In the acknowledgements, maybe? That doesn't feel quite right, either.

Maybe there's a simpler answer than any of this. Maybe he should express himself in the pages of the novel itself, write an ending that communicates to Jess how much he cares for her, how much he's learned from her. They haven't finished the book entirely; there are pages outlined but not yet written. There are more characters and relationships not fully fleshed-out that he could get some mileage out of. He'd have to be careful not to be too obvious, not to be too cheesy – not to harm the book itself in pursuit of reconciliation. But it feels doable.

Okay. Time to get to work.

Chapter Forty-One

JESS

Jess is starting to wonder if coming to this taster class was a mistake. She's distracted by thoughts of the book's ending (and, if she's honest, also by the attractive French teacher). It feels like exactly the wrong time to be starting something new, even if she's glad to be focussing on something other than her complicated feelings about Alex. She needs to concentrate, and to fight her natural tendency to flit from one task or one hobby to another. Part of her wonders if she is only doing this to escape from having to untangle the knot of The Alex Situation, as she has taken to referring to it in conversations with Lily and in her own internal monologue.

Jess already knows how her learning French is likely to end: she'll be excited for a few weeks, thrilled to put her first few sentences together, then the real work of learning will start, and she'll lose interest, and think about taking up cross-stitch or pickleball or the cello. Still, though, escapism aside, it feels important to face what she's been running from her whole life: that her dad did in fact exist, and part of her is inextricably linked with him. It feels, maybe, like growth. Like taking her head out of the sand at least a little bit.

She's been thinking about her conversation with Lily, about her claim that anything worth having requires work, and sometimes that work is inconvenient and painful. Maybe this connection to her dad – to Jess's own DNA, her own heritage – falls into that category. And besides, this *is* just a taster class. By the time it properly starts later in the year, the bulk of the editing work on the novel will surely – *surely*? – be done. She'll have space in her brain and in her timetable for something new. Another reason to stay put, to not go rushing off on adventures – a reason to add to Ivy, and her grandparents, and maybe, if they can figure things out, to Alex.

She forces herself to tune back in. They are going round the class, each person sharing their connection to French, why they've chosen to learn it or refresh it at this point in their adult lives. Jess's heart begins to thump. She has a choice, she knows. She can brush it off with a laugh, as she usually does with difficult things. She thinks about saying, *I want to be able to flirt with the hot men when I'm next on holiday*, waiting for the others to chuckle, watching the teacher for signs of blushing. She could say, *I'm hoping to win the lottery and get a second home on the Riviera*. But when it gets to her turn, she surprises herself.

'My dad was French,' she says. 'I never knew him, and I thought it would be nice to have more of a connection to him.'

Jess's heart is so loud now that she is sure everyone can hear its unsteady rhythm. But nobody else in the room seems unduly concerned: the only response is some sympathetic *mmm*s, and the concerned, furrowed brow of the tutor, which once upon a time (last year, perhaps) might have annoyed her and put her off sharing anything that wasn't light-hearted ever again. Her ears are ringing, and she can barely hear what others have to say.

Alex, she knows, would be proud of her. He's on his own journey processing his past, and he knows these small victories shouldn't be taken for granted. She knows, too, that thinking of him in these seminal life moments, wanting to share even the hard stuff with him, can only mean one thing: that she's more deeply in love than she realised, and that what they have is worth fighting for.

* * *

Lily's advice was well and good, but Jess is still smarting from Alex's walking away. And anyway, what is she supposed to do? Really, it's up to him to contact her. He's the one who walked away. She doesn't want to nag, and a text saying, *Are you okay?* could feel to him like nagging, like she's saying, *Where are you? Have you got over your sulk? Are you ready to discuss this like an adult?* Especially because, deep down – or maybe not even that deep down – that is how she actually feels. She could overcompensate with emoji, and hope that covers any buried passive aggression, but she doesn't trust him to read the right thing between the lines. Especially as she's not sure what the right thing *is*, what it is that she actually wants to tell him. Sometimes, *Grow up*, is what she beams at him telepathically across London. Other times, it's *I love you! Come back to me*. But mostly, she just misses him. She misses their creativity bouncing off each other, misses working with him on their book, talking about its characters, which have become so real to her.

She opens the text on her computer, scrolls up and down to her favourite parts: the witty dialogue Alex finally let her include, the new characters she introduced and developed. It's glaringly obvious, to her, which parts are her writing and which parts are his, but it's the job of a good editor to smooth that out, and she trusts Nathan to do it well. She's proud of the work they've done together, even in its unfinished, unpolished form.

And maybe this is the answer. Maybe she'll write her own ending to the book. The characters who were exchanging coy looks as they waited for help from the emergency services, looking for any distraction from their fear, their hunger, the sharp pain from their injuries. Maybe she'll write them a happy ending, one in which they hash out their differences and discuss how to resolve conflict like grown-ups. It doesn't matter if it doesn't make it into the book; it can just be a message to Alex. *See, this is how it's done. This is how adults communicate. This is how I wish we would communicate. See how they say* I love you *by the end of the story? By the way, why haven't we said that to each other yet?*

In their book, many beautiful things have come from the wreckage of the crashed plane. Reconciled spouses, a renewed faith in God for one character, and fresh determination to live life differently and with purpose for others – to pursue that art career, to write that book, to go back to college and finish that degree. And now, this love story.

Everyone's life is a plane wreck in some small or big way – Alex with his anxiety, and his pain from having not been looked after the way he would have wanted as a child. Even Jess, though she's buried it and run from it and papered over it with fun and with books and with Netflix – she hasn't exactly emerged unscathed from her childhood, from growing up without a dad and with an often absent mum. But out of the wreckage of their two lives, maybe hope can emerge. Hope, and love.

She just needs to get the ending right.

Chapter Forty-Two

ALEX

The journey from Alex's flat to Nathan's office is becoming a little too familiar for Alex's liking. Not that he minds seeing his old university friend – in fact, he'd like to see more of him, but preferably over some bottles of wine and a cheese plate rather than in a sterile office, with the stress of a looming deadline hanging over his head like the sword of Damocles. He probably should have figured out ahead of time that mixing work and play, friendship and business, would come back to bite him, but here we are. Specifically, here we are at the exit to the Northern Line, having carefully avoided the dirty seats by standing all the way from Hampstead to London Bridge. Alex promises himself a browse of Borough Market on the way back, a stop at Monmouth Coffee to pick up a bag of their Ethiopian blend, and a chorizo roll from Brindisa. The thought of these things fortifies him. This isn't necessarily going to be an easy meeting, and he needs to know a reward awaits him when it's over.

'So,' Nathan says, indicating the armchairs in the corner. The armchairs that Alex has spent far too much time sitting in these past few months. Perhaps more time than he has spent in his therapist's office, which is saying something. The hours there have felt interminable. The hours here, too.

'So,' Alex says back. 'You summoned me?'

'I did. Because you're not replying to my emails.'

'I must have missed them in my inbox.'

'You're a terrible liar.'

'I'm a fiction writer, Nathan. Lying's what I do for a living.'

Nathan sighs. He clearly has no patience for this today. 'So, anyway. I summoned you, yes. Because Jess has sent me what she says is a finished copy of the novel. But I thought it was a little odd that she sent it to me without reference to you, especially as she'd previously indicated that she'd taken it as far as she could. It sounded like maybe you'd washed your hands of the book and left her to finish it.'

'That's not the case at all.'

'Glad to hear it.' Nathan catches Alex's eye and refuses to look away. Alex considers it a challenge – one in the face of which he refuses to back down – and holds Nathan's gaze. He can tell Nathan is waiting for him to say more, but Alex has always outdone his friend in stubbornness. He's always outdone most people in stubbornness.

'So I take it you've seen the ending she's written, then?'

'Why are you so sure Jess was the one to write it?'

Nathan twirls his wedding ring one way, and then the other. 'Because it's my job to scrutinise writers' styles? And also because . . . Well, if you haven't read it, I don't want to spoil it.'

'What makes you think I haven't read it?'

'Because if you had, you wouldn't be so nonchalant about the whole thing.'

Alex readies his air quotes. 'I'm not *nonchalant* about her having sent it to you without checking with me first, I'll tell you that much.'

'When was the last time you had a conversation with her?'

Alex does the mental maths. 'Oh, a few weeks ago.'

'As I suspected.'

'What does that mean?'

'I think you should read her ending and then judge for yourself.'

Nathan opens his drawer and places a thick wad of paper on the desk. He takes a few sheets from the top of the pile and slides them over to Alex. 'I'll wait,' he says.

This all sounds very ominous.

Alex feels self-conscious; it's one thing having people listen to you read out loud – something he is used to – but it's quite another to have someone watch you as you silently take something in, trying to keep your features under control so that they don't betray the stomach-clenching emotions passing through you.

Because Jess's ending is . . . not subtle.

As a book's conclusion goes, it is not great. Too obvious. Too unnuanced.

But as a message to him, it is loud and clear, and that's what he needs. Jess has obviously figured out that subtlety would be pointless, lost on him.

We have to figure out how to talk about difficult things, says one character to another. *Life is full of difficult things. Hopefully not as difficult as this plane crash, but still. I know I paper over the cracks by putting on a brave face and looking for the bright side and the fun. And I know conflict makes you anxious. But you're more resilient than you give yourself credit for. And we have to figure this out if we want it to work. And I want it to work. Do you?*

Alex swallows hard. He turns the page for the response.

I do. Of course I do.

Alex has read enough. He clears his throat. 'Well, anyway. I've got my own version of the ending, as it turns out. If you would like to see it.'

'Of course,' Nathan says, not bothering to hide his grin. 'I'd love to. I imagine it will be very enlightening. Email it to me, would you?'

'No problem,' Alex says. And then he says some other things, and so does Nathan, but he won't be able to recall, later, what any of those things are. He needs to get out of there, drink some water, count to ten and do his grounding exercises so that he can bring his pulse down and think clearly enough to get himself back on the Northern Line. Maybe he won't get any coffee from Borough Market after all. Caffeine seems like the last thing he needs right now. He is perfectly stimulated as it is.

Outside the door, he slumps against it. His knees feel as weak as they did when he was a teenager, in the grip of his first crush.

'I'd move, if I were you,' Nathan calls from inside the room, his grin obviously still there, audible in his voice. 'Health and safety, and all that.'

He's not wrong. If this were a cartoon, and Nathan were to open his office door – something which is not exactly beyond the realms of possibility – Alex would end up flattened against the opposite wall, a pancake that would gently slide down until it landed in a crumpled heap on the floor. Not that Alex landing in a crumpled heap is an unlikely scenario, after this turn of events.

Chapter Forty-Three

JESS

Jess didn't expect Nathan's response to her sending in the finished book would be a simple, *Please come and see me at your earliest convenience*. She feels as if she's been called to the headmaster's office, about to be given a detention for etching the name of a boy on the underside of a wooden desk (she can neither confirm nor deny that this has actually happened to her).

Was her ending that bad?

Maybe it was. It's possible she was more focussed on sending Alex a message than she was on actually writing an ending worthy of the rest of the book, which as a whole is really rather good, if she does say so herself.

She knocks on his office door more timidly than she usually would.

'Come in,' says a voice that doesn't sound gruff or angry. She relaxes a little, takes a deep breath. This will be fine, right? It will be fine.

'Hi,' she says. Her voice comes out shaky. Not such a bad thing: it communicates to Nathan that she knows she has messed up. She hovers nervously next to the chair opposite his desk.

'Sit, sit,' he says, so she does.

She waits for the verdict.

'So, the ending.'

Get to the point, she wants to shout. This was always the worst part about being called to the headmaster's office. The waiting for the axe to fall.

She can't bear it anymore. 'You hate it.'

Nathan seems to be suppressing a grin. 'No, no. I don't hate it at all. I think it's a great . . . outcome.'

He's hedging. Jess waits for him to elaborate.

'I think you both know that the ending needs to be rewritten. The most important thing about each part of a book is that it serves the story. And this ending – well, it's serving something else, isn't it?'

Her cheeks burst into flames. At least that's what it feels like.

'What do you mean?' she says, for the sake of saying something, and then she cringes, because she doesn't want to sit here while Nathan explains her own feelings to her.

He raises his eyebrows and slides some pages over to her.

She doesn't recognise these, but she reads them anyway; her cheeks, impossibly, are getting hotter as it dawns on her that this is an ending Alex has written just for her. Lines of dialogue jump out, slapping her in the face, which must be why her face is increasingly burning.

You're my family now. You're the one I put first, regardless who else needs me, or thinks they need me, or has just got used to calling me whenever they need anything.

I know I'm not perfect. I know I need to work on my anxiety and get better at working through difficult issues.

I project my own fears onto others sometimes. I know that. I'll work on that, I promise.

Jess's eyes prickle with the tears that threaten to fall. She chews her lip, swallowing around the lump in her throat, willing her emotions to settle.

'You've taught him well,' Nathan says. 'Those are some lines worthy of a full-on romance novel.'

She's not sure if this is a compliment, but she says, 'Thank you,' anyway. Or at least she tries to. It comes out like a squeak.

'He needed to loosen up, as an author but also as a person. I really hope you two can make it work.'

Jess nods. She wishes she had the wherewithal to verbally spar, to be funny in this moment and diffuse the cringe she feels. But all she has is gratitude, and also a desperation to get out of there, and go and find Alex. To get those difficult conversations out of the way, but maybe first to do some other things.

'So once you've figured that out, maybe you can rewrite this ending?'

From deep within, she manages to summon her voice. 'I think that can be arranged,' she says.

'Good,' he says. 'Keep me posted on everything.'

Jess is pretty sure she won't be doing that. 'Maybe

not everything,' she says, recovering her smile. 'But we can write you a better ending.'

'Glad to hear it,' Nathan says. 'I look forward to reading it.'

'I look forward to writing it,' she says. And then she gets up and goes before she embarrasses herself further.

* * *

'So apparently we need to rewrite our ending,' Jess says, when Alex opens the door to his flat. She's caught him in baggy shorts and a T-shirt – perhaps these are his pyjamas. Or perhaps he is relaxing into more casual clothes. A new Alex. She liked the old one, but she can live with this one too. Although, *live with* is maybe a bit premature. They've got a lot to work through first.

'Ah. So you got that memo, too, then?'

'Apparently we weren't very subtle.'

'And we need to be *subtle*.' Alex uses his fingers to mimic air quotes, a cover quote on a book. 'So,' he says, looking her up and down in a way that suggests he has missed her. Or perhaps just checking to see if she has brought writing supplies. 'You're here to rewrite the ending.'

'In a way,' she says, locking eyes with him. It's pathetic how much she's missed him. It's only been a few weeks. They're still standing in the doorway, kept close together by the walls. Neither of them apparently wants to move from this forced proximity. 'I think we should talk. But I also think I want to—'

Alex leans forward, and his lips land gently on hers. She doesn't finish her sentence.

'Talking can wait,' he says softly, brushing her hair away from her face and kissing her more deeply. He pulls back, remembering his manners. 'If that's okay with you,' he says, a note of desperation in his voice.

'It's very much okay with me.'

* * *

Afterwards, Jess pulls her T-shirt back on, while Alex makes tea. She should probably have thought this through better, what she was going to say. It feels like there's so much, and she doesn't know where to begin. Maybe she should have brought writing supplies after all – her trusty, battered notebook for brainstorming. What would she write at the centre, surrounded by a bubble? *A better ending*, probably.

'So,' Alex says, handing her the tea. 'Where do we start?'

'I was just wondering that too.'

'Let's maybe start where we left off,' he says, shuffling back into bed and pulling the quilt over both of them. 'Or where *I* left off. When Ivy was over.'

Addressing this head on. This seems like a good sign, an indication that he's changed. That he's not going to run away from difficult conversations.

'Okay,' she says. 'That sounds good.'

'First of all, I want you to know that I wasn't faking feeling unwell. Sometimes, when my anxiety peaks, I can't even see straight. Or I feel sick. But anyway, I was talking to my therapist about it.' This is a good sign too: he is working on himself, becoming more self-aware. 'And I realised that I was feeling defensive of you. That I put so much of my life on hold for other people for so long, and I was angry on your behalf, that you were going to miss out on things because of looking after Ivy.'

Jess takes Alex's hand and traces the outlines of his fingers with her own. A gesture of affection, yes, but also a way to keep herself grounded, keep herself calm, keep herself from wanting to run away. 'I get that. It's not the same thing, though. You and me – we're different people.'

'Of course. And the reason it hurts so much is because it triggers stuff from my childhood, things about not having had the attention I needed. You didn't have that. Well, not in quite the same way.'

She knows, now, though, that she needs to process her own childhood. Stop assuming she's fine, when she's only fine as long as she's running – to fun, to books, to anything that distracts her from pain. 'I always say I don't miss my dad because I don't remember him, but I think growing up without him definitely did have an impact on me. That, and a mum who kept trying to escape her grief by going on adventures.' Jess shuffles onto her side to face Alex, but also to move, to do something with the nervous energy coursing through her. 'It's not that I was unloved or anything. My time with my grandparents was always special. But I probably needed my mum more than I realised.'

'I'm really glad to hear you say that,' Alex says. He turns on his side to mirror Jess. The affection in his face calms her a little. 'I've been worried about how much you suppress everything. When I met you, I thought you were one of those people who've never had anything bad happen to them, and that was why you seemed to just float through life, enjoying it and insisting on happy endings.'

'You thought I was an airhead. Go on, admit it.'

'No, I . . .'

Jess cocks an eyebrow. She has been practising doing this in the mirror for years, and this is the first time it's worked at an opportune moment.

'Okay, fine. But in my defence—'

'Oh, this'll be interesting.'

Alex rakes his hand through his hair. 'In my defence, all I knew about you was that you were an influencer, and all I knew about influencers was that some of them are . . . kind of shallow?'

Jess whacks him on the arm, playfully, but also hoping to hurt him just a tiny little bit.

'You think that's a good defence?'

'I see now that I was wrong.'

'Good.'

It's a chance to move away from the serious conversation, but Jess surprises herself by not taking it. 'You know, my mum was so young when my dad died. She probably thought, *Life can be taken away from me at any time. I want to enjoy it while I can.* And I think I picked up on that.' She swallows hard, the sadness her mum never let her see now manifesting as a lump in her own throat. She looks away from Alex, composing herself. 'My mum was really good at cheering me up when I was growing up; she'd make popcorn, we'd dance around the kitchen, watch silly films together. But my grandma always asked me questions and got me to talk about how I was feeling. Maybe that's why my weekends at her house were so important to me, too. Her love language was listening. And I really needed that.'

'Yeah. That makes sense.' He searches out her face until she meets his eyes. *I'm safe*, those eyes seem to say. *It's okay that you're telling me this.* So Jess takes a deep breath and keeps going.

'The problem is . . . all of that means that I haven't always been a great friend. I'm great at planning birthday surprises and throwing dinner parties and recommending the perfect book. But my best friend has some tough stuff going on, and I didn't even know, because I don't like to ask about the hard stuff. And also maybe she didn't want to tell me, because I don't know how to listen – I only know how to distract people. But that's not always what they need.'

'Sounds like we both have a lot of learning to do, still.'

'Despite your advanced age.'

'Hey.' He doesn't rise to the bait, beyond a wiggle of his eyebrows, and that alone feels like a sign of growth. 'Anyway,' he says, moving swiftly on. 'We can learn together. How to be better people.'

'Better friends,' she says, finishing her tea and settling back down into bed, her head on Alex's chest.

'Better partners.' His voice vibrates through her.

'Better family.'

Alex kisses the top of her head. Something she has always found so calming. It's affectionate, soothing. It doesn't demand anything from her – whether that's a kiss back, or anything more than a kiss. It says, *You belong here. You're home.*

'All of it.'

Family, she thinks. She is going to get to know his big, messy family. He's drawn her diagrams – to help her remember who's married to whom and who used to be married to whom, which nieces and nephews belong to which branch – and she has tried to commit them to memory, but she needs to put faces to names. She's looking forward to that.

And she's trying not to get ahead of herself, but she's looking forward to her and Alex having a family of their own, too – whatever that looks like. Ivy will be part of it, at least some of the time; maybe most of the time as her grandparents age. But Jess and Alex have space to get to know each other before that happens, space to build a strong enough foundation to welcome a child, whether that's Ivy or their own. Her stomach unexpectedly backflips at the thought of this – of having a baby together – when she wasn't even sure it was something she wanted just a few months ago.

She knows she is getting ahead of herself. They haven't even said *I love you* yet. The kiss on the top of her head feels close to it, but she'd like to hear the words. Once upon a time – all of maybe two weeks ago – she would have swatted that feeling away. Pushed it down, kissed him, distracted both herself and him with activities that don't require love, just attraction.

But she's going to be brave.

She can do it with adrenaline sports; she can do it with adventuring around foreign countries where she doesn't speak the language. Even starting to learn French has felt brave.

And if Jess wants Alex to say it, maybe she has to say it first. Maybe the vulnerable child in him, who always came second, needs her to go first. It feels scary. But like Lily said, relationships are hard work. All relationships, even the good ones. Maybe especially the good ones. Maybe that's how they get good in the first place.

It would be bravest, she knows, to move her head from his chest, to manoeuvre herself into position so she can look straight at him as she says it.

But, baby steps.

'Alex,' she says, clearing her throat.

'Mmm?' His voice vibrates through her. It feels like their bodies are one body when this happens. Like if something happens to one of them, it's happening to both of them.

'I think I . . .' She's wimping out. She can feel it. She clears her throat and starts again. 'I—'

'You?'

She knows he knows what she is going to say. But that doesn't mean he's going to make it easy for her. The smile she can hear in his voice tells her all of that.

'I love you.'

Phew. That wasn't so hard. And now that it's out, she can feel her whole self relaxing, turning liquid.

'I'm glad,' he says, and she finds herself holding her breath. Is this going to be one of those 'Thank you' situations, like Ross at the airport in *Friends*? Is it going to be 'I love spending time with you too'?

But no. It isn't.

'Because I love you too.'

Those words, vibrating through her. If there's any better feeling than that, she doesn't know what it could be. Not even skiing down a black run comes close. Or diving off a high board, meeting the pool with a splash and a surge of adrenaline.

She doesn't expect that, the thrill of it.

Maybe settling into a relationship with Alex could be the biggest adventure of her life.

It is, she decides as he nuzzles into her neck, kissing her, certainly worth a try.

Jess: I jumped off the diving board

Lily: Glad to hear it. Unless you broke your neck. Then it's bad

Jess: I didn't break my neck. It was a lot more pleasant than that

Lily: Well, that's good news. Give me all the deets. Unless you don't want to. That's fine too.

Jess: Maybe later, over wine?

Lily: Not wine.

Jess: ??

Lily: 🍷❌

Jess: Is there something you want to tell me????

Lily: Got some good news of my own.

Jess: 👶🎉🍼👼

Lily: 😊

Epilogue

JESS

Jess is buzzing by the time the first guest arrives at the bookshop for the launch. It doesn't hurt that this first guest is Lily, thrilled to be out of the house without baby in tow for the first time since he was born. The process of publication, it turns out, takes as long as a pregnancy, and then some. After Jess and Alex's careful structural edits, the copyedits and proofreads all took time – as did the arguing on the merits of Oxford commas and em dashes – so this has been a big year for both Jess and Lily, both of them assuming new identities: mother, published author. Jess came into her own, planning a baby shower – balloons, a handwritten book for congratulations and advice, home-baked cookies and brownies – and Lily has apologised a hundred times for not being able to reciprocate. *I'm lucky if I get to wash most days*, she's said more than once. *So I think baking for your book launch might be a bit beyond me at this point.* Jess has been over to hang out, to hold the baby while Lily dives into the bathroom for a few welcome minutes of refreshing water on her body, so she knows

Lily isn't exaggerating. It seems relentless and nonstop, motherhood, and she feels vaguely ashamed for all the times she has compared writing to pregnancy and babyhood.

Honestly, writing a book, even co-writing a book with an arrogant author you initially can't stand, is a walk in the park compared to what Lily has achieved with her body, and is achieving now – keeping a human alive. Whenever Jess wants, she can close the laptop and walk away from the manuscript she is currently working on – and while it may feel like a wrench when other obligations drag her away, nobody is actually going to die because she doesn't pay attention to it for a while.

But Lily assures her that motherhood is worth it, that she'd do it all over again in a heartbeat, despite her terrifying tales of the emergency C-section and its aftermath. She seems more exhausted than happy, but there's an air about her of having, not exactly relaxed – because looking after a tiny person is anything but relaxing – but loosened into her new role, like her whole life was waiting for just this.

And that, Jess realises as she looks around the bright blue bookshop – filling with friends, Alex's family, her bubbly mum already on her second glass of fizz – is another way in which pregnancy and writing *can* be compared. She, too, feels like she was made for this. Another chapter in her life – what feels like the main event – has begun, and that's something she has in common with Lily.

'How are you doing?' Alex is next to Jess, suddenly,

his arm on the small of her back, his low voice close to her ear.

'I'm very, very happy,' she says. This is true of tonight, and it's true of life in general – the life she and Alex are building together. They don't share a flat yet – they're currently in a stalemate when it comes to the whole Hampstead vs Pimlico conversation – but once that is resolved, it won't be long until they move in together. *I love you* has become part of their daily vocabulary, whispered into phones late at night when they're not together, and energetically demonstrated when they are.

'I'm very happy too,' Alex says now.

'I'm glad,' she replies.

Lily clears her throat next to them.

'Hello,' Alex says, acknowledging her properly.

'Hello,' she says. 'And congratulations. To you both, obviously, but I've already congratulated Jess, so.'

Alex does a little ironic-but-not-quite bow. 'Thank you,' he says. 'I think it's my best book yet.'

Now it's Jess's turn to clear her throat. 'Your?'

'Well, it's ours, obviously. But of the books with my name on the cover, it's the best one.'

Jess narrows her eyes in mock severity. 'Fine.'

'I think,' Lily points out to Jess, 'that there's a way to view that as a compliment.'

Alex thanks her with his eyes. 'Exactly. I'm at my best when we work together. Is what I was trying to say.'

'Fine,' Jess says again, less grudgingly this time. Then Alex leans down and kisses her on the forehead, and all traces of grudging are washed away. It's not hard, honestly, because her heart is an over-inflated balloon, ready to pop at any time. She gasped when she arrived at the shop – to the left of the door, the whole window is filled with copies of their book, and swirly white writing invites customers to come in and browse 'Alex Maxwell's brilliant new book – co-written with talented debut author Jess Martin'. In the shop, now, more and more people are milling around, picking up a glass of fizz and browsing the shelves. She recognises friends from Instagram, can't wait to speak to all of them. And over in a corner, a familiar face: the brunette from the Godalming pub.

'Go,' Lily says, when she notices her looking over. 'No need to babysit me. I'll do my own milling around.'

Jess is grateful.

'Hi,' she says, when she's taken the few steps needed to reach Cassandra. 'I've met you before, right? In Godalming?'

'Hello. Yes. Congratulations, by the way.'

'Thank you.'

'You can tell me now,' she says, leaning in for confidentiality. 'Are you two together?'

She looks over at Alex, talking animatedly to one of his sisters. It's safe, she decides. It's not like it's a big state secret, and anyway, people will have guessed by the end of the evening.

'We were still figuring it out when we were in Godalming,' she says. 'But yes. We are.'

'Well,' Cassandra says. 'Congratulations on that, too.'

There seems to be no hint of resentment in her voice. Jess takes her well wishes at face value. 'Thank you,' she says, and right on cue, Alex approaches.

'Ten minutes till the speech,' he says into her ear, and she waits for him to recognise Cassandra. But he probably has so many fans who've randomly stopped him in restaurants. Or maybe a touch of face blindness.

'You remember Cassandra?' she says eventually. 'From that pub in Godalming?'

'Of course,' he says, instantly all charm. 'Nice to see you again.'

Jess sees it then – the look in Cassandra's eyes, part admiration, part attraction, part disappointment and crushed hope. She feels a little sadness on her behalf, but only a little. They've worked at their relationship, she and Alex, in the last year. Jess has memorised Alex's family tree and visited all of its branches; she's tried her hardest not to suppress difficult emotions and to face difficult conversations that need to be had. Alex almost never leaves in the middle of arguments anymore, and the combination of meds and therapy has helped get his anxiety in check. Their relationship is good, and not just in the bedroom. Not even just in the writing department, though they've already been signed up for a second book together. They've learned and grown, and they're both better people as a result. Lily was right – relationships aren't easy, and this one hasn't always been, either. But even in the rough moments, something about Jess and Alex feels *right*.

'Nice to see you too,' Cassandra says, recovering her composure and her bright smile. 'I can't wait to read this book.'

'We hope you like it,' Alex says, putting his arm around Jess. Jess tries not to think about why he is doing this – to mark his territory, to spell out he's taken, or simply as a mark of affection that she's overthinking.

Nathan taps a spoon against a glass then, calling them all to attention.

'Thank you, everyone, for coming. We're delighted to be launching Alex Maxwell and Jess Martin's joint debut. It's been a long time coming, but we hope you'll think it's been worth the wait. It's getting great reviews – *The Independent*'s called it: *The start of an exciting new partnership*, and the *Sunday Times* has said that *Alex Maxwell is back, and he's better than ever*. I think we all know why that is.'

Nervous laughter from Alex, dawning realisation and accompanying *oohs* in the crowd. Raised phones for photos, Bookstagrammers enthusiastically vying to be the first to share this particular bit of tasty publishing gossip now that it's official.

'And I'm thrilled to announce – and Jess and Alex don't know this yet – that the book will be straight in at number two on this week's *Sunday Times* bestseller list.'

'Two?' Alex mutters. 'I suppose that's not bad for a book that's not about murders.'

But there's a buzzing in Jess's ear, and she barely hears him. She didn't hear anything after *Sunday Times* bestseller. She doesn't even think before she puts her arms around him, hugging him hard, and then – sod it – kissing him. She's been at enough book launches to know this isn't the done thing, but it's hard to care in this moment. Nathan laughs, with perhaps a little bit of second-hand embarrassment. Phones are unashamedly raised even higher now, the crowd leaning in at just the right angle to get the best photograph, the one they might even be able to sell.

Jess doesn't mind.

It's been a long road, getting here. With the book, with their relationship. Both of those things deserve to be celebrated.

And if other people want to celebrate, too – whatever that looks like: champagne, selfies, gleeful Instagram posts – then let them, she thinks. Let them.

Acknowledgements

Sitting at a desk making up stories doesn't seem like it should be hard work, yet somehow it is. So I'm very thankful for everyone who's supported me through this process, as well as through the last seventeen years of slowly carving out a writing career for myself.

A lot of the same names turn up again and again in my acknowledgement sections, and with good reason. The long-time faithfulness of friends is so important, and I'm grateful for it. For Becky Bennett, who believed in me before the start of this project. For Rebecca Kabat, whose encouragement kept me going through the early faltering drafts of novels very few people have seen. For Jaime Amrhein, Sonia Faletti, and Sandra Vanderbilt, my greatest cheerleaders. For Emily Ribeiro, for wise and caring support. For Blake Dennis, my lifelong friend, the Elinor to my Marianne.

For Brian and Chitra, for keeping me sane through the drafting of this book, and providing me with a safe and lovely home to live in and great company while I wrote it.

Also, thank you to Maddie Wilson, for kind

encouragement and edits delivered gently and thoughtfully, and to Daniela Nava – get yourself a copy editor who responds to your writing with GIFs from *Schitt's Creek*. Thank you to all the team at Avon/HarperCollins for all the work of marketing, publicising, and securing translation deals for my books, and for my translators and audiobook narrators, whose names I don't yet know at the time of writing – vital parts of the process who so often go unsung.

Thank you to all my friends at CCL, whether old or new, who buy my books, read them, review them, and recommend them. Thank you for letting me bore you with my long-winded explanations of the publication process and for caring enough to pray for me and to check in with me about how it's all going.

And thank you to you, the reader, for spending a few hours with my words and the characters I've created. I hope you've enjoyed yourselves.

Loved *Losing the Plot?*
Don't miss *Bookishly Ever After!*

Two rival bookstore owners. One chance for a happily ever after . . .

A cosy, hilarious bookish romcom, perfect for fans of Emily Henry and Lucy Vine.

Already read *Bookishly Every After*?

Why not visit the *Big Apple Farm*!

The perfect book for fans of low-spice, small town romance!